FRAGMENTS

Trevor Sparrow

Disclaimer: This is a work of fiction. The names, places, events and incidents in this book are either a product of the author's imagination or are used in a fictitious manner. Nothing in this novel really happened as described. None of the people, events or places in the text are real. Any similarities you think you see are coincidences, nothing more, nothing less.

Copyright © Trevor Sparrow 2025
All rights reserved
ISBN 9798310788015

Fragments

Beware that, when fighting monsters, you yourself do not become a monster... for when you gaze long into the abyss, the abyss gazes also into you.

Friedrich Nietzsche

For Christine.

Best wishes
Trevor Sparrow
15 · 11 · 25

Chapter 1.

1979

20th October - Saturday
Somewhere in Northern Ireland.
Lobster.

"Christ" he muttered "what happened to him?"

The Special Branch officer peered into the room through the vision slit in the door. The interrogation room contained a table and three chairs, all bolted firmly to the floor. A single unshaded bulb dimly lit the scruffy yellow painted walls and green floor tiles. Two men sat facing each other across the table. He recognized the army officer from previous interrogation sessions. His specialty was high value prisoners, this could be interesting. The prisoner sat opposite, handcuffed to the table and hooded. The sound of the door opening made the prisoner flinch. He let out a little cry.

Joining them in the room, the policeman could hear quiet sobs coming from beneath the hood. He studied the trembling man, noted the hands clenching and unclenching, and the mud-stained clothes. He was uninjured, but soaked in water, vomit and somebody else's blood. His trousers were gently steaming where the prisoner had pissed himself. Judging by the smell he had also shat himself. Over everything there was a spattering of someone's brains, globs of flesh and fragments of hair.

He looked from the trembling man to his army colleague. To ask his question he merely needed to raise an eyebrow and give the slightest nod of his head in the prisoner's direction.

"Evidently," replied the soldier, giving studied pause for effect "this gentleman has incurred the displeasure of the Sandman."

Chapter 2.

2024

10th June - Tuesday
Economic Intelligence Unit, Victoria Street, London.
Nicholas.

Nicholas French was a member of His Majesty's Secret Service. To the very small number of people outside the Service who knew this, he had done little to dissuade their notion that his days were spent abseiling from helicopters and confronting super-villains at gunpoint.

In reality, his entire three-year career had been spent commuting to Victoria on the tube. In an open-plan office over the railway station, he worked from 9 'til 5 at his computer. The office nominally seated 20 people, but since COVID its sole constant occupant had been Nicholas. His immediate boss, Ms. Fiona Perry, occupied a glassed-in office at the end of the floor. It was painfully quiet.

Nicholas specialized in Forensic Financial Surveillance, FFS or "for fucks sake" to its detractors. Using state of the art software and almost unfettered access to banking systems he mapped the flows of money from dodgy paymaster to corrupted recipient.

The current task in hand was deja vu all over again. For some time now his focus had been the Government's backbench MPs. He had been asked to look at the regular monthly payments made from a New York based lobbying group to a rather nondescript back bencher.

The lobbying group had three sources of funding. One was in New York and the other two in the Caribbean. Careful tracking back revealed that the primary funding source for all of this money was a Polish businessman. This gentleman seemed to have no obvious source of income. He made frequent trips to the Cayman Islands presumably carrying suitcases full of cash. The cash, in various currencies, went into anonymous accounts held with two of the less inquisitive banks. Suitcases full of cash failed every "smell test."

The next step was to try and get to the source of the funds being laundered. Polish intelligence had tagged the businessman as potentially being a member of Russia's FSB. Intriguingly, the MP in question had been claiming expenses for language tuition. The regular lessons were paid for by direct debit and when Nicholas looked at the receiving account, he noticed corresponding matching payments to an account held by the Russian Embassy in London. The Russians were indirectly charging the British taxpayer for their intelligence gathering meetings with the MP. Cheeky bastards thought Nicholas.

Nicholas emailed his report to Fiona and went to get a coffee. On the noticeboard in the kitchen area someone was advertising the Civil Service Scottish Dancing and Reeling Society, "ALL WELCOME."

"Which circle of hell is that?" he mused aloud.

Fiona had somehow materialized behind him. "Highland flings not your cup of tea, Nicholas?" she asked. "Thanks for the report on the MP, it's gone up the line, no immediate action, but can you save it away for a rainy day? I'm beginning to think we would be better off trying to identify the MPs who are not funded by someone else's intelligence service rather than those that are."

It was just then that Nicholas noticed that the organizer for the Scottish dancing was Ms. F Perry. Damn.

Back at his desk Nicholas tidied the file up, put a summary into the electronic registry: "MP Daniel Kowalski, FSB compromised." One day, that file would probably get accessed and the opportunity to hold Cabinet rank would go someone else's way.

Nicholas now had nothing to do for the rest of the week. It was essential to appear busy, so he started to devise a full banquet of "work that is not work." Amuse bouche: revised dress code and guidelines. For starters: Online Health and Safety awareness training module. Second course: Online Modern Slavery awareness training, … dessert…

Whether it was revenge for dissing the Scottish dancing or just some management instinct for spotting idle hands, Fiona was on his case and had appeared at his desk.

She read from a list: "I need you to have prepared a registry search, ready for Thursday afternoon, setting out the following:

One: Everything we know about Martin B Collins, American Citizen, whereabouts unknown, particular emphasis on late 70's early 80's.

Two: Any information specific to Northern Ireland for the period 1979 to 80 designated Operation CLARET.

Third: Any information on an agent, officer or asset using the workname SANDMAN.

Finally, Nicholas, this report will ultimately be for American eyes, so no whimsy or flourishes, thank you."

No need for her to channel Professor McGonagall thought Nicholas.

Registry was the great all-knowing database. It held every electronic document generated by the various organs of the British secret state. There was also a generous helping of information from the secret states of other countries, both friendly and hostile. Its limitation was that searches into the dim and distant paper-based past could only be made once the documents had been scanned, turned into text and properly classified.

Nicholas started to run searches against the Registry database. It came as no surprise to Nicholas that his initial searches didn't turn up much.

Martin B Collins was a complete blank. There was no Operation CLARET listed for Ireland.

The search results for Sandman were more promising. The database search for work name SANDMAN turned up half a dozen entries, all of them in ancient GCHQ transcripts. Nicholas studied the documents on his screen. Evidently the security services back in the 70's had taken an interest in two individuals. GCHQ had codenamed them SONNY and CHER. The individual they called SONNY was a lawyer in Northern Ireland. A sharp-eyed policeman, detailed to keep an eye on SONNY had noticed that he would leave his office and make calls from a nearby phone box. Odd behaviour for a man who already had a phone in his office. Clearly, and as it happens correctly, he suspected that his office phone was being listened to. The line to the phone box was tapped in its turn and the calls recorded, transcribed and eventually archived.

Nicholas worked his way through the scanned documents that recorded the calls. CHER was a woman living somewhere in the Republic, peripherally connected to the IRA. SONNY was providing her with a weekly update of names of people arrested, how they had been caught, names of police officers, gossip and rumours. The two knew each other well and there was a lot of mundane personal stuff in the calls as well. CHER was having problems with her car, which eventually broke down and needed a new gearbox. SONNY purchased a microwave oven at some point and there was discussion about different recipes. At first

GCHQ believed this to be potential codewords, possibly bomb making, but over time it emerged that it really was about a microwave oven. The calls stopped in July 1984, when the file says that CHER was killed in a road traffic accident.

Nicholas listed out the intercepts that had mention of SANDMAN:

December 1979. SONNY tells CHER that "persons unknown" had killed someone referred to as "Murph", possibly Murphy. He had been found dead in a burnt-out car in a lay-by. CHER mentions that "Murph" was a volunteer and was supposed to be doing a job. On the transcript an unknown hand had annotated this as "possible placing of car bomb?" SONNY had said that it wasn't an accident. The body was badly burned but appears to have at least one bullet wound to the skull and maybe two in the chest. SONNY reports that he had overheard someone say it might be connected to SANDMAN. CHER asks what he knows about SANDMAN, but SONNY knows nothing more.

January 1980: CHER has an update on the SANDMAN. Two lads driving from the North to Dublin had been stopped by a Brit roadblock. When the lads get a bit mouthy with the soldiers, one of the squaddies at the checkpoint said, "you should watch out, or the Sandman will get you." The other soldiers laughed.

October 1979: CHER says that she has been told that two volunteers found dead in a burnt-out car may have been killed by the SANDMAN. She says she has been told that there are photographs of the two bodies taken before the fire. It seems both were shot first. The source of the photos says that an unknown person, codenamed SANDMAN by the Brits did the shooting. SONNY says he is aware of the two bodies in the car, but says it is being described by the police as an "own goal." They seem to think it was an attempt to lure an army patrol onto a car bomb that went wrong. Nobody has mentioned SANDMAN in connection with it. SONNY agrees to ask around.

November 1979: CHER asks SONNY if he has heard anything about the whereabouts of two unnamed volunteers. One is described as "one of our friends." There is concern that the "friend" has vanished without trace. SONNY agrees to ask around. The transcript is annotated to say that this call is referred to on a subsequent occasion, where "SONNY believes SANDMAN may be involved in the disappearance."

September 1979 SONNY has been asked by someone local if he heard anything to do with a "friend" who has gone missing. Could the SANDMAN have been on the ferry from Dublin? Someone onboard (Gerry or the Jerry?) boarded the Ferry OK, was seen talking to a young woman at the bar, but did not get off at the other end. No trace of him or his bag. Question: could the SANDMAN be involved? Could the SANDMAN be a woman? CHER promises to ask around.

August 1979 CHER asks SONNY if he has heard more about Paul? Paulie? SONNY tells her that Paul was being detained. Under questioning he was doing ok at first and sticking to his story. Then he was shown a series of photographs, one of which was of him being given a pistol. There were a lot of compromising photographs, which seemed to really upset him. SONNY didn't get to see the compromising photographs, but he heard that Paul was pleading with the police not to show the pictures to his parents. The photos came in an envelope marked SANDMAN. SONNY heard that when the Army went to Paul's house they went straight to where the pistol had been hidden in the garage.

Nicholas was disappointed, this was slim pickings, and it hardly reflected well on the Service that the only information he could find on the SANDMAN was overheard gossip.

The only other snippet of information on the Registry system was that there was a file awaiting scanning and indexing, marked "SANDMAN – DET. Newry. Died Motorcycle accident February 1980." Nicholas had not heard of the designation "DET" before, so a quick Google search was needed to enlighten him. It turned out that "the DET" was the British Army's Special Reconnaissance Unit. It undertook secret and highly risky undercover work in Northern Ireland during the Troubles. Nicholas sent a file retrieval request. He marked the request TOP PRIORITY – URGENT.

Time to go home.

Chapter 3

2024

11th June - Wednesday
Economic Intelligence Unit. Victoria Street, London.
Nicholas.

When in doubt, Google it, was Nicholas's approach. The great all-seeing intelligence database had its advantages, but Google was great for filling in the gaps. According to the internet, Martin Brogan Collins was the eldest son of the Collins dynasty of Boston, Pittsburgh and New York. Martin Collins was last seen in New York in the summer of 1979 and the internet gave a broad spectrum of theories as to what happened next. He had been kidnapped by a gang hoping to extort money from the family, he had been abducted by aliens in a UFO, he had died at a drug fueled orgy or he had gone to live in a monastery under an assumed name. Before his disappearance he was romantically linked to one of the Kennedys. It was speculated that he had been trying to get his pilot's license at the time of his disappearance. Another speculation was that he was planning a visit to Antarctica.

Brogan was such a weird name that Nicholas looked it up. Brogan is derived from the Gaelic for shoe, fitting because part of the Collins fortune was also derived from shoes. Who knew?

His younger sister Marcia, heir apparent to the family fortune, was a Congresswoman, closely connected to the US president. The Collins family was immensely rich, its wealth controlled by the father.

Diverting as it was, Nicholas emerged from the internet rabbit hole with enough to provide an inconclusive paragraph with which to pad out his report.

Just after 10.00 one of the receptionists appeared carrying a sealed courier file. For the first time in three years, Nicholas had a physical file to look at rather than an electronic document. The file was cardboard, dusty and faded. It was held together by several elastic bands, which had gone hard over the years and snapped when he tried to remove them. The file was titled SANDMAN – DET and had been annotated in a different hand, "killed in motorcycle accident - February 1980." The file was reassuringly bulky, but completely uninformative.

This was unlike any file he had seen before. The inside cover sheet bore the photograph of a tabby cat, and every field of the summary had been completed with the phrase NOT KNOWN. Turning the pages revealed a copy of Amateur Photographer magazine, some blank copier paper, two copies of the Evening Standard and a dog-eared edition of Punch magazine. All were dated February 1980 and dated in the sense that Punch's jokes had not worn well with the passage of time. Amateur Photographer Magazine seemed appallingly sexist and there were rather more pictures of naked pre-teen girls than could be justified on artistic grounds. If I'm caught with this, I will be sent for a week's sexism awareness training mused Nicholas.

With just a date of death to go on, Nicholas decided to go at the problem a different way. He searched the Passport Office database of births, marriages and deaths. Narrowed down to just January to March 1980 the numbers came down appreciably. Filtering the file on road traffic accidents got the numbers down further, with the last cut being just motorcycle accidents. There were twelve, one of whom might fit. SANDMAN's motorcycle accident might have been outside the UK, he reasoned, but this gives me something to go on. He listed the twelve names as an appendix to the report.

The next topic to tackle was Operation CLARET. There was nothing if he focused the search on Ireland, but CLARET had covered a number of different operations over the years. A quick Google search and a dive into the internet revealed that Britain had engaged in a secret war with Indonesia in the 1960's. Unauthorised, officially deniable cross border incursions into Indonesia by British special forces were given the sobriquet CLARET.

Also unauthorized was an attempt to inspect the undersides of a visiting Soviet cruiser in 1956. An hour of research got Nicholas to where he would have been in seconds if he Googled it. He would not be able to link the dead frogman of operation CLARET to Northern Ireland.

Chapter 4

2024

12th June - Thursday
Economic Intelligence Unit. Victoria Street, London. Nicholas.

Nicholas had returned from lunch at the Subway sandwich shop. For the next hour or so anyone looking at his screen would have seen a spreadsheet of fiendish complexity. He was trying to work out how many combinations of sandwiches he could have chosen from. There were seven types of bread, available toasted or not, eight cheeses again toasted or not and about a dozen types of meat. There were twelve salad items and twelve different dressings. Total number of permutations came out at 4.6 quadrillion, or did it? He was checking his maths when he noticed Fiona on her way towards him. He instinctively knew that neither Fiona nor indeed taxpayers in general would be enthusiastic if they learned what he was up to, so he closed the spreadsheet quickly.

"What was in the file you had sent up from the document archive" she queried. He showed her the file which she went through page by page. "Very interesting" she observed, implying the opposite. "Still on track for tomorrow morning?"

Nicholas reassured her "Yes, absolutely."

He returned to working through the list of fatal motorcycle accidents that had taken place in 1980. After some digging, he realized that two records were both odd and similar. Both deaths, one in February and one in March, took place in Sandwich in Kent. Just as he was thinking about Sandwich permutations, some co-incidence! Both were described as due to excessive speed, with no other vehicle involved. The February death was an adult male, the March one an adult female. A check on both names revealed that both had died once before, as children. "Fake identities" he mused. Further searches came up blank. "If this is all the digital world can tell me," he mused aloud "I will need to descend into the analogue abyss."

Fiona had heard him, "Do tell…"

Nicholas explained that he had exhausted the records held on the various databases and that he now needed to get access to the as yet unscanned paper records held in various archives. Fiona immediately suspected Nicholas's motives. The main archive was close to the big shopping mall at Westfield. She suspected that rather than working, Nicholas wanted to skive off and spend the day drifting round the shops.

Chapter 5

2024

13th June - Friday
Economic Intelligence Unit. Victoria Street, London. Nicholas.

Next morning, he emailed Fiona five solid pages of report, mostly cut and paste from internet sites.

About ten minutes later she summoned him. With airy hand gestures she conjured an imaginary powerpoint presentation into the air:

"This needs a second draft:

POINT ONE: we hold NO information in respect of Martin B Collins.

POINT TWO: we have NO record of any Operation CLARET in the context of Northern Ireland

POINT THREE: we hold NO information regarding any person using the workname SANDMAN.

Not more than fifty words. Also, this time, spell check it before you send it to me."

Reeling from the verbal bulleting, Nicholas obeyed and a little while later Fiona went past his desk on her way to the management floor. She gave him a thumbs up, so presumably all was well.

On her return she stopped at his desk. "We are meeting the Americans on Tuesday, so wear a suit and tie. In the meantime, follow up on those motorcycle deaths in 1980. See what you can find out about the DET's personnel and activities in Ireland and if you need to, get down to the document archive and see what files they hold. Most of this history stuff will probably never make it into the scanning process."

Chapter 6

2024

13th June – Friday (afternoon)
Economic Intelligence Unit. Victoria Street, London.
Nicholas.

Nicholas had travelled, deep in thought, to Shepherds Bush. He had a season ticket that covered this zone, but why not put in an expense claim for the fare on the tube anyway? What would Fiona do if she caught him? "The punishment is death!" He hadn't intended to say that aloud, but aside from the man sat opposite, nobody reacted.

Nicholas was strangely excited about getting access to the archive. He needed to dig into the paper records for this current enquiry, because the digital trail had gone cold. What he also knew was that the archive was a gold mine of interesting stuff, no longer relevant to current operations, but fascinating anyway.

He had been told that the document archive in Woodstock Road was difficult to find. On his phone he could see that Google Maps identified a Secret Service Document Archive as being at the end of the road. On a chain-link fence was a sign bearing an enormous heraldic crest, part lion, part fish, and which read "Secret Service Document Archive."

Nicholas presented himself at reception. The bored looking scruff behind the desk held out a tray. "All firearms, exploding pens, grenades, etcetera, please" he requested, "we know how deadly you double 0 agents can be."

"I'm not 00 anything" protested Nicholas.

The scruff's smile confirmed that this was one of his little jokes, "Well there's a surprise, phone please."

Nicholas did as he was told, and Scruff led him through the corridors to the archive office.

Apart from the scruff on reception, Miriam was currently the sole occupant of the Document Archive. She had joined the Service three years previously, graduate entry and on the upward trajectory towards greatness. Last Christmas, whilst still ascending, she had headed out to the office party. Her blonde hair had been pinned up, her make-up immaculate, a glittery sheath dress showed off her slender figure to advantage. The amount of cleavage displayed was just the right side of provocative. A smart new pair of high heels had taken her to a smidgeon under six foot in height. In her own estimation, she looked stunning. Bright and bubbly, she was going to make an impression.

It is a matter of record and much gossip that Miriam had left the party that evening with her career prospects trending down, big time. She had transitioned from shimmying glamour to projectile vomiting, center stage on the dance floor. The violence of projection, the quantities involved and her subsequent tumble from her heels, made her downfall the stuff of office legend. When a vacancy in Documents materialized soon after, her exile to Shepherds Bush was inevitable. She had, however, learned a valuable life lesson: when mixed in industrial quantities, mince pies, cherry brandy and vodka should not be taken together, particularly on an empty stomach.

Miriam looked up at Nicholas as he was led into the office. "Good afternoon, Mr Bond" she purred in her best fake Russian " we have been expecting you."

"I'm not Bond" responded Nicholas, falling in with the joke a little too late " um..I'm French, Nicholas French." His attempt at a Sean Connery accent was unconvincing.

Miriam switched to an atrocious 'Allo 'Allo style French accent. "French eh…Zen walk wiz me to zees interesting files, wot we have."

 Nicholas realized where he had seen her before: "Christmas Party" he blurted.

"Fuck you" came the reply. That rather killed the mood and Miriam reverted to her natural accent, which marked her out as a Londoner.

The files in question were from the same archive box as the SANDMAN file he had received the day before.

"These only turned up by chance, if you hadn't requested the SANDMAN file, they would probably have been destroyed. They are from a batch supplied by the Army and seem to date from the 80's. Judging by the box, it's been through various document stores before it came to us."

She took him through the first few files. "These all relate to vehicles, purchased, maintained and long since sold or scrapped." She put those to the side.

"These two are more interesting." The first file bore the title: ICEMAN DET Newry. Written below was "Died March 1980 – Motorcycle accident." Inside was a photograph of a tabby cat, the same details sheet marked NOT KNOWN in every field and a selection of periodicals. There was Punch from December 1979, Cosmopolitan January 1979 and two copies of Exchange and Mart. "The Cosmopolitan is interesting reading, but frankly this file tells us nothing."

"The SANDMAN file was the same" said Nicholas, "whatever these files held originally, it appears that someone wanted to cover their tracks."

Miriam handed him the last file. It simply bore the title LOBSTER. Like the others, inside it had a picture of a tabby cat and more magazines and papers. "So far as I can tell, these are the only files which were doctored in this way."

"But look" said Miriam "the LOBSTER file is different from the two DET files. It looks more like the MI6 folder from back then. Something links SANDMAN, ICEMAN and LOBSTER. Something that happened in Ireland in the late 70's. Perhaps MI6 had an interest in LOBSTER, which they concealed. To make it watertight the other two identities had to be hidden as well. Do you have any clues as to who LOBSTER might be?"

Nicholas made his way back to the office. He was slightly startled by the smile and wink he got from the security guard at the door. Both women on reception winked at him. As he got into the lift, he could hear them behind him, cackling with laughter. The Unit Director and Deputy Director joined him in the lift. As they both exited to the next floor, both turned back and gave exaggerated winks. Unnerved, Nicholas headed back to his desk.

Fiona came over at once. "Did you, by any chance, hand your phone to the receptionist at Woodstock, without locking it first?" Nicholas couldn't remember, but Fiona was pointing at his screen. The message header read "Tinky Winky is off games." An email, with his name on it, had gone to everyone in the Department. "I have contracted an exotic sexually transmitted disease and will be unavailable for romantic purposes, Love and Kisses, Nicholas French, WINK! WINK!" Nicholas stared at it, feeling sick." "Someone in Communications Security had just sent round a message headed, "Lock your devices, don't be a winker."

"This will haunt me forever" thought Nicholas.

Chapter 7

2024

29th June - Sunday
Port Solent, Portsmouth Harbour, England.
Pauline.

Port Solent sits at the top of Portsmouth Harbour. Just across the water is the flinty stone walled Porchester Castle, built by the Romans. By contrast, Port Solent is a modern marina, brick-built shops, restaurants and houses encircling the harbour. Double locks protect the moored yachts from the vagaries of the tides and the surrounding buildings give shelter from the wind.

One such yacht, Sea Bear, was currently tied up to a pontoon. The yacht was chartered out most weeks. She bore the battle scars of previous charters, of pontoons hit and other sundry bumps and bangs. Nevertheless, she sailed well, was comfortable and well equipped. Her current occupants had chartered her for well over a month now and Sea Bear was beginning to feel like home.

The suntanned lady sitting in the cockpit of Sea Bear was happy to chat with anyone. Simply ask "where are you from?" and you would not get away before you had been told the whole story.

Pauline Thomas was an Australian, a Cronulla girl, meaning she had been born in the Sydney suburb of Cronulla, nearly sixty years ago. She went to school in Cronulla, supported the Sharks and surfed from the beaches. Like her parents, before her, she was a keen sailor and member of the Cronulla Sailing club. Glorious weekends were spent doing up the old clubhouse, enjoying BBQ's or sailing Botany Bay and the Australian coast.

She had met her husband, Pete, at the club. He was a newcomer, moving to Australia from the UK in his twenties. Shy, he kept himself to himself, but she liked him. They drifted together, often literally as they crewed on the same yacht and winds could be light. Pete was a policeman, a trainee at first. Once he had passed out of training, he was initially based in Sydney.

In 1986 he successfully applied for transfer to Cronulla and they married. As her father had shouted at the wedding "about bloody time." Pete did well in the force, was promoted and finally retired in 2023. As a couple, they had never been outside Australia, usually their holidays took them to Darwin, Melbourne or sailing out in the Whitsundays. Now they had come to the UK, on the big retirement holiday, long dreamed about. The plan was to take in the world capital of sailing, Cowes and the Solent.

With them was their daughter, Jenny, now in her late twenties. Pauline had just the one child, as Jenny had "bloody near killed her, I was thirty hours in labour before they popped her out!"

Now the three of them were living on Sea Bear and exploring the Solent. They had spent nights in Cowes itself, visited the Island Sailing Club with its flags and historic dining room. The Hamble, Beaulieu River. Southampton Water and Osborne Bay had all passed under their keel. Pete and Jenny were down below, planning a route to Brighton. Jenny had heard it was a modern Sodom and Gomorrah, so worth a visit.

Chapter 8

2024

30th June - Monday
Port Solent, Portsmouth Harbour, England.
Pauline.

Taking advantage of the east running tides required a very early start, so as dawn was breaking, they radioed ahead, motored the yacht from its berth and into the lock. The channel leading through Porchester lake had barely enough water in it for their draught, but with a close eye on the chart plotter they left Porchester Castle behind them, passed the moored aircraft carrier, then HMS Victory and the Royal Dockyards. With the tide starting to push eastward they reached the Solent Fort at Spithead and headed out beyond the Owers. As the sun rose higher, the wind picked up and they pushed forward under full sail in a comfortable Force 3. It was still chilly, so when Pauline appeared on deck it was to bring hot coffee and not the cold beer that would be called for back home. As the Millennium tower at the entrance to Portsmouth Harbour began to recede into the distance, Pete was looking back at the Solent, "Bloody expensive, but worth it."

The wind was picking up quickly now, a force 4 or so, then after about twenty minutes up to force 5, they reefed down and pushed on. Away to the North they could see the low-lying promontory of Selsey Bill and further along the coast, Worthing. There were dark rain clouds over the land and the wind was strengthening. The waves were getting bigger, so the whole boat was pitching more. Pete moved around below decks putting away any items that might fly about.

Once they had passed the Outer Owers buoy, they were well clear of the potentially treacherous shallows that lay off Selsey Bill. They could now steer a direct course to Brighton. Away to their right were huge wind turbines, making up the Rampion Windfarm. "I suppose you should expect a lot of wind wherever you see a windfarm" remarked Jenny. By the time they had reached Brighton Marina the sea had become rougher, and the wind came in fierce gusts that made the boat heel. They furled away the jib, dropped the mainsail and motored towards the entrance. "We'll sort out fenders and lines once we are in the shelter of the marina" called Pete, "let's not take any chances."

They had phoned ahead the night before, to book a berth. When Pete went below to call on the VHF the marina office was expecting them and answered with instructions to take berth 8-13. "Look for pontoon 8" Pete had called up from the cabin. Pauline maneuvered the yacht into the fairway next to pontoon 8, but it looked as if every space was taken. To make matters worse, she couldn't see the numbers for the individual berths.

"What number are you looking for?" called a man who was sitting in the cockpit of one of the boats tied alongside the pontoon.

"8-13" she answered.

"It's on the other side of the pontoon" the man replied. "Turn round and come into the next fairway along, I will stand on the end of the pontoon to take your lines." The man left the cockpit and headed along the pontoon, together with a second, younger man who had been in the cockpit with him.

Pauline neatly swung into the berth and Jenny handed the center spring to the older man. He quickly cleated it off and then Pauline handed him the stern line.

"Are you all right? Pass me the line." It was the younger man calling up to Pete who was stood on the bow. Pete was stock still, clutching the rope to him. He gasped and then fell backwards onto the deck.

Jenny ran to him and prised the rope from his hands. "Dad, dad, what's wrong with you?"

Pauline killed the engine and went forward. The two men tied the boat off and stood by, looking concerned. Pete was dazed. They helped him below and Jenny made him a cup of coffee. Gradually, sipping the coffee, Pete regained his composure.

"Should we call an ambulance?" The older man asked, "Has this happened before?"

"No ambulance" muttered Pete. He looked from the young man to the older and then back again. Looking directly into the older man's eyes, Pete seemed to be questioning what he was seeing. He looked hard at the younger man again. "It's uncanny, I see it now...he's just like..." there came a look of realization. "Oh my god", he turned to the older man "you must be... the Sandman?" he said.

The older man looked back, but did not reply.

The younger man had introduced himself as Andy. He offered to show Jenny to the marina office, so she could sign them in. The two of them sorted out the connection to the shore power, then hatched a plan to go into Brighton together on the bus.

Once they were gone, the older man, who had introduced himself as Martin, had returned to his own boat. It was called Wanderer. Pauline and Pete joined him and there was a chance to introduce themselves more fully. Martin showed them over his boat, which was not quite as big as Sea Bear, but still comfortable for two people. It was a more traditional design, long keeled and cutter rigged, he had explained.

Once they had gone back aboard Sea Bear, Pauline and Pete sat together. "What happened Pete?" she asked. "Why did you call him Sandman?"

Pete was guarded, "he reminded me of someone I once met, before I came to Australia. It just took me by surprise. The lad Andy is the dead spit of the person I met all those years ago. It was like seeing a ghost and it just startled me. It's nothing."

Pauline was intrigued but knew not to push, she knew nothing of Pete's life in England before he had emigrated. All he would ever say was that he was raised in an orphanage and that he had a tough childhood. If she kept asking, he clammed up and looked away. In time she learned not to ask. When they were first married, he would have terrible nightmares, twisting and turning, sweating and mumbling. "Please don't, no, no, please don't" he would slur, covering his sleeping face with his hands. He would start, awakening with a look of absolute terror in his eyes, then, seeing her concerned face, relax and sleep again.

Pete would simply not talk about the nightmares. As time passed, they eased and eventually subsided away to nothing. Little details of Pete's past would sometime slip out, but she said nothing and kept her counsel. When Jenny was little, she had heard Pete tell her that her hair was like his mother's. Another time he mentioned that Grandad had been a fisherman but realized that he had slipped up and said no more. One evening after a really bad day at work, he had drunk a little too much and staggered to bed worse for wear. "A fine fucking birthday this has been" he had told her. "Strange," she had thought, "his birthday was still three months off."

Chapter 9

2024

30th June - Monday
The West End, London
Geraldine.

There is shopping which is mundane, and there's shopping which is self-gratifying retail indulgence. Geraldine was shopping and it was very much the latter category that applied. She had a half day and was doing what she did best, spending money on herself.

Yesterday was her day at the Spa Covent Garden. She had been going there since the 80's and loved the ambience. In those days she had not looked entirely out of place amongst the slender ballerinas and celebrities who were her fellow patrons. Since then, she had swelled to three times her former size. Everything had got bigger. Yesterday she had been starved, massaged, scrubbed, treated and polished. She had emerged feeling renewed, confident that, yet again, she had turned the clock back. A more dispassionate observer might have thought "mutton dressed as lamb", if so, it was a very ample serving of lamb.

Geraldine always travelled by taxi and expensed it to the Service. Anyone else would have been hauled over the coals for this sort of extravagance, but her role as a Controller allowed her to submit her expenses as an undocumented subset of other operational expenses, so she could come to no harm.

First stop was Charbonnel and Walker, purveyor of luxury chocolates, in the Royal Arcade off Old Bond Street. They had greeted her there like an old friend, for indeed this was one of her favorite destinations. While the taxi waited, she had agonised, considered and finally settled for the Boit Rouge, Fine Milk and Dark Chocolate, with alcohol, which was priced at £160.00. To her mind that was a modest, mid-range box of chocolates, almost economical, so she added £15.00 worth of Peter Rabbit chocolate Bunnies to top things up.

Next stop was Rigby and Peller in Conduit Street. Yesterday, the girl at the Sanctuary had suggested she might consider "going up a size." In reality, this had been tact in the extreme. Last year's bra had been adequately dimensioned on its day, now the battle was lost by some margin. She emerged after about an hour bearing her collection of newly acquired finery. It was pretty enough to have delighted Marie Antoinette yet possessed a structural integrity that Isambard Kingdom Brunel might have endorsed.

Next stop was in Chiswick. The new bike lane had introduced chaos to the High Road and the taxi driver was at his wit's end trying to find a parking place.

Geraldine wandered into the antique shop, drifted around looking at various items. The owner, Gregory, seeing she was there, came over to help. He drew her attention to a Victorian letter writing set. It was a polished mahogany box, with brass hinges and an escutcheon engraved with "Letters." Inside it was lined with green baize and subdivided into spaces for paper, envelopes, writing implements and stamps. Geraldine liked it, haggled the price down and then agreed to purchase it. She paid cash. At her request, the shop owner wrapped the box.

She returned to the taxi just in time to catch the driver telling a parking warden to "fuck off back to Poland." She smoothed things over, but not before the warden had in his turn told the taxi driver to "fuck off back to Turkey." London is cosmopolitan and diverse; what racism there is, tends to be imprecisely calibrated. Neither had identified the other's ethnicity correctly, making the insults sting even more.

Geraldine had breezed into the Service's office in Victoria. The man on security detail had embarrassed himself when he made the obligatory bag search. He didn't admit it until afterwards, but he had not immediately realized it was a bra and knicker set he was looking at. As he started to inspect the items, he realized he was getting a somewhat fierce look from Geraldine. He moved things along without even looking at the other items.

Back in her office Geraldine considered her priorities. A chocolate Peter Rabbit was devoured. She unwrapped the wooden box. Inside it was £2,000 in cash and a luggage label. The label bore numbers, laid out in groups of four. From the bottom drawer she took out a well-worn book. Using the book, she decoded the label. She then discarded the label and her transcription of it in the secure document disposal bin in the corridor.

Meanwhile, the owner of the antique shop had performed a similar decoding job, on Geraldine's message to him. He had found a luggage label between the banknotes with which she had paid him earlier. Her message read "Get me Tickets for Wimbledon men's final."

That night a member of the office services team collected the secure document disposal bin from the corridor outside Geraldine's office. He wheeled it down to the basement. He did not take it to the shredding area but took a detour to an anonymous meeting room deep in the building. He knocked on the door. When told to enter, he wheeled the bin in and unlocked it. "Will that be all, ma'am?"

"Yes, thank you" the woman seated at the desk replied. "Same again tomorrow, remember, not a word of this." Her ice blue eyes contemplated him coldly.

As he walked away, he thought "there is no chance of me saying anything about this to anyone." The woman was smart, friendly and affable. She also managed to convey an air of absolute ruthlessness.

Fate is fickle. The woman in the basement was checking up on Geraldine because the Director of the Economic Intelligence Unit liked cars. Bernard ran his little outstation in Victoria effectively, but in the Service was seen as an odd bod. He had no field or international experience to call upon, just a background in tracking down financial and computer fraud.

Bernard was the man who would be called in when it was necessary to "follow the money." He had developed a nose for where the money went, which was usually on pointlessly expensive items. He had a fine eye for watches and handbags, scarves and shoes, big boys' toys of all descriptions, that didn't quite go with the individual's earning capacity. When it came to explanations for unexpected wealth, he was cynical. Every tale of a rich recently deceased relative in Switzerland or a lucky bet coming home got his antennae quivering.

A blue Mercedes AMG GT63, with all the trimmings cost well over two hundred grand. Bernard had seen it whilst on a day out in Whitstable. The car was not that unusual, but what had caught his attention was who was driving it. He had taken a quick picture on his iPhone and forwarded it to someone he trusted. The accompanying message was one character "?".

Chapter 10

2024

31st June - Tuesday
Trafalgar Square Hotel, London.
Fiona.

The two CIA operatives looked like school kids, thought Fiona.

"Pleased to meet you Ms. Perry, Mr. French." They introduced themselves as Peter Griffin and Lisa Simpson.

"Worknames, I presume" Nicholas had asked.

 "Yeah, we didn't realize you got those TV shows over here" answered Peter, "it's been awkward, we just had to pass it off as a co-incidence."

"Coincidences are suspect" intoned Nicholas recalling the mad professor's lectures in training.

Fiona smiled, "you've seen our response to the CIA's list of queries, we have drawn a blank I'm afraid."

Lisa was ready for this. She looked as if central casting had supplied her rather than the CIA. She had perfect teeth, big brown eyes and dark hair, that looked almost black. Her skin suggested healthy outdoors woman rather than bookworm. "Yes, thank you for replying so promptly. We would like to share some information with you on a confidential basis, in the expectation that it may help us to move things along. Are you familiar with the M60?"

"Well yes," Nicholas was puzzled, "it's a ring road around Manchester, it's in Lancashire."

Lisa looked at him like he was an idiot. Nicholas was on the point of saying "don't use your fucking Paddington Bear hard stare on me missy...", but he realised that discretion should be the better part of valour in this instance.

In a slightly exasperated tone, Lisa read from her iPad: The M60, officially the machine gun, Caliber 7.62mm, is a family of American general-purpose machine guns firing 7.62x51mm NATO cartridges from a disintegrating belt of M13 links. There are several types of ammunition approved for use in the M60, including ball, tracer and armour piercing rounds."

"It was adopted in 1957 and issued to units beginning in 1959. It has served with every branch of the US military and still serves with the armed forces of other states. Its manufacture and continued upgrade for military and commercial purchase continues into the 21st century, although it has been replaced or supplemented in most roles by other designs, most notably the M240 machine gun in U.S. service."

Lisa placed a photograph of an M60 machine gun on the table in front of them.

Nicholas feigned recognition, "Ah yes, that M60, the machine gun. Not in Lancashire, and…."

"And," continued Lisa, "as you know, we are seeking to trace the movements of Martin B Collins, who the White House are greatly interested in finding."

She placed a picture of Collins in front of them.

"We have established that on 14th June 1979 Martin Collins purchased 10 M60 machine guns and a significant quantity of 7.62mm belted ammunition for use thereof. Our colleagues in the FBI have discovered that the consignment was initially delivered to a Charleston address."

Peter took up the story. He was in his late twenties, hair cut too short, slightly overweight. Like a shaved hamster in an expensive suit, thought Nicholas.

"There is the suggestion that the arms were then placed in a container that was shipped initially to Liverpool. Subsequently that same container was taken by road and ferry to Dublin. We believe that Martin Collins travelled on that same ferry and would have been in Dublin at the beginning of August '79."

Nicholas and Fiona leaned forward in anticipation of a picture of the ferry, but that, sadly, had eluded the CIA.

Lisa now read from a prepared statement, "it is our understanding that Collins met with senior Republicans during his visit to Dublin. He was present at a number of social events and rallies."

"What are your sources?" asked Fiona.

Lisa continued: "Since this operation was initiated by the Office of the President, we have had the full co-operation of the FBI, CIA and other agencies. This enabled us to track the purchase and shipping of the M60's. The Irish authorities, after a request at the highest level, provided full co-operation. They confirmed Collins' presence in Dublin. The Irish authorities have discreetly engaged, on our behalf, with former members of the IRA, who have confirmed the details."

"Engaged discreetly?" said Fiona.

"Yes, they wanted tickets for the Rugby World Cup. In exchange, they told us everything we wanted to know. We got them a box and about twenty of them went over to France at our expense."

"Go on…"

"Well, it seems that in 1979 Collins was a wealthy, enthusiastic young man, wanting to do his bit for the freedom fighters. The IRA saw him as a cash cow to be milked. He pushed hard for a chance to fight the Brits. The IRA didn't want him killed, so they came up with a plan to keep him happy with no risk. There was concern that he might go off on his own, do something silly and get killed or captured. From what they said, he was indiscreet, idealistic and stuck out like a sore thumb. If he went North, there was a strong chance of him being picked up. There was also a pragmatic consideration. If they didn't give him a chance to "do his bit", then he might well find his way to another group of freedom fighters, taking his cash and guns with him."

"They sent him up to the border with a young man, a volunteer considered to be sensible, a safe pair of hands with no track record of military activity. The idea was that they would be able to get up to the border area without attracting attention. The plan was to pick a remote area, without witnesses or the risk of running to the authorities and stage an attack for the American's benefit. They were to fire on the Brits at long range, hopefully with no risk of return fire and then run for safety. The two of them headed off to Armagh in a van, taking one of the M60's and enough ammunition to make some noise."

"Go on…"

"They were never seen again."

"So, what happened? "Asked Fiona

"We believe that someone using the workname SANDMAN was involved. The Irish Special Branch were tapping a phone line between Dublin and the North. The contact in the North mentioned that the SANDMAN had been active at around the time of the disappearances."

Lisa handed over another picture. "This is Eastney Barracks, home of the Royal Marines Museum. It's now closed, but it was possible for us to look at its online archive and view items in its collection. We led the curator to believe that we were potentially providing funding for a joint exhibition about the US Rangers and the British Commandos."

"Our particular interest was one exhibit, a M60 machine gun, captured in Northern Ireland, by 40 Commando in 1979. The serial number had been posted online when the Museum's collection was catalogued. It came up when we searched using the original sales record from the manufacturer. We examined the gun held in the collection and were able to confirm that the serial number did indeed match one of the batch supplied to the IRA by Collins. The curator didn't know how it came to be in the collection. He was happy to put us in touch with an ex-marine who he thought might know about its capture."

"And what did the ex-marine tell you?"

"Nothing yet, when we reported back, we were told to contact you guys so you could send someone along. We have arranged to meet him in Poole tomorrow."

"No problem, we will send along a couple of people. Nicholas, you take it, and we'll find someone to go with you."

Chapter 11

2024

30th June - Monday
London's South Bank, opposite Parliament.
Miriam.

Miriam had been summoned to Thamesbank House. She had been signed in and sent to the senior management suite. As she sat waiting to be called, she recognised the feeling of impending doom. Miriam had only ever seen Bernard Chester, the Director once before and that was at the Christmas party. His look of surprise as she vomited over him, plagued her nightmares. She began to worry that a repeat performance might be coming on. "Think, relax, control the emotion" she thought to herself.

She could clearly recall the day during her training when the instructors had driven them through the Welsh rain and parked up. They couldn't see what was happening outside, but one by one, the trainees were motioned to jump down from the lorry. Through the canvas sides, those who remained could hear yells, followed by a splash.

When her turn came, Miriam had been led to the parapet of a bridge. About 60 feet below was a river, which had created a pool below the bridge. The member of the training team had said to her, "when I tell you to jump, you will jump, remain upright, keep your knees together or the water will rush up your fanny and blow out your eardrums, do you understand?" She had nodded. There was a pause. Logically, she reasoned this must be safe, otherwise there would be a pile of bodies down there and she could see the previous jumpers all sat watching on the bank. Still a pause. There was a terrible feeling of anticipation. She looked at the trainer. He said nothing. Why the delay? She looked down again. "Jump!" There was a terrible feeling of doing something stupid and unnatural, but she jumped. The feeling of falling made her whole-body tense. She hit the water and found herself plunged deep in the cold depths. She swam to the side and clambered out. "Eardrums intact?" one of her fellow trainees had asked. She had grinned.

"Just before that jump, that's how I feel now", she thought. A framed Japanese woodcut hung on the wall. She studied it, a calming distraction.

After a few minutes the P.A. had shown her into the Director's office. When Miriam entered, he was sat behind his desk. He got up and ushered Miriam over to the meeting table. A dark haired, immaculately dressed woman was sitting at the table, looking at her intently. The woman had piercing blue eyes, Miriam tried to meet her gaze but found she could not; she looked down. No introduction was made, but evidently this was someone to be taken very seriously.

Miriam was conflicted. Should she apologise for the Christmas party or simply wait until spoken to. Somehow her brain was telling her to do both.

"Miriam" began the Director, "can I ask if you have applied for employment outside of the service recently?" She hadn't seen that coming.

Honesty was the best policy she decided, "That's correct, I have applied for roles at JP Morgan and Citigroup."

"What led you to decide to look outside the Service?"

"Um, well, I felt I had damaged my prospects within the Service, due to an unfortunate incident."

"What did you do? The woman had asked.

Miriam paused. She closed her eyes at the memory. "I was sick over the Director and about a dozen others at the Christmas party. I was re-assigned to archives immediately afterwards, I am so sorry, desperately sorry, I was so ill afterwards I thought I might die, in fact, I hoped I would."

The woman turned to the Director. "Why do I never get to go to these parties, it sounds like a wild time was had by all."

The Director was smiling, "I ended up dancing the night away in a pair of trousers borrowed from someone else, who was about twice my size. I looked like Charlie Chaplin." Miriam was pleased to see he could smile about it now. On the night he had looked as if he was about to have her killed.

The Director continued. "Miriam, you're not going to get either of those jobs. Despite your erm…projectile indiscretion, we have something of significance for you to do. Something which is vital to the safeguarding of the service."

Miriam was a little surprised, particularly by that last phrase, which she had assumed was only said in spy novels. She nodded her agreement before she knew what it was. For a moment, lurid possibilities flashed through her head, Iran, Pakistan, Moscow…

"Miriam, you will already be aware that we are dealing with a request for information about one of our operatives from back in the 70's, called SANDMAN. This request comes from the US President, via the PM, so we must take it seriously. Now I can tell you that, no matter how carefully the files are searched, you will find nothing of value on SANDMAN."

Miriam explained that Nicholas had visited her, the files they had found and the mysterious absence of detail in the files for SANDMAN, ICEMAN and LOBSTER.

The Director was pleased. "That's excellent, Miriam, you will join the team working on this and let's take it through to a point where the Americans are happy. However, that is not your prime purpose in this. What I am now telling you will not be repeated to anyone outside this room. You will report only to this lady, you will keep no records. Am I clear?" Miriam nodded her agreement.

The woman introduced herself, after a fashion. "Miriam, my role in the Service, is to identify potentially hostile individuals and to neutralise the threat they pose." She gave a wry smile, "sometimes you will hear me referred to as a ratcatcher."

She was watching for Miriam's reaction; seeing agreement, she continued, "I want you to work with your colleagues to satisfy the American interest in SANDMAN. You must help them find out what they need to know, being careful to ensure they only learn what we want them to know. To everyone it will appear that you are just a useful extra person to have on the team, to help with the logistics. Behind the scenes, you will work for me. My agenda is different. I want to know why they have an interest in SANDMAN, who initiated the enquiry and find out what they intend to do with the information."

Miriam was about to ask a question, but the woman pressed on. "Anyone showing an interest in SANDMAN is suspect. It may seem like ancient history, but some aspects of SANDMAN's work are still relevant today. What you need to know is that, thanks to Bernard, the ratcatchers are currently looking hard at a member of the service. This individual has two characteristics that we find intriguing: firstly, a lifestyle inconsistent with their salary and secondly, a continued curiosity about SANDMAN. This individual has no reason, operational or otherwise, to have access to information on SANDMAN. Now that we are looking more closely at this person, it has been realised that they have been trying to get access to information on SANDMAN off and on over many years. We need to understand why and specifically, on whose behalf."

Miriam was thinking about the files she had found for Nicholas. "Can I ask who you are looking at, surely it can't be Nicholas French?"

Bernard was amused "Definitely not Nicholas, this investigation goes back a long way. Nicholas is working under instruction to help the Americans. He knows nothing of the ratcatcher's involvement. We'll keep it that way, so Nicholas can play the investigation with a straight bat."

Miriam was already thinking about where the investigation might lead. "The files were annotated to show that SANDMAN and ICEMAN died in 1980. If we don't have records, where is this likely to get us?"

"We believe that SANDMAN and ICEMAN are both alive somewhere. We are certain about ICEMAN, who is hiding in plain sight. We have lost track of SANDMAN, we don't have an accurate identity or location to go on."

"They both were involved in a project that was run in the late 70's during the Irish troubles. It was a covert surveillance program, but the team made up of SANDMAN and ICEMAN went rogue. Their brief was to be covert and unobtrusive, definitely no active measures. Then bodies started popping up all over the place. They started to work to a different agenda, one we never really understood."

"The other file you mention, LOBSTER, relates to someone who was not a member of the team, but an IRA member they handed over to the Army. LOBSTER is in long term witness protection, new identity, the full works."

"May I ask what happened?"

"To be candid, we don't really know. SANDMAN and ICEMAN believed that they were compromised and that their identities had become known to the opposition. They never explained what made them think this, however they started to cover their tracks very effectively. It's possible that they gave themselves away because of something they did. It is also possible that someone within the Service gave them away. The problem is that very few people within the Service would have known about them in any detail. For a while we believed they were both dead, but in time we realised that one of them was alive and had assumed a new identity."

"They dropped out of sight, but not before they had given us enough information to roll up one of Moscow's most ambitious and deepest penetrations of the Service, the Government and the media. That coup has remained one of our most secret successes. It's also a complete mystery as to what happened. They were tasked to operate against the terrorist threat in Ireland. We know that is where they were operating. Then without warning they disappear, leaving a trail of bodies and supplying enough surveillance information to put us on the trail of a sophisticated Russian penetration operation here in the UK

"Our success in dealing with that Russian network has been one of our most closely guarded secrets. Within the service only a handful know what happened and no one knows how it was done. Only the PM at the time was told and none of her successors were informed. From what we know, Moscow has an almost pathological interest in this affair. Their network which was blown was called Crocodile. We think that Moscow believes that someone on their team blew Crocodile and if that's true, that someone could be very high up by now. Maybe even the top man, or maybe one of his trusted oligarchs."

"Why don't we just leak the information and blow whoever it was out of the water? asked Miriam.

"There are two answers to that question. We don't know who it is. We were never aware of the Crocodile network until SANDMAN and ICEMAN gave us the initial lead. How they knew what was going on, we were never told. If someone in Moscow told them, we have no idea who it was or why. If it was a source in Moscow they never revealed themselves again. Some of our best minds have looked at this and it remains a mystery."

"What's the second reason?" asked Miriam.

"By creating uncertainty in Moscow's mind, we inject distrust and distraction. It also makes them take silly risks."

"I don't fully understand, what risks?"

"Think of it from Moscow's point of view," continued Bernard "if you knew that somewhere here in London was the scratch for this particular itch, might it not be worth setting someone to work to get access to the files and find out. Miriam, your job is to get involved, see what hares are set running and see who takes an interest. Over the years, a number of requests have been made to see the files on Crocodile. They are always refused. It is a secret that is passed from Director to Director, because some of the assets are still in play. For the time being, all you need to know is that the information on SANDMAN, ICEMAN and LOBSTER is within the Crocodile files."

Miriam was thoughtful, "I see, so the ratcatchers are looking at a potential mole within the Service. You hope that the renewed interest in SANDMAN might make the mole take risks and incriminate themselves?"

"Correct, I prefer the term embedded penetration agent, but if you must, yes, a mole. Your job Miriam is to play along. If there is a mole..." The Director banged his hand on the tabletop, "whack a mole." He mimed a pistol being fired.

Miriam took this to be bravado. Admittedly, the Director was part of the Top Team in the Service, but he ran a small part of it, which was made up of geeks who never went into the field. She doubted the Director had the authority to have anyone bumped off, let alone someone in the Service, mole or not. Furthermore, it was against the Service's stated policy to be bumping anyone off. Miriam exchanged looks with the dark-haired woman at the Director's side. She had remained impassive throughout. Now there was the faintest hint of amusement in her expression. The ice blue eyes betrayed the merest hint of a twinkle.

Chapter 12

1979

10th April - Tuesday
The Shannon Hotel, Capallmara Beach. Eire.
Moira.

The Northwestern coastline of Ireland is a place of extremes. When the sea is angry the surf piles up in foaming rollers from the Atlantic that thunder onto the beach. Those nights, the wind screams and plucks at the roof tiles. Yet on other days, peace itself reigns; calm and soft, gentle breezes, warm sun and quiet starry nights.

The Shannon Hotel was a place apart. It had been built in the 19th century when Victoria ruled Ireland. It lay on a granite fist of land, jutting into the Atlantic. The fist of granite was sand fringed, hence its local name, The Beach. To the confusion of most, the Hotel was nowhere near the River Shannon. It was named for its founders, the Shannon family. Save for an old stone circle it was the only construction on the headland. Locals would say it was "on the island", not technically true since there was a sandy neck of land connecting the headland to the village. Its remote location, about four miles beyond the village, gave it a certain discreetness which in turn made it popular with a particular type of clientele. For the gentleman from Belfast or up from Dublin and wishing to enjoy the favours of a lady who was not his wife, it offered every opportunity to avoid embarrassment. Should a gentleman happen to meet another gentleman of his acquaintance there, then the less said the better.

As ownership passed down through generations of the Shannon family the hotel became more respectable. Sturdy brickwork and well laid slates had stood the test of time. Less so the windows, for when the wind blew, they rattled and jumped while the nets and curtains danced in the draught. The woodwork on the balconies and soffits needed paint. Inside, some areas were newly painted and smart, but most were scuffed, faded and flaking in places. There was never enough money to do the whole place at once and it showed.

As to the clientele, the beaus and their floosies were long gone. When guests stayed, they were families in the summer, commercial travelers or builders who had taken on jobs locally. There was a bar, with limited opening hours, strictly for guests and the food of a somewhat bland and repetitive nature. For the gastronomically adventurous wanting more than hearty fare, there was salad cream and tomato sauce on every table.

A previous Mr. Shannon had been a staunch Republican. In consequence the current Mr. Shannon inherited an echo of his forbear's customers. More out of custom than any other reason, various elements of the IRA leadership would congregate at the hotel once a year for a get-together, or in corporate terms, an away day. These were not fighting men. Typically, they talked about fundraising rather than fighting. It was all very relaxing and jolly. At the end of the day little groups could be seen walking out over the sands, to shed socks and shoes to paddle in the sea.

Moira Shannon had just turned fifteen and was helping her parents at the hotel in the role of unpaid chambermaid. Moira was at an awkward age and knew it only too well. Since Christmas she had grown and now her clothes didn't fit properly. Her mother had put off a trip to the shops in Sligo saying, "Moira, these'll do for now, you've still got some growing up to do before we go spending money." Her mother didn't mean to wound, but that stung. Moira had known exactly what her mother was saying. She hated that she hadn't grown like the other girls. She was becoming tall and skinny and flat. She had no curves at all. When she stood in front of the mirror on bath night, she still looked more like a little girl than a woman. To make things worse, her mother still cut her hair into a little girl's pudding bowl fringe and bob cut. Flat too, no curls.

Moira had tucked herself away out of sight in a corner of the garden. On her knees her well-worn copy of "The Finucane Diamonds, A Sister Susan Crime Fighter mystery" lay open. Sister Susan was not like the nuns from school, but like Maria from the Sound of Music. From the corner of the garden Moira could see the old signal tower that faced out over the sea beyond the village. In her mind's eye it was just like the tower in the story. As Moira chewed her bookmark, Sister Susan faced the tower, then she was ascending the dark staircase that led up the tower. She had seen the jewel thieves' signal flash out over the waters. Revolver in hand,

Sister Susan climbed upwards... Moira's attention was taken by the sound of a vehicle approaching.

From the village with its solid little houses, whitewashed walls and deep-set windows, had come the sound of a wheezy, straining engine. Moira had watched as the yellow and white Volkswagen camper van gasped its way along the unmade road that led from the village towards the hotel. It was making heavy weather of the potholes, rolling, lurching and crashing. The two occupants seemed not to mind, they were singing "Summer Holiday" and whooping at each bump. "We're all going on a summer holiday, no more working for a week or two, fun and laughter on a …. this must be it." The van had reached the end of the road, literally as the track ended at the hotel carpark. She followed the van into the carpark and watched the young couple get out. He was tall, slim and bearded, she was blonde and pretty. They stretched and looked out over the beach.

"Thalassa Thalassa, the wine-red sea" sang the woman to the tune of Summer Holiday. It didn't quite scan, they smiled at each other. As they started to unload bags and cases, Moira walked over to them.

"Hullo there" said the woman looking directly into Moira's face, "who are you then, pretty one?" "You have the loveliest blue eyes, I bet you've already broken a fair few boys' hearts." Moira nodded, but in truth she doubted she had.

The couple checked into the hotel. They had called ahead and booked a large double room for ten weeks. Surrounded by bags and camera cases they signed the register as Alex Manning and Isobel Elliot.

"Not married?" Moira's mother had asked. It didn't really matter, the register had pages of Mr and Mrs Smiths who hadn't been married, let alone Smiths.

"Don't let the names fool you, I'm keeping my name," laughed Isobel, and they both waggled their hands to show wedding bands. "We are newly hitched and fancy free."

Alex and Isobel were photographers who had been commissioned to take photographs of the West Coast. They were English and the publisher was looking for the outsider's eye. Moira helped them carry bags to the room, showed them how to fill the bath from the water heater and warned which windows opened and which did not.

"Look at that view", Isobel told her, "You are so lucky to live here."

Moira looked and as she did, she noticed someone skulking behind a bush in the hotel garden. Fortunately, Isobel had not seen the skulking figure and turned back into the room.

Isobel had noticed Moira's book. "Sister Susan, new to me" she said opening the page at the bookmark. She read a little and looked at Moira with exaggerated seriousness. "Do all the nuns round here carry revolvers and go round shooting lanterns from crooks' hands?"

Moira suspected she was being teased, "Only when forced to confront a gang of desperate jewel thieves. Anyway, she wasn't always a nun, she's a crack shot, can pick locks and drives a car as fast as any man." Moira explained Sister Susan's back story, her devotion to the faith and her uncanny ability to spot the clues that the police had missed.

"Very commendable, it's good to know that if I had any jewels, and if they were stolen by desperados, I could call on a gun toting nun to get them back. It looks like you've read this book a hundred times. If you want something different you can always borrow one of mine" smiled Isobel.

A skulking man in the garden was also taking an interest in the new arrivals. In his own mind, Callum was a player. The main man. To everyone else he definitely was not a player. He was a small-town crook. He was a nuisance to be tolerated and avoided where possible. His father had been the relatively prosperous owner of a small building company. Soon after Callum's birth his mother's health had broken, the marriage fractured and in time, the family home had crumbled too, through neglect. His mother had gone to a place in the mental home and his father drank himself, by way of delusions to a place in the graveyard.

As a child, he had been a bully. Even to this day grown men remembered their childhood anger as Callum had knocked them to the ground, stolen a chocolate bar or smashed a toy. Grown women remembered him as the hair puller, spitter and snail thrower of their childhood. He had been a big child, stocky, strong and quick to punch.

After school, no job held him for long, a petty criminal looking for a gang to join. In time, the biggest gang happened upon him, and he became the IRA's man in the village. He remained a bully. He would go round collecting "for the cause" and if anyone seemed too reluctant there would be threats and sometimes more. Even the stoutest waverers would be cowed when they saw the pistol pushed into his waistband. He was now a very big man; acne had scarred his face in his teens and his hair worn in a greasy mullet ensured he precisely fitted the most frequent description of him: a fat ugly bastard. Although he was only 29, too many beers, pie and chip suppers and fags had given him the body of a forty-year-old well on his way to a first heart attack.

The family house had been bulldozed and a mobile home installed in its place. It was set well back in the dunes behind the village. From there Callum called Dublin once a week. He would give his contact an account of what was going on locally. It was always nothing to get excited about at all, but the man would listen, thank him and then pass the message up the line that all was "quiet at Capallmara Beach."

Today's call had been different. A young English couple had arrived at the hotel, and they seemed to have equipment with them.

"What sort of equipment?" asked his contact.

"I don't know, perhaps cameras" Callum was uncertain he had only got a glimpse as they had unloaded.

"I think you should keep a close eye on them" came the instruction "let me know when you find something." Once Callum had rung off, his minder passed on the message "all quiet at the beach."

Callum had positioned himself in the garden behind a bush. He watched the window of the couple's room, but he could not see in. He saw Moira and the English woman appear at the window for a brief while, then nothing for ages. It was getting dark, and the room light came on. At this angle all he could see was the ceiling.

"Callum, what are you doing?" It was Mrs Shannon; she had been to the village and come up behind him unnoticed. She looked up towards the window. The English girl was at the lighted window. She had just pulled her jumper over her head and was now taking off her t shirt.

"How dare you" snapped Mrs Shannon "you should be ashamed of yourself. Get away from here and if I see you around here again, I will call the police", The noise had bought Mr Shannon to the door, and he was looking hard at Callum. Callum slunk away, cursing for not having said anything, not able to think of what he could have said.

That night Mrs Shannon dreamt the dream again. She was in the stone circle, surrounded by darkness. She felt that someone was watching, someone in the shadows, she turned, but his slimy hands took her. She was dragged. Down into the water, into the kelp. The voice was saying "there's a strong chance we will lose both mother and baby." She was in pain, terrible pain, she was drowning. She was fighting for breath. Now she was awake, hot and sweating.

Her husband was looking at her. "The stone circle, the hospital when Moira was born?" he asked. She nodded and tried to get back to sleep. That dream always came when something bad was going to happen.

The next morning after breakfast Mrs Shannon had taken Isobel to one side. "I'm sorry to tell you this dear, but last night we scared off a peeping tom who was watching from the garden. He was watching you when …" Mrs Shannon mimed a jumper being taken off.

Isobel looked shaken, "Oh, I didn't think to close the curtains, I'm so sorry Mrs Shannon." "Did you get a good look at him?" Isobel moved closer and whispered "was he…..um playing with himself, do you think we should tell the police? You have a young daughter to think about."

In truth Mrs Shannon had not looked to see if Collum was "playing" or given any thought to whether Moira might be at risk. Now it was put to her, it came to her that yes, he might have been and yes, Moira might be at risk. Her concern had been the hotel's reputation, such as it was.

Later that morning, Mr Shannon came up to Callum outside his mobile home. "You will stay away from the hotel; you will stay away from my guests, and you will stay away from my daughter "he had firmly stated. Callum had protested that he was under orders from Dublin, but Mr Shannon had been equally adamant, "if I tell them, that my wife caught you in our garden with your dick in your hands, spying through binoculars on a young girl as she took her top off, they will take a dim view. Did they ask for a report on the wee English girl's tits? I have friends in Dublin too, you know. What if the English complain, had you thought of that? I do not want the police sniffing round my hotel looking for a flasher. Do not push your luck."

Moira had bumped into Callum later in the day. She was moping about in the dunes, and he came up to talk to her.
She found him to be creepy but was curious about his strange behaviour in the garden. "Why were you watching the English couple yesterday?" she had asked.

His reply surprised her. "I've heard from Dublin that they are spies; we must watch them and find out what they are doing." It all sounded implausible, but Moira had agreed to keep an eye on them and report back. She copied down Callum's phone number and agreed to call every evening. Moira had been happy to help. It was what Sister Susan would do if there were spies about and up to mischief.

The young couple were away most of the day, taking photographs. She had taken the pass key, gone through their room, careful not to disturb anything and found nothing. She had reported back to Callum that they had some clothes, guidebooks, some books about the Romans and some camera lenses. They kept themselves to themselves.

"Good work" Callum had said. "Follow them and see what they get up to."

Chapter 13

1979

20th April - Friday
The Church, Capallmara Beach. Eire.
Father Francis.

Word soon spread around the village that the English couple from the hotel were taking pictures. People with cats, was one version of the story. The west coast was the other. Father Francis had heard both versions, so wasn't surprised to find a man wandering round the churchyard, taking pictures.

Father Francis had greeted the young man "Is it cats you're looking for; I have one that's a Saint."

The man looked puzzled, introduced himself as Alex and the two of them sat on the bench by the church door.

A large tabby cat jumped up between them. "This is Saint Columba, my cat" explained the priest. "When I first came to the Parish, he just appeared, a tiny kitten, which tells you how long I've been here as he's getting to be quite an old cat now. He's the most calm and peaceful cat you will ever meet. He's good as gold, even with the Sunday school children, he sits and listens to my sermons, never misbehaves."

Alex had asked if he could take a photograph or two for the book. Father Francis held up Saint Columba so that they faced him cheek to cheek.

After a few pictures, Alex stopped, laughing "Got it" he said. "You'll see when I show you the picture."

Every now and then the couple sent off a parcel of film. A week or so later a parcel would arrive marked Photographs – do not bend. One of these pictures in hand, Alex walked up to the church and found Father Francis fixing a pew that needed the seat screwing down. Alex had handed the print over and the priest burst out laughing. Alex had caught man and cat both staring into the lens with the same expression. Father Francis was delighted and accepted the print graciously. There would be no question of payment Alex said.

Later that day Father Francis had walked along to Finn's and asked if he could frame a picture. Finn was a glazier by trade, but picture frames was a sideline.

"Would it be a cat picture by any chance?" Finn had asked. There on Finn's worksurface were about a dozen pictures of people he knew with their cats. One of the fishermen was shown holding out a sprat and his black cat reaching up to take it. In another the postmistress was touching noses with her cat. The young English couple have been busy. Everyone had the same question, "Do you think my one will make it into the book?"

When the priest handed the print over Finn had laughed, "that will be in the book for sure." "Tell me Father" he asked tipping his head to one side with mock seriousness "remind me which one is the priest and which one the cat?"

When Father Francis collected the framed print from Finn he was told an interesting snippet of gossip. The two English had gone into a pub further up the coast. When the girl behind the bar had asked what they wanted, one of the old men sat in the corner had called out, "we don't take orders from the English here." The man was probably just joshing, but the place had gone silent. Cool as a cucumber the young fella turns around and asks if he will get a drink, if he orders in Gaelic. Now the fella asks in Gaelic, but the funny thing is he can't remember the word for beer and ends up asking for a pint of fish. Quick as a flash his wife tells him "You've asked for a pint of fish" and corrects him. The old boys in the corner think the fish thing is a good laugh. Then she calls up to the barmaid that she may have to have beer as well because she doesn't know the Gaelic for the drink she wants.

"Ask for it in English dear, and I'll translate" calls one of the old boys."

"Bacardi and Coke" she says.

"That would be Bacardi and Coke" says he, and the whole place bursts out laughing. In no time at all, people were talking to them, giving them ideas for photographs, having their portraits done. "I'll tell you; it sounds like those two could charm the birds out of the trees if they wanted to."

The print of himself and St Columba, took pride of place in Father Francis' study. He would show it to visitors, tell the story and try to catch the way Finn had said it; "Tell me Father, remind me which one is the priest and which one the cat?"

Something about it made him reflect. He'd never thought about it before, but from his first day in the parish the cat had been his constant companion. It would sit and watch him while he worked. It would look intelligently at him when he talked to it. As a little joke he used to say grace over the cat food when he put it in the bowl. If he forgot, the cat would sit patiently looking up at him. Saint Columba would only eat once grace was said. When the sun shone Saint Columba would be in the church. His favourite spot was a patch of sunlight cast by one of the upper windows. As the sun moved, the patch of light would move in a slow arc across the floor and the cat would stir, move and settle to be always in the beam. On cold nights the cat's presence on the end of the bed was a comfort. "It's strange to think it, thanks to you Saint Columba, I have never been alone here."

Chapter 14

1979

10th April - Tuesday
The Shannon Hotel, Capallmara Beach. Eire.
Moira.

Moira was trying to keep the couple in view. She had followed them, keeping to the dunes as they walked along the broad sweep of the empty beach. Beyond the hotel there was no path and the beach curved away to a small cove. Once, a small coaster had grounded in the cove and the wreck's rusted red skeleton remained. Beyond the cove the cliffs began and there was no beach, only tumbled rocks. A tree had been washed up into the cove; the bark stripped by the waves to leave it white and skeletal at the water's edge. The couple headed for it and disappeared out of view. After a while she crossed the sand in a crouching run and peeped round the tree. They were both naked and the man had a camera in his hands. The woman was sitting with her back against the tree.

"Hello, Moira" she called, standing up and approaching her, "are you spying on us?"

Moira was embarrassed and flustered. Isobel was smiling at her. Neither of them made the slightest effort to cover up, Moira didn't know where to look.

"As you can see, we have nothing to hide" continued Isobel. Alex walked away towards the sea. "Are you eyeing up my fella" asked Isobel playfully. She had tilted her head on one side and looked in Alex's direction. "He's skinny, but he has a nice bum."

Alex had turned back towards them, "Come on in", he called.

"Nice flat stomach and..." Isobel laughed and smiled at her. "Come on in, can you swim?" Moira hesitated. "Please yourself" came the reply as Isobel scampered down the beach. Moira watched as the two of them splashed around in the water, swam a short distance into the waves and just mucked about like big kids They were so carefree. For a moment Moira considered stripping off and joining them, but memories of standing naked with the other girls in the school showers after hockey came flooding back.

Alex and Isobel dressed and the three of them strolled back up the beach.

"Let's go for fish and chips" Alex had called back, and he set off ahead.

Isobel gave Moira a knowing look, "Did we embarrass you? Didn't know where to look, did you?"

"Isobel", said Moira "I'm sorry if I seemed shy, I don't know much about boys, I was a bit confused about what might…. happen. "
Isobel looked at her in mock horror, "I should think not, oh you silly goose! did you think we were going to have an orgy on the beach? "

Over fish and chips, they chatted about photography, the Romans, the book they were planning and just life generally. When they parted, when Isobel gave her a peck on the cheek, Moira realised she was just a little in love with Isobel.

Moira told them the story of how the hotel came to also have a fish and chip counter. It seemed an odd combination, but it came from a boyhood passion for fish and chips on the part of Moira's father. As a young man he had travelled to Whitby in England and been apprenticed to a famous fish and chip shop. He had carried the knowledge back to the hotel, won over Moira's grandparents to the idea and converted an outbuilding into the chippy. He had set up his own little business. He had become a careful buyer of potatoes, so woe betide anyone trying to fob him off with anything but the best. Similarly, the fish had to be absolutely fresh from the sea. To set Mr Shannon talking about which oil to fry in was to lose a good half hour, after which you would come away no wiser, but at least aware of the choices. The chippie only fried on two days of the week, Friday and Saturday. A little queue would form, clutching shopping bags and passing on gossip.

In a rare lyrical moment Mr Shannon might tell a customer that they were at the meeting point of land and sea, to enjoy the best of both. "Coming together at the liminal place, potatoes from the fields behind us and this fish is from just beyond those waves there" pointing with his tongs at the sea. Neither was strictly accurate as the cod came from much further away and the potatoes from the other side of Ireland by lorry. It was true in spirit, which is what counts.

One morning the hotel took call after call on the phone. It seemed as if half the world was calling to say that a dead whale had come ashore and did the English couple want to come to photograph it for the book. As the morning wore on and the phones continued to ring, Mrs. Shannon would simply answer with, "if it's about the wee whale, they are already on their way."

The English couple came back pleased with their whale pictures. As the camper van sputtered up to the hotel, it was in darkness. While they were out, Moira had been in their room looking through their pictures, sneaking through their things when the lights had gone off with a bang, which had made her jump.

Alex and Isobel had managed to get the lights back on, they seemed to know a little about electric lighting from their photography studies. "What you have there Mr. Shannon, is a fuse box and wiring that are fifty years out of date. We've patched it as best we can, but you should think about getting someone in to look at it."

A new fuse box and wiring were purchased and for the next few weeks the power was off and then on most days. The electrician was busy with other jobs, so Alex did some of the work as a favour to the Shannons. Between them they rewired the hotel, room by room. Alex seemed to enjoy the work. According to the electrician, Alex was doing a good job of the wiring, well up to professional standard.

Moira continued to spy on the couple. She crept into their room and looked through the boxes of pictures that came back from the printers. There were some amazing pictures. Isobel had photographed two women looking out to sea, as their husbands set off in their fishing boat. They looked like statues carved with worry.

Alex and Isobel came down to breakfast one morning and realised that the Shannons were noticeably upset. The news was there in the paper, John Wayne was dead. He had been a great favourite with the family, as he had stayed in their hotel, together with others from a film crew. They had been making the film "The Quiet Man" at the village of Cong, which is down in Galway. Some of the filming had been nearby and for that brief time, the Shannon Hotel had been abuzz with Hollywood glamour. Mr. Wayne had stayed in the best bedroom and Maureen O'Hara in the second best. It was back in 1952, but Moira's parents had both met Mr. Wayne. It was recalled that film people drank like fishes and were rather pushy, but their presence was the topic of endless fascination for the locals. Now, Mr. Shannon had dug out a framed picture, signed by the man himself, wreathed it in black crepe and placed it prominently in the dining room.

Moira was beginning to feel guilty about spying on Isobel and Alex. She told Callum that she didn't think they could be doing anything wrong. Callum told her to keep looking.

That afternoon the three of them had walked down to the cove. Isobel had a cassette player and while the batteries lasted, she played Joan Baez and Joni Mitchell songs. Alex and Isobel stripped off and played in the waves. Isobel had handed her the camera and asked if she could photograph the two of them. The camera was a heavy Nikon camera, Isobel told her how to hold it and which button to press.

"You're not going to do... anything, are you?" Moira had asked.

Isobel had widened her eyes in mock horror, "What is it with you and orgies on the beach?" she asked, "you have too much imagination for one so young." They had stood arm in arm before her, smiling. "Say cheese." Click.

Moira continued to search through their room whenever they were away. She looked at the photos but could see nothing suspicious. There was one photo that she really liked. Alex had photographed Isobel by the old tree on the beach. The tree was bleached white by sea spray and sun. Isobel lay on her back staring up into the sky with her arms and legs draped over the tree branches. Apart from her upturned chin her face was hidden, her hair spread on the sand. Her naked body was laid out for the camera, every detail, every curve. Moira wanted her own body to be like that. She took the photograph and hid it in her room. Sometimes when she was alone, she would take the picture from its hiding place and trace a finger along the shapes of Isobel's body.

Moira had taken Isobel and Alex to see the stone circle. They walked around the stones taking photographs. Moira knew that couples who wanted a baby would come to the circle on the night of the full moon. If you were lucky a baby came, if you were not, a creature called the sprite would come and drag you into the sea. When she explained this to Alex, he had asked if this was where she had been conceived. She had never given the subject any thought, so shook her head, blushing.

Moira had become fascinated by the camper-van. Sitting in it, while Isobel boiled the kettle on the little gas stove, she had fantasized about traveling the world in a little van of her own. She imagined herself cooking corned beef fritters, beans and instant mash in some exotic location. Just like Isobel, she could sleep in the van, cook in the van, drive to exciting places; it would be ideal.

Isobel had punctured the bubble of her fantasy. "Have you thought about where you would take a bath every now and again or do your washing? What if you meet a handsome young man and want to take him back to your place? Although without that bath, perhaps the young men won't be interested. There's a lot to be said for staying in hotels and one day I suppose you will be the proprietor of the Shannon Hotel."

Chapter 15

1979

14th June - Thursday
The Shannon Hotel, Capallmara Beach. Eire
Moira.

The English couple were coming to the end of their time for photographs when a slightly strange pair stayed at the hotel. They did not arrive at the same time, but Moira was sure they were together. They both gave Dublin addresses for the register. The thin man was in his twenties and dark haired. He was skinny, with ill-fitting clothes, as if he had borrowed someone else's suit for the trip. The woman was younger, but quite glamorously dressed. Her name was Siobhan. They did not talk to each other, ate breakfast at separate tables and kept apart. It was strange how they seemed to be together, but apart. There seemed to be recognition, an understanding that passed between them, but they were secretive and behaved as if they had never met. Moira overheard her father speculate that they might be having an affair. In the night Moira heard Siobhan leave her room, creep along the corridor and knock on the thin man's door. After a while, she heard the bed springs creaking. Then the woman crept along the corridor back to her room.

Next morning when Siobhan went down to breakfast Moira slipped into her room using her pass key. On the dressing table was a pair of leather driving gloves and a shiny black clutch bag. Moira looked inside. To her horror it contained a small black gun. Moira immediately left the room, only to find Siobhan coming back along the corridor.

"Good morning" said Moira, "just checking on the room." Her voice sounded nervous and shifty. The woman looked at her in a strange nasty sort of way but said nothing.

Moira had no idea what to do. What if they are here to kill Alex and Isobel? She imagined Isobel lying naked, like in the picture, but shot dead. After an agony of indecision, she finally went to Isobel and Alex's room, knocked and, getting no reply, unlocked the door with her pass key. She stepped into the room to find they were both still in bed. They were awake, under the sheets and looking at her.

"What's wrong?" asked Isobel.

"I think you should hide" blurted Moira, "I think they are here to kill you...."

Chapter 16

1979

15th June - Friday
Somewhere in Northern Ireland.
Siobhan.

Siobhan was waiting at the wheel of the car, engine running and ready to go. Her hands poised on the wheel. The new leather driving gloves were a nice touch. She flexed her fingers slightly to admire the way the leather caught the light. It made her look stylish. She had chosen a deep red shade of lipstick. Her mascara and eyeshadow carefully applied to complete the image of femme fatale on her first mission. She had chosen a grey trench coat, belted at the waist. She was thinking that she might buy a beret for her next mission, maybe in peach or a light yellow.

Her first mission! She had driven to the Shannon Hotel and made contact as directed. She had gone to her room as planned, but that night she had been unable to resist the urge to go to him, to hold him, to give herself to him. Theirs would be the pure burning passion of fighters for freedom, snatching one moment together amid the danger. "I suppose it was brief", she thought, "but he seemed startled to see me. The bed creaking like that didn't help either. It would have helped if he had taken off his vest."

It had been awkward at breakfast, they sat at different tables as planned, but the thin man kept looking across at her. It was either lust or puzzlement, or maybe both.

She had called the local contact about the girl that was snooping in the room. "Could she have been a tout?" she had asked. On the phone he had said he knew who she was and would deal with her.

Once they were in the car, it all seemed better. The thin man was calm. She had driven carefully, as instructed, crossed the border without difficulty and at the first filling station made sure the fuel tank was topped up. He had watched from the car as she went into the garage and paid for the petrol, taking the notes from her new clutch bag.

"I like your purse" the girl behind the counter had said. She told the thin man about the girl liking her purse.

"It's very smart" he had said.

She had driven slowly up to the agreed handover point. Two people were waiting, smoking cigarettes next to a light green car. The thin man got out of the car and greeted them. They spoke briefly with the thin man, there was a pause while the three men looked around carefully to make sure they were not being watched. From the boot of the light green car one of them took out a long object, wrapped in a blanket. The thin man unwrapped the bundle, a rifle fitted with a telescopic sight. He checked the rifle, loaded it with a clip of bullets and came back to their car. The boot opened and he placed the rifle inside. He said "off we go" and Siobhan drove carefully to the alley where they would rendezvous afterwards. She parked and watched him walk away; the rifle wrapped in the blanket tucked under his arm.

She wondered if she would become famous, like the Price sisters. Crazy Prices she had heard them called, heroines of the armed struggle.

It was irritating that even after what had gone before, she only knew him as the thin man. "Perhaps I'll ask on the way back" she thought "after all we have shared.... "

She looked up.

A beat-up old Volkswagen camper-van was slowly reversing into the alleyway. It looked like the one from outside the hotel. She could not afford to be blocked in, so she sounded the horn. The VW bus briefly stopped and then lurched back towards her. She wound down the window and shouted, it was no use. The van continued until it gently hit her car. "Get out of the way" she yelled.

Alex appeared from behind Siobhan's car and shot her twice in the chest using a silenced pistol. She looked at him, her eyes bulging, her mouth working silently. Alex then shot her through the forehead. He reached into the car, took her handbag, arranged her hands on the wheel and backed away to hide behind the nearby wall. The VW moved off around the corner.

At an upstairs window about two hundred yards away, the thin man waited, watching the main street that led from the police station. He had re-arranged the furniture, moving a table to give a firm rest for the rifle. He had half opened the window, just enough to clear the rifle barrel. He partially pulled the curtains. The room was now dark. Through the telescopic sight he observed as the members of an army foot patrol moved down the street.

He had set the sight to 400 yards, close enough to ensure a hit, not so close that the patrol would be able to accurately return fire. He waited, heart pounding, until he judged they were about 400 yards away. He selected his target, placed the crosshairs on the soldier's head, stilled his breathing and fired. The soldier slumped to the ground. The rifle kicked as he worked the bolt and fired three more times. In the excitement, he had aimed too quickly, the bullets went high, scarring the walls above the soldiers as they scattered for cover. No more hits, time to go, before the soldiers started to shoot back. He wrapped his rifle in the blanket and ran, crashing down the stairs, through a small courtyard and down the alleyway back to the waiting car.

Breathing heavily, he jumped into the passenger seat.

"Let's go, let's go." He panted. He looked across and realised in horror she was dead. "What the…."

In that instant Alex had walked up to the car and fired two bullets into the thin man's chest. "And one for luck" he said as he aimed at the forehead and squeezed the trigger. The thin man's head jerked backwards, and he fell sideways onto Siobhan. Alex reached into the car. He took the thin man's wallet from his jacket pocket.

The VW van re-appeared. Isobel carried a jerrican of petrol which was quickly shifted into the car between the two bodies. Each corpse was quickly photographed. Then the VW van wheezed away. The fire quickly spread to the spilled petrol, for a moment the flames flickered over the corpses. Siobhan's hair briefly flamed and shrivelled. Then the petrol in the jerrican caught, the car and its occupants were consumed in a massive fireball. Black smoke poured upwards.

Back in the street a deadly hush had fallen. After the thin man had fired at them, the foot patrol had all taken cover. Now they were crouched, pulses racing, in doorways and behind walls, taking quick looks up the street and popping back into cover. One soldier ran across the street to a better position. No shots came. The patrol warily scanned the windows for the sniper. It was deathly quiet. A woman came to the window of her house, drawing the curtains to get a better view. Her movement attracted the attention of a soldier in the street outside. He quickly took aim. She ducked out of sight. He held his fire, instinct telling him that a middle-aged woman in a pinny and curlers was unlikely to be shooting at him.

One of the soldiers ran to his downed mate who was sprawled on the pavement groaning. There was no blood. The spent bullet had lodged in a spare self-loading rifle magazine in the soldier's smock pocket. By some strange chance the thin man had knocked the sights on his rifle awry, probably whilst it was in the car boot wrapped in the blanket. With the rear sight pushed up, it had shot low, and his first shot had struck a kerbstone many yards in front of his target. The bullet had ricocheted up with most of its energy dissipated, hit the rifle magazine and bent it like a banana. Apart from being winded and the soreness from an ugly bruise, the luckiest squaddie in Northern Ireland was unhurt and now had a story to tell.

A column of smoke burst upwards from behind the houses further down the street. People came out of the houses, shouting that the fire brigade should be called. There was a car on fire with people in it.

Chapter 17

1979

16th June - Saturday
Callum's Mobile Home, The Dunes, Capallmara Beach. Eire.
Callum.

Callum was on the case. The day before, the two volunteers had been killed in the north and it looked like they had been betrayed by a tout. They had stayed at the Shannon Hotel. Siobhan's call to him and her suspicions about Moira being in her room seemed to make it all fall into place.

The plan had formed as the day wore on and by afternoon, he had decided to grab Moira, bring her back to the caravan and interrogate her. He had started the interrogation well enough. "Are you a tout?" he yelled.

"No" came the reply.

He shouted louder. She cried. He hit her. She whimpered. Callum hit her again. He threw her onto the bed.

Moira screamed "No" again and again.

Afterwards, as it started to get late, Moira pulled on her clothes and crept away. Teary and sore, Moira had set off down the beach track towards the hotel. Callum was sat on the mobile home's bed feeling very pleased with himself. He was about to get a beer from the fridge.

There was a timid knock on the door. "What's wrong, you silly bitch, have you come back for your knickers?" He had torn her knickers off and now they lay on the floor.
Callum opened the door to find he was looking straight down the barrel of a silenced pistol. It was the English woman, Isobel. "Hands behind your head" she ordered. "Get onto the bed, lie face down."

Callum hesitated.

 Move or I will shoot you in the face" hissed Isobel, there was no doubting she meant business. He obeyed and lay face down, trying to peer back at her.

With the gun aimed straight at Callum's face, Isobel used her free hand to pull off one of Callum's socks. He started to turn to see what was happening.

"Face down" she hissed. Callum felt a sharp pain in the sole of his foot. "Lie still."

As the contents of the hypodermic took effect, Callum felt incredibly drowsy. He closed his eyes. Breathing became an effort. As his breath shortened, he was dreaming in vivid colours. It was the garden at the rear of the old house. His mother was sitting on the back step. She was bent double, her face cradled in her hands. She was crying, hiding her sobs behind her apron.

Callum called to her," Mammy."

She looked up. He could see her eye had been blacked, her cheek was bruised. "Oh Callum" she sobbed "Callum dear." Everything was grey, darkening, then nothingness.

Callum was dead.

Isobel had bit her lip when she heard Callum mumble for his Mammy. She checked his pulse, then put the sock back on. She systematically worked through the mobile home, removing any trace of herself or Moira. She leaned over the gas stove and nicked a small cut into the gas hose then worked it back and forth until it split. She placed a kettle on the hob and turned the ring beneath it on, leaving it unlit. She went to the door, locked it from the inside and slipped away out of a window at the back of the caravan.

That night Mrs. Shannon stood outside her daughter's room. She could hear the sobs from within. She could not bring herself to knock. After a while she went away. That night she dreamt that she was dragged from the stone circle by the sprite, down into the sea, to be trapped in the confessional, and it was filling with water. She fought to get free. Waking she found her husband nursing his nose where she had lashed out and hit him. Something bad was about to happen.

Chapter 18

1979

17th June - Sunday
The Shannon Hotel, Capallmara Beach. Eire
Moira.

The next day passed with much unsaid and Moira had felt very alone. Her mother had been behaving strangely, watching her, bringing her tea and fussing over her, but not saying anything. Moira wondered if her mother had guessed.

The thin man and Siobhan had not come back. After a few days, the Shannons cleared each room. The thin man had left a few toiletries, nothing more. Siobhan had left more: some shoes, underwear, a dress and a cheap novel, "Deadly Passion." They boxed up the items, ready to forward them on. Mrs. Shannon had sent postcards to the Dublin addresses they had left on the hotel register, but no reply ever came. Years later the two boxes were still in the hotel storeroom, unclaimed.

The English couple were gone for a few days. When they returned, the Volkswagen camper had gone, replaced by a pale blue Hillman Imp. "The poor old bus was so rusty that the suspension pulled away from the body, we nearly lost the wheel" Alex had told Mr. Shannon. "Scared the living daylights out of us when it happened. No garage would repair it, so we had to raid our savings to buy the Imp"

Alex and Isobel went down to their favorite spot on the beach. They were lazing beside the tree, reading, when Moira appeared.

"I need to show you something" she said. She stood in front of them hesitating, then took off her blouse and bra. She turned away from them, and they could see she had been beaten. There were welts and bruises. It was possible to make out the impression of a belt. She had been hit very hard. Moira then stepped out of her skirt, and they could see her legs and buttocks had also been beaten.

Isobel went to Moira, "You poor thing, who did this to you?" she asked as she helped Moira back into her clothes.

Moira choked out the name "Callum."

"Then you must go to the police" said Isobel softly. "He can't be allowed to do this and get away with it. When did it happen?"

Moira shook her head "I can't go to the police, there's worse, I think I might be pregnant. Everyone will know..."

"In that case, we will go with you," urged Isobel, "The man's an animal, he must be locked up or no one will be safe."

"Callum's dead, they found him dead the next day."

Isobel looked directly at Moira, "Did you kill him? It will be OK; no court will punish you if they see what he did to you."

Moira shook her head, "It's not me or anyone. They are saying he died because there was a small gas leak, it was an accident. He was gassed in his sleep."

They led her gently back to the hotel. Alex and Isobel sat and talked with Moira's parents. It was clear that Mrs. Shannon knew something bad had happened to Moira and at first, she had wondered if they, Alex and Isobel, were involved. But she had reasoned that they had left early that day and would have been far off by the time Moira had been hurt. Isobel was explaining that it might be good for Moira to have a change of scene and if they agreed she could accompany Isobel on her trip to London in a week's time. Mr. Shannon had not seen the point, but clearly his wife had an inkling why a young girl might take a trip to London. Mrs. Shannon prevailed, and the arrangements set. Moira was both relieved and delighted.

There was one further awkward topic. Callum's funeral was set for the following week, and a good turnout was expected. Mr. Shannon had explained that Callum had some very unsavoury friends, who could be very dangerous for an Englishman with a camera. Alex had seen the point and agreed to be a very long way away for the week of the funeral. He even agreed to clear the room, allowing them to fit in another paying guest for the week.

Chapter 19

1979

18th June - Monday
Victoria, London
Moira.

It all fell into place. Alex set off first, driven to the nearest railway station by Isobel. She then returned, they loaded up the Imp and set off to meet the ferry. Isobel had said she was worried that it might be a rough crossing on the ferry. Before they left, she gave Moira some tablets. "These will ward off the seasickness" Isobel had told her. The pills gave Moira a headache, but she reasoned it was better than being seasick.

Thankfully, on the ferry, it became evident that Moira was not pregnant, just a little late.

They stayed in a small hotel in Victoria. For Moira, who had never travelled far before, it was a real shock. It was loud, the noise of cars, buses and trucks filled the day and night. The streets were crowded. The buses were full, the tube a crush. She had never seen so many people before. Moira was overwhelmed. Isobel took her round showing her the sights of London: Tower Bridge, the Thames, Westminster Abbey and Parliament.

Then there was a day of shopping, culminating in the purchase of a smart denim jacket in Topshop. Isobel had taken her to a restaurant in a cellar just south of Oxford Street. Moira had never seen anything like it. There was one enormous pizza for them to share. They cut it into slices with a knife that was a wheel on a handle.

Chapter 20

1979

20th June - Wednesday
Bloomsbury, London
Moira.

The next day was Isobel's choice of where to go; she took them to the British Museum. As they went in, Isobel touched the nose of the Lion face that was set in the door. Moira followed suit and she saw others do the same.

"You must pat the lion's nose" Isobel had insisted, although she didn't explain why.

Isobel went straight to the gallery of Roman treasures. Some of the things were beautiful beyond Moira's expectations.

"Look here" said Isobel, "this was made nearly two thousand years ago and for most of the time since, it has been lost in the ground."

Moira looked at the face, set in the bottom of a bowl, hair formed a wreath around the beautiful face. The expression was strange, staring, intense, mysterious. Was it a man or a woman?

Isobel read aloud the label beneath the bowl. "First Century AD Patera; If he or she lived and is not just an artist's dream, then the person portrayed here is long gone, turned to dust. Yet we look at her as if the picture was made yesterday."

"It's a sad face", said Moira, "but I love it. It's as if she knew that one day this would be all that was left to remind the world that she existed. This little green frying pan is all that's left."

"Don't let her beauty fool you, this is a cruel face", said Isobel, "This is Medusa. Her hair was a nest of snakes. Anyone who looked into her eyes was instantly turned to stone. It's a message from the grave, beware of appearances, don't look into the eyes of the monster." Isobel smiled; she touched the tip of Moira's nose with her finger. "Maybe this face you see in the mirror is hiding evil within, the darkness in your soul." Isobel laughed as Moira looked solemn. "Perhaps it was buried with her to make sure her grave was undisturbed, or maybe she just wanted to go to the underworld with her favorite frying pan in her hand."

Moira looked again at the label; dug from a grave in 1880. She imagined the Roman woman, lying cold and dead for all those years and then someone digging into her grave to take the bowl.

"That pizza we had yesterday, would have been familiar to two Roman ladies out on the town" Isobel added. "Except that the Romans didn't have tomatoes, they didn't reach Europe until the sixteenth century, however, the tasty dormouse topping was authentic. Those Roman ladies would have had flatbreads, with cheese and honey-soaked deep-fried dormice. To go with it we might have had some sauce made from rotted fish, which the Romans loved. For dessert we could have had giant snails, specially bred and kept in big jars where they were fed on milk."

Moira loved to hear Isobel talk about history, although she began to suspect she was having her leg pulled, especially the story about eating dormice and snails.

As a child, Moira had read the story of the town mouse and the country mouse. Isobel had taken her to a hairdresser. They sat side by side as they had their hair "done." An exquisite bearded young man with manicured nails had fussed over her, called her darling, combed and cut her hair carefully.

He said how much he loved her eyes. When he went to get her a coffee, she leant over to Isobel and whispered, "He's lovely."

"You're barking up the wrong tree there, sister" whispered Isobel's hairdresser, raising her eyebrows and looking to one side. She asked Isobel about it afterwards and Isobel called her a goose. "She meant he would be more interested in a boyfriend than a girlfriend."

"Oh!" she realised; "I really am the country mouse!"

Chapter 21

1979

21st June - Thursday
Oxford Street, London
Moira.

Their next trip was to Selfridges where they drifted from counter to counter on the ground floor. They sniffed at the perfumes. They considered various shades of lipstick. A lady consultant had emerged from behind one of the counters and offered to "make them over." It was awkward trying to keep still as someone poked around with a little brush so close to your eyes, but Moira willed herself to keep still, as liner and mascara were applied. Moira blinked at her reflection in the little mirror that the consultant lady held before her. With her new haircut and make-up, she looked like a different person.

Clutching the little bag of makeup items that Isobel had bought for her, Moira followed Isobel as she quickly walked down Carnaby Street and into the backstreets.

"We are going to the cinema", Isobel told her.

Back home the nearest cinema was a long drive away, so it had been a rare treat to go. For Isobel's benefit she listed the films she had seen, "there was Bambi, the Wizard of Oz, The Sound of Music, Oklahoma, Summer Holiday...."

The cinema was not what Moira had expected. A narrow doorway had led to a flight of stairs that emerged onto a small foyer. An unsmiling, hard-faced woman sat at a desk. "I shall call her Mrs. Hardface" thought Moira.

"Two for Caligula, please" Isobel had asked.

The woman looked dubious. "Are you sure you know what this film is about, dear? We cater for a special clientele only. It's not gone on release yet, so its uncertified."

"Yes, I understand," said Isobel.

"I don't think you do" came the reply, "it's explicit, the full on..."

"That's alright," smiled Isobel sweetly "we've probably done worse ourselves."

"Really? You don't fool me" replied Mrs. Hardface.

"Moira, show the woman your legs and bum" said Isobel, sounding exasperated. Moira meekly lifted up her skirt, turning to let the woman see the bruises and welts.

"Arabs, they pay well," Isobel advised "but will do stuff even your Romans hadn't thought of. They're all going to see this film, so we want to do some research. Fun way to spend your holiday, spend the money while the bruises heal."

Mrs. Hardface had been all sweetness and light from then. She had taken Isobel's money and ushered them to the cinema. It was small, with only twenty seats. The chairs were like armchairs; "these are comfy" Moira thought.

There were only three other customers, all men. One man came over to sit behind them, but straight away Mrs. Hardface shone a torch on him and told him to move back to where he had come from. "Leave these ladies be, or I will chop it off" she had told him ominously. "You don't want him getting your hair all sticky" she had told them. Smiling, she went to the little projection booth at the back and the film began.

Moira whispered to Isobel, "I can't believe you told her we were a pair of prostitutes."

"We're in London, we can be anyone we want" came the giggled reply.

"Did you see anything you liked?" Mrs. Hardface had asked as they came out afterwards.

"Lots of ideas," Isobel had replied, "that dance was wonderful; I can see them going for that. Of course we can't all look like Helen Mirren, but the clothes could be run up quite cheaply. And one other thing, before things get going, lock all the knives away! That's one fantasy I don't want them to act out!"

She asked Moira the same question, but Moira's mind was in a whirl. She had just watched, sex, murder, blood, gore, mutilation, orgies and didn't know what to think.

Isobel answered for her "I think Moira has taken a fancy to Malcolm McDowell, even if she did just watch him hack some chap's plums off ."

Mrs. Hardface grinned broadly, "He is a bit of a moody duck, but I can see why you like him. Well, good for him, I say. I can think of a few of our clientele who deserve the old chip-chop."

As they emerged back into the daylight, it was beginning to rain. "Why did we go and see that?" Moira asked as they walked along the pavement.

Isobel stopped, at once serious. She held Moira firmly by the arms and brought her face close. Unblinking, Isobel stared at Moira. Now there was a hardness in her expression that made Moira want to look away. Isobel had become like the face in the Patera, beautiful, yet fearsome.

Isobel spoke quietly, but forcefully, "To know the world, we must know what people are capable of. The more power is given, the greater the opportunities for evil. Caligula thought he had the power of a god. Look what he did with it. Callum thought he had power over you. He did what he did. Look how they both ended. Dead!"

Moira didn't know what to say. She could not avert her gaze. Isobel held her spellbound, it was frightening her. For a moment, Moira saw the monster that lay beneath the smile.

The cold, hard face of the abyss was before her. It made her want to cry.

Then the mood changed, like a sunrise. With a hug and a peck on the cheek, Isobel was smiling at her. "Also, I wanted to watch an orgy or two. It can be so very quiet, living at the Shannon Hotel. We need to wake the place up! Make it more like ancient Rome. What would your Mum say to that?" Isobel was teasing again. They walked on, scattering a flock of pigeons up into the drizzle.

Chapter 22

1979

21st June - Thursday
The Salisbury public house, Covent Garden, London
Moira.

They were going to eat at a fish restaurant called Sheekey's, just off Leicester Square. They were early and the table was not ready; they went into the pub on the corner. Moira was fascinated by the place. It was as if they were in a Victorian palace of lights, mirrors, woodwork, brass work and varnished mahogany.

Isobel bought them each a Bacardi and Coke. Drinks in hand they tried to find somewhere to sit. At the back of the room, there was a table big enough for four, occupied by a couple who were deep in conversation. There were two spare stools, so Isobel asked if the couple minded them "perching on the end."

For once it was Isobel who was surprised and Moira who got the first words in "Caligula, Caesonia"

"I live" came the reply, for indeed it was Malcolm McDowell and those his final lines from the film they had just watched. They all laughed.

"You were incredible, so beautiful" Moira gushed to Helen Mirren. "We've just watched the film and here you are." The actors were puzzled. How could they have seen the film it couldn't be on general release? Moira told them about the little cinema.

"Did you have your dirty macs on? "asked Malcolm.

"No, but some of the audience did!" replied Moira. "For some parts of the film, I just closed my eyes, it was more than I was expecting", she admitted.

"Nothing to be ashamed of" came Helen's reply "I was there! At times I had to look away myself! There were things I thought were anatomically impossible...I couldn't believe my eyes!"

There was a little more chatter about filming in Rome, then Helen asked, "would you like us to sign something?" This is how celebrities ask ordinary folk to pack it in and go.

Isobel took the hint, dug into her bag and produced a small book. The cover was edged in purple and bore the picture of a Roman coin with an anchor and dolphin. It was The Twelve Caesars, by Suetonius, a translation by Robert Graves. "I was going to give this to you later, as a present, Moira, but it would be nice to get it signed. "

She handed the book over, together with a pen. Malcolm signed first, chuckling to himself, then Helen. With that they drank up and headed back to Sheekey's for a fish supper.

When Moira received her gift that evening, she read the messages in the front: "With love from Isobel and Alex" and below that, "with love from Gaius Caesar Augustus Germanicus, the God, Caligula and Milonia Caesonia, his wife" and below that "Helen" with a pair of kisses.

"The two loveliest people in the world and the two worst monsters," Moira mused.

The next day Isobel took her to see Grease, then Star Wars. She had heard about both films, but not dreamed she would see them both in one day. After the films, they had eaten Chinese food at a restaurant near Leicester Square. Moira had tried to use chopsticks, not very successfully. Seeing that Moira would otherwise end up hungry, Isobel had asked the waiter for ordinary cutlery.

On their final day they had gone to an amazing shop called Liberty's. Moira had never been in a shop like it. There was stuff from all over the world, it was like an oriental bazaar, all crammed into an old half-timbered building. There was a whole room full of silk scarves, another with chunky jewelry. The place smelt of sandalwood and perfume. Moira whispered to Isobel, "it's so exotic…I love it."

Then they walked along Carnaby Street, looking at clothes. Moira spotted a statue looking down at the shoppers from a first-floor window.

"That's Shakespeare", Isobel had told her. They ate at a restaurant called Cranks. It only sold meals for vegetarians, no meat at all. You could see straight into the kitchens. When Moira realized that they didn't wash the dishes by hand, but instead put them into a machine, her amazement was complete. The country mouse had seen her first dishwasher!

That night, while Isobel slept, Moira stood at the window of their hotel room. She looked down at the street outside. There were few people about, but the noise of traffic, police sirens and dustbins being emptied kept her awake.

Moira watched as Isobel tossed and turned, unsettled in the bed opposite hers. Isobel's night was troubled. Guilt gnawed at her. Her mind replayed the events of the previous week. She had guessed that Callum would question Moira. She had followed at a distance, as Moira was taken to Callum's mobile home. She had been listening outside the mobile home as Moira was beaten and raped. Moira had suffered, while Isobel agonized about what to do.

When Isobel had finally made up her mind, she had gone back to where the VW camper-van was hidden. With a quiet fury she had dug out the pistol, phenobarbital and a syringe. From that moment she had determined that Callum would die. The plan was simple, but brutal. Moira could not know that Isobel was a killer; she must wait until Callum let Moira go.

Isobel found that no amount of treats and films could ease the guilt she felt. She hated herself for her delay outside Callum's mobile home that day. Moira had suffered more, because Isobel decided to wait. That decision to delay, logical to protect the mission, now made her despise herself. To make it worse, in her dreams, Callum called for his mother as he lay dying. She kept reliving that moment, over and over again. Like a little boy, "Mammy." Now she felt almost as if she had killed a child, no matter how many times she tried to remember he was a grown man and a rapist at that.

Chapter 23

1979

22nd June- Friday
The Church, Capallmara Beach, Eire
Father Francis.

Father Francis had not known what to expect for Callum's funeral. The man had few friends, but on the day the church was more than half full. "Where do you find friends like these" he thought, "it's like the cast of a gangster movie." Not a single woman here, only men, he noticed. "A funeral without at least one woman in tears says a lot about how the man lived his life."

This was the first time Father Francis had been called to officiate at a paramilitary funeral and had phoned the bishop for guidance. "The man's dead, send him on his way without a fuss and don't make waves," was the message. The police seemed to be giving the church a wide berth as well.

A good priest can deliver an acceptable eulogy for someone he knows little about, cares for even less and nobody else has got a good word for. It's just part of the job. As Father Francis warmed to his task, he realized that only one member of the congregation was paying any attention. It was St Columba. The cat had already heard him rehearse his lines in the study, so he had cut things short, with nobody the wiser. The congregation seemed pleased to be let out with so little time served.

An honour guard had been formed. Young men in berets, dark glasses and combat jackets, who had formed a line at the graveside. Their volley of pistol shots over the grave startled pigeons and gulls into the air, swooping and whirling about the Church. The coffin was lowered into the grave. The lads did well, given Callum's weight, to make it a graceful descent.

"Do we bury the flag with him or not?" someone had asked.

"Not, I would think" he had replied. There was a pause while the tricolour, now somewhat muddied, was rescued from the top of the coffin. Father Francis intoned the familiar words; a few handfuls of soil were thrown onto the coffin lid. A small wreath was placed. Callum was laid to rest.

The prospect of sandwiches and drinks drew the mourners away to the hotel. Soon all was quiet. Finn would be along later to fill the grave. He had offered to add grave-digging as a sideline to the glazing business. Father Francis, knowing the man needed whatever business he could find, had given him the job.

The funeral was a success in ways that nobody in the congregation realized. Every conversation in the hotel bedrooms and every phone call had been recorded. Had they known that the hotel had been re-wired by a young Englishman and that he had placed little electronic boxes in every room, they would have been more guarded in what they said. But they were none the wiser and the boxes listened. Every conversation would be stored by the boxes, transmitted over the phone lines in the early hours of the morning, to be transcribed and assessed over the coming weeks.

Every face had been photographed. Long after Finn had finished filling the grave, a shadow emerged on the darkening hillside and stretched aching limbs before slipping away. Only St Columba, with his cat's eyes, might have noticed the shadowy figure in the gloom, the camera with its long lens slung over his shoulder.

Chapter 24

1979

22nd June - Friday
The Shannon Hotel, Capallmara Beach. Eire.
Anna.

One of the guests at the funeral had taken Mr. Shannon to one side and told him that they would be sending someone down, to dig around. Callum's death had coincided with something strange happening over the border; they wanted to re-assure themselves that all was well.

It was a young couple who turned up. Anna was dark-eyed, raven-haired and strikingly pretty. Eion was fair of face, with intense blue eyes, strongly built. Together they looked like a pair of film stars or a fairytale prince and his princess. The Shannons took a real shine to them. They were polite, quiet spoken and a delight to have around. Mr. Shannon had taken them up to Callum's mobile home. They had ducked under the police tape and explored thoroughly. They looked behind the cooker where the pipes could be seen to have perished and cracked. Mr. Shannon had been surprised that so small a crack could have been deadly. They imagined Callum, tired, maybe drunk, lying on the bed as the room slowly filled with gas. They noticed that Callum had covered the one air vent, probably to keep out the draughts.

Sitting outside, they asked Mr. Shannon about the English couple. He had been watching them, concerned about them, he said. Mr. Shannon was not one to speak ill of the dead, but he explained that Callum had been caught spying on the English woman, using binoculars to watch her undress.

Mrs. Shannon's encounter with Callum was recounted, including the telling detail that he had his dick in his hand. Mr. Shannon had then told them that Callum was a strange and lonely type, who had a reputation as a peeping tom. When they asked if it was just the English woman he was interested in, Mr. Shannon was able to tell a little story. On the headland was a stone circle, which was known to be the local "lovers' lane." Unfortunately, Callum was known to sometimes lurk there; spying on the couples who went there.

"A justified reputation?" Anna had asked.

Mr. Shannon was embarrassed to admit it, but when he and Mrs. S. were there, he thought he had caught a glimpse of Callum watching them. "Of course, that was over 15 years ago" he added, "so Callum was a lot younger."

Back at the hotel they went through the English couple's possessions. Whilst Alex and Isobel were away, they had left some boxes and a suitcase to be stored. In the storeroom, Anna and Eion looked at the photographs, noting where the

English couple had been. They looked with interest at the picture of Isobel naked on the beach. Unfortunately, not one of the pictures showed the English couple's faces. They read the letters from the publisher, looked through the books and came away no wiser. Mr. Shannon packed everything away afterwards, guilty at having intruded into his guests' privacy for no reason.

Anna now turned her attention to the sparse collection that Siobhan and the thin man had left. She questioned the Shannons closely. Had these two guests been together, had they arrived in the same car? Did they leave together? It transpired that they had arrived separately but left together. It seemed to Mr. Shannon that the thin man couldn't drive, but Siobhan could.

Mr. Shannon aired his theory that they were lovers concealing an affair. Had the English couple and these two met or spoken? Mr. Shannon had hesitated, then remembered that the English pair were away most of the time, so these two couples never met. In the end, Anna concluded that nothing untoward had happened at the hotel.

Chapter 25

1979

29th June - Friday
The Shannon Hotel, Capallmara Beach. Eire.
Moira.

The weekend after Callum's funeral Moira and Isobel were back at the hotel. The Imp bumped its way along the track, throwing up dust as they sang over the noise of the engine. They had gifts from London for her parents. Moira had bought aftershave for her father and perfume from Selfridges for her mother.

They had admired the new haircut, noticed the eye shadow and the new jacket was a source of wonder. Tales of Grease, of the dishwasher, the giant Pizza were recounted. Mrs. Shannon had quietly taken Isobel into one of the rooms, closed the door and grim faced, asked the inevitable question.

Isobel watched the look of relief spread over the woman's face at her reply. "She was never pregnant, she's been hurt, but not in that way" Isobel had told her. "It was that man, Callum, the peeping tom, he beat her."

Mrs. Shannon was not a woman for showing emotion. Now she bear hugged Isobel to her and cried. "If I'd gone away with her, the whole village would have put two and two together and got five. I didn't know what to do, so thank you, thank you, thank you."

Mrs. Shannon wiped her eyes. "You don't know what we're like here. I knew that she had been hurt, but if I asked her what had happened, I didn't know what to do. She's a good girl. I couldn't have lived with the shame of people whispering and pointing at her. I didn't want it to be true and I didn't want her to lie to me and I wanted to be a good mother."

"What we should do, is have a nice cup of tea" suggested Isobel, "and never talk of this again. From what I hear, Callum gassed himself and that's the end of it"

Moira had seen that her mother had been crying. That evening Moira came to Isobel's room. "What did my mother say?" she asked.

"She thinks that you're too young to be wearing the eye shadow" came the reply. "But she likes the hair and jacket"

Moira was not amused, "Don't tease me, this is serious, what will she tell the priest when she goes to confession. I must live here, I want to get married here, what if people find out?"

Isobel sat her down, "I told her that Callum had beaten you, but you had not been touched, "down there" in any way. So, you could never have been pregnant. As for confession, don't tell anyone what happened. You know what happened, your God knows what happened, don't get anybody else involved. You need to learn to only tell people what they need to know."

Moira left, but something was still troubling her.

Alex was back at last. Moira went with Isobel and Alex on a trip to photograph the old kelp factory. It was only a shell, the roof long gone and the interior overgrown. Ferns and moss grew where once the kelp had been sorted, cut and processed. It was sunny, but there was enough chill in the breeze to make them seek out a sheltered spot. There Isobel settled down against a bank of grass.

Moira moved gently alongside her and tentatively put her arm around Isobel's waist. She barely seemed to notice her, then shifted to put her arm around her. Isobel was engrossed in her book and Moira lay still, secretly thrilled at being cuddled up with her. In a while, Alex joined them and motioned for Moira to budge up. There was just enough room for the three of them to lie comfortably together. Alex was half asleep, Moira contented and, in the middle, Isobel, deep in her book. Somehow that felt better.

Isobel put down the book. "Alex, I've been thinking about the Rex Nemorensis."

He looked at her over the top of her book "you think this is the sacred grove of Diana?" he asked with a smile.

"No" she replied, "think about it, I can understand people wanting to be the King, but once you were the king, your life became paranoia and fear. Always wondering who you could trust. That way madness lies. Why would you want to be king, if you thought about what it could do to you?"

Moira had never heard of the Rex Nemorensis. Alex explained that it was Latin for the King of Nemi, a sort of high priest who lived in a secret grove dedicated to the Goddess Diana. The Grove was near to a beautiful lake in Italy, which had been a great favourite of Caligula's. Only a runaway slave could become the King, by killing the previous King. Each King was always armed with a sword, constantly on the lookout for a challenger who might want to kill him. Isobel quoted "he holds his reign by strong hands and fleet feet and dies according to the example he set himself. It seems that Caligula took an interest in the King and arranged for a stronger rival to be found. The old King was overthrown and killed, and the new one took his place. Of course, Caligula probably appreciated the King's plight better than most. He had become Emperor by smothering Tiberius, now he didn't know who to trust and who was out to kill him. That way lay madness and ultimately the madness was the pretext for his own assassination."

Moira was feeling uneasy. The talk of challenging a rival to the death made her wonder if Alex was angry about her cuddling up to Isobel.

Alex said, "I suppose the answer is, to know when to leave the grove, walk away, turn your back on it. Continue the journey along another path." He closed his eyes. "We could sail to Byzantium…."

He sighed, then quietly recited the poem.

"That is no country for old men.
The young in one another's arms,
 birds in the trees – those dying generations
 at their song the salmon falls, the mackerel crowded seas...."

He leant over and kissed Isobel, "to Byzantium, before the madness comes."

She kissed him back, "to Byzantium..." she whispered "and mackerel crowded seas..."

Moira concluded that they were talking about something else, not her.

Isobel brought her face up close to Moira, watching her closely.

 "Moira" she asked, "What if there was a sacred grove, one that promised you knowledge, perhaps the knowledge to right wrongs, would you want to rule it? Wouldn't it be worth it, taking just one life to gain that knowledge?"

"I don't think so" said Moira after a pause, "I'm not sure I like the idea of killing someone."

"Not even Callum, just think, if Callum had been the King of the Grove, could you have poisoned him, or stabbed him or pushed him off a cliff?"

Moira shuddered at the thought of Callum and realized the answer was yes.

Isobel continued, "When we set off for London you knew you might have to kill your own baby, for the sake of your future. Wouldn't it be so much easier to kill someone else? Someone who deserved it? Think how exciting the Grove could be, always wondering what was going on behind your back, sword always at the ready, the thrill of combat against a deadly rival. I think you would make a great King of the Grove."

They walked back to the hotel. Alex told Moira that he knew that one day she would find the right person. It was just unlucky that her first experience of the grown-up world had been with such a monster of a man. When dealing with people, and especially men, she should assume nothing. Never go against your gut instinct. She nodded, she should never have trusted Callum. She should not have believed his spy story or gone to his caravan when he called her. Alex swung his arm round in a great sweep, "Somewhere out there is someone who is just right for you, all you have to do is find them."

Alex and Isobel had one last day at the Hotel. The pictures had all been posted to the publishers. The bags were packed and ready for an early start in the morning. Moira had followed them down the beach, to the washed-up tree and as usual found them, naked on the sand. Isobel was reading her copy of Suetonius.

Moira had her own copy of Suetonius with her, the one with the signatures. "Snap" she said, holding it up for Isobel to see.

Isobel smiled up at her, "no more Sister Susan I see, we can compare notes on the corruption that absolute power brings…" Isobel stopped.

Without the slightest hesitation Moira had undressed completely and turned to Alex.

"I've been thinking over and over about this, I want a white wedding." she said. "When the time comes, I want to walk to the altar in a white dress. I want the village to see me in a beautiful white dress. I want my friends to see me in that white dress."

She had completely puzzled them.

"What if I go to the altar in a white dress and then on my wedding night my husband looks at me and he can see I'm not a virgin?"

They both burst out laughing.

"Oh, you goose!" shrieked Isobel "is that what's been worrying you?"

"You could turn the lights off", offered Alex. "Or make him wear a blindfold. Or both wear balaclavas on backwards"

Isobel chimed in "or throw sand in his eyes at just the right moment. Or both put buckets on your heads"

"You silly thing!" Isobel took Moira by the arm. "Just tell him you are, men will believe anything you say." Isobel stood next to Moira and they faced Alex. Isobel addressed him solemnly, "Are you the only qualified man present?"

"I believe so, these are my credentials."

"I shall take that as a yes! We are both virgins, never been kissed and off to the church, clad all in spotless white, do you believe us?"

Alex pointed a finger at Moira "Yes" and then, squinting at Isobel, pausing for effect "maybe….perhaps…Yes! I believe you."

Isobel and Moira ran towards the sea shouting and laughing. Alex picked up the camera. Just as they splashed into the waves, he took their picture.

The next morning, they were gone.

Moira hoped they would return next spring, but they didn't come back. Moira read Suetonius over and over again. The Sister Susan books gathered dust; Moira saw the world differently now.

Chapter 26

1980

12 May – Monday
The Church, Capallmara Beach, Eire.
Father Francis.

Father Francis had seen the photograph book advertised, sent off a cheque with a cover letter and waited. It was just as Spring was turning to Summer that it came. The next day he went to call on the Shannons at the Hotel.

Together they turned the pages of the book. There he was, one of the first pictures was the one of him and St Columba. The caption read, "Remind me Father, which one is you and which is the cat?" There was Finn in his shop, the post mistress with her cat, then some pictures of the crowd on the beach when the whale had come ashore. There were landscapes, they had caught the wildness of a storm, a great rolling wave with the spray bursting off the top like a shower of diamonds. There were the three old boys in the pub, the fisherman talking, the two wives watching as their men launched their boat into the waves.

Father Francis paused before turning the page, "the next few pictures are more artistic, um, personal to them" Moira saw it was the picture of Isobel sprawled naked on the sand, by the limbs of the washed-up tree. On the facing page was a naked back view of Alex looking out to sea. Both Shannons waited for a cue from the priest as to what their reaction should be.

"I know priests are not expert in such matters", he began, "but these are beautiful pictures of a young couple, natural, relaxed, confident, a delight." They were all happy to agree.

The priest adopted a more somber tone. "I'm sorry to say that there's bad news in the book." He turned to the foreword of the book. He read "This work was commissioned as the first collaboration between Isobel and Alexander Manning. They spent the first year of their marriage documenting the West Coast of Ireland. It is a place they grew to love, for its wildness and its people. This book is their epitaph. Isobel and Alex died together in a tragic traffic accident, on their wedding anniversary 12 March 1980. We have lost two bright souls."

It was as if her world had burst apart. Moira fled to her room. On the bed, she held her copy of Suetonius against her face. She cried until she could cry no more.

There was a gentle knock on the door. It was her mother. Could Father Francis see her for a moment. He came in, sat quietly beside her and said, "Moira, I would like you to have the book. I know how much they both meant to you"

She thanked him, wiping her eyes.

"Moira, there's one last picture in the book that I didn't show your parents, but I thought you would like." The final picture in the book was of the last day on the beach. There was the clear sky, the expanse of sand and the thin strip of the waves. Isobel and Moira were running, hand in hand, backs to the camera, naked towards the surf. Alex must have taken the picture as Isobel leaped the first wave. It was as if she was taking flight, pulling Moira upwards.

"Like a pair of angels ascending" he said quietly as he left the room "I will pray for Isobel and Alex, and so should you. It will help"

Father Francis opened up the church one morning a few weeks later to find Saint Columba sitting before the altar. The cat was looking unwavering up at the figure of Christ on the cross. A shaft of morning light illuminated the Cross, the Christ and the cat looking upwards, in the most beautiful light. If the English couple could be here to see it, that picture would have made it into their book, he thought.

Later that day, he noticed that Saint Columba was lying still on the stone floor. The patch of light had moved on and the cat, unable to follow, had passed into the shadow. It was the stillness of death, and the priest gathered up his cat. He walked to the altar and looked up. "Thank you for the life of my friend, oh Lord, please, I beg you Lord, take him into your care."

A priest sees a lot of grief and mourning. Francis had seen many grieve: a wife as her husband's breath stilled on the hospital bed, the mother told her child had fallen from the cliffs and died, the wives of fishermen lost in a storm, never to be found. He had watched a young man, made mute by the loss of wife and baby daughter. There were so many that he had become practiced at mourning with them. He could look into their faces, say the words, shake the hand or touch the arm, express condolences. "Thank you, Father" they would say, wiping away the tears or fighting them back.

Yes, he had seen the pain of loss, but now he felt it. He mourned Saint Columba, he grieved, it hurt in a way he never could have expected. He missed him achingly. He wanted to keep his friend, but now he must give the fur one last stroke, wrap the stiff body in a clean pillowcase, place it within an old bible chest and carry it to the graveyard. There, Finn was waiting. He had dug a new grave in a corner of the Churchyard. They would never fit a person into that space, there was just enough to bury the cat. Crows cawed from the rooftops.

In time Francis added a small cross. The taste of grief stayed with him, and he missed his cat. He was offered a kitten as a replacement but declined. Sat at his desk, he looked at the framed picture and reflected on his pain. How could someone make another person suffer this? He thought about the gunmen who had come for Callum's funeral. They inflict this, they thrive by this, they justify making some mother, some father, some husband, some daughter, some son, to suffer this pain. It was as if a light from Heaven had flashed around him. He was angry.

One Sunday, Father Francis, preached about the nature of loss, of mourning and grief. He had a mission. He spoke out against the men of violence. The men from Dublin realised they should not come back that summer; they would not be welcome.

The machines listened and transmitted. They recorded little fragments of hope; of the slow journey to peace, but the road ahead was long.

Chapter 27

2024

10th June - Monday
Globe and Anchor Guest House, Poole, England
Miriam, Nicholas.

It was just coming up to 2.00 when Nicholas parked outside the Globe and Anchor bed and breakfast in Poole. He had picked Miriam up from Shepherds Bush just after 9.00 and they had driven down at a leisurely pace. Miriam already suspected that Nicholas was up to something, but she was happy to get out of the archive for the day. Nicholas had briefed her on the way down, but frankly it seemed like a wild goose chase. That they had stopped for a quick lunch at a pub confirmed her suspicion that this was a joy ride.

The Americans, Lisa and Peter, were about five minutes late having got lost in Bournemouth. Introductions over, they knocked on the door and were greeted by former Regimental Sergeant Major Roy Strong. He was a friendly, smiling bear of a man, strong in name and in nature, upright and tidy.

The guest house reflected the man too, it was immaculately clean, comfortable and bright. Any notions that they were heading for a doss house were quickly dispelled. The lounge had a small corner bar, plaques on the wall and prints showing marines in action. Miriam was looking at the regimental plaques in place of honour above the bar, "so you were in Forty Commando and Four Two?" she asked.

Roy immediately warmed to her, picking up on her use of Four Two not forty-two. "That's correct, I started in Forty and was moved over when I made Sergeant."

Miriam's father had been a Major in Four Five and her elder brother had served two tours in "Afghan" in Forty. When Roy learned this, it was as if Miriam was part of the commando "family." He would be happy to tell her anything.

The Americans were introduced, and their potential funding of the Marine Museum explained. Roy could probably have ranted about the inequities of closing Eastney on the promise of a site in Pompey, only to have the funding cut, for a good hour or two.

After five minutes, Miriam decided to cut to the chase. "Roy, how did the M60 machine gun come to be in the Marine Museum. Where did it come from?"

"Well," said Roy, "it was late '79 and at the time I was a lance corporal, in charge of a sniper team at one of the border outposts in South Armagh. Bandit Country. You were always on your toes there and it was dangerous. One day a Wessex landed on our pad and a scruffy long-haired type wearing civvies and carrying a camera bag got out. Our sergeant took one look and barks out "Who the fuck are you?"

"This chap didn't bat an eyelid, smiles and says, "Delighted to make your acquaintance, charmed, I'm sure." Before anything more can be said, one of the officers appears, gives everyone the evil eye, meaning "Shut it" and takes our guest away."

"Later on, a couple of the snipers and I get to sit down with the chap. He carefully briefs us on various features on the other side of the border. The general message is that he will be on the wrong side of the border for a day or two and if anyone shoots him by accident he will be mightily upset. He says he will be in a Ghillie suit and armed with an SLR, so if you see someone who fits that description, hold your horses! We were not allowed to shoot across the border, unless fired on, but he clearly was taking no chances."

"The armourer later tells me that this guy drew a rifle, stripped it down and then returned it saying it was a piece of shit. When he got a rifle that he was happy with, he sat for a while cleaning it. I noticed he took two mags and carefully reloaded them, putting a tracer round two up from the bottom. That's a good trick, 'cos if you are in a firefight, when you see that tracer round go, you know it's time to swap mags. Clearly this guy knew his stuff."

Lisa was getting impatient "Who was he?"

"All in good time, so as I was saying, we sat together in the briefing, and I called him Sir. He looked at me a bit strange and said "not Sir, just call me James." I think I called him Sir because I thought he was an officer and I thought I knew him from somewhere. At the time I couldn't place where. It was a while before I remembered, but I think we had been on the same course together."

"His name was James? Is that first name or second?

"Probably neither" replied Roy. "I thought that he had another name when he was on the course, these sneaky beaky guys sometimes used fake names. Especially if he was going over the border, he wouldn't want the IRA or GARDA to pick him up and recognise his name. We called him by his callsign, which was Sandman."

"Sandman was James?"

"That's right. Anyway, that night Sandman went over the border. The next morning there was a short sharp burst of shooting, then it went quiet. We all stood to and waited. We couldn't see anything, but after a little while, we heard that Sandman had asked for a small party to go over as he had something for us."

"We sent four blokes and Sandman guided them to his location. We covered them until they were out of sight, but there was nobody else about. I later heard one of the blokes say that the Sandman was hidden up and one of them nearly trod on him, he was so well hidden."

"When they got back Sandman handed over the M60 to the armourer. All the blokes were interested in having a look at it, it was an unusual bit of kit. A touch on the heavy side, but you wouldn't want to be on the wrong end of it! We took it back to the UK when the tour finished, and it was tucked away in the armoury. Eventually someone had the idea of putting it on display and sent it away to the museum. I think it was de-activated at about that time."

Miriam asked "Where did the M60 come from, you said Sandman took an SLR. How did he come to have an M60? Who was doing the shooting?"

Roy replied, "Some things are best forgotten, this was sneaky beaky and we were told to keep our mouths shut."

"I quite understand, perhaps this will help you recall" said Miriam, holding out her SIS pass for Roy to see. "This all took place over 40 years ago. We all have the appropriate clearance to discuss these events."

Roy was hesitant. "Just to be clear, I didn't go over the border. Some of it was talked about, but we were warned off even talking about it amongst ourselves. I did see the squad and Sandman come back with the two men."

"Did you get a good look at them, could you describe them?"

"Not at all, one of them had a hood over his head and was covered in blood and stuff."

"and the other one?"

"Well, he was wearing a fancy camouflage jacket and yellowish boots, suede like desert boots. Oh, and he didn't have a head…"

Peter Griffin asked, "Are you saying he was dead?"

Roy looked patronisingly at Peter, "That tends to be the case when someone has their head chopped off." In a sing song tone, he continued "He was not only merely dead, but really most sincerely dead."

Miriam recognised the reference "from the Wizard of Oz, the coroner…"

Roy beamed at her.

Miriam pushed for more, "Chopped off?" she asked

Roy was unsure, "I only got a quick look as they tucked him into a body bag. Could have been blown off or maybe shot at close range, hard to say. I suppose only the Sandman could answer that question for you, he was the only one there when it happened."

"About half an hour later a Wessex flew in, picked up the Sandman, the prisoner and the body bag. We never saw anything of them again."

"Could the Sandman have shot him?"

"Maybe, I know that when the Sandman handed back the SLR, he apologised to the armourer for having been snippy with him previously about the first weapon. He said he was pleased with the weapon he had taken with him and that he had fired just two rounds, which was odd because we had heard a long burst of firing in the morning. Probably 50 rounds or so. Of course, the armourer was delighted. Not just with the M60, I don't think anyone had ever apologised to him for anything before. He was singing the Sandman's praises for a while"

"Did you ever come across the Sandman again, do you know what unit he came from?"

"Never heard or saw him again. He wasn't a regular, not a policeman, not SAS or SBS either, we would have been told. He might have been one of your lot, Miriam"

Lisa wanted to go back to the Sandman's name. "You said that James or Sandman, was an alias and that you had been on a course with him. Where and when was that."

"I'm not sure it's the same man, but I was on a sniping course at Oakhampton and he might have been there at the same time. I think I might have a photograph of the course members somewhere if you don't mind waiting while I look."

While Roy was out of the room, Lisa turned to Nicholas and Miriam. "Are you saying that Sandman is definitively not part of British intelligence or the military? How come he turns up on a helicopter, operates across the border and it looks like he trained with the marines?"

"That's about the size of it" replied Nicholas "we have absolutely no information on Sandman. This is all completely new to me."

Roy returned with a photo album and after a few minutes searching turned up a group photograph of six men. One man was holding a small blackboard bearing the words "RM Sniping course, Oakhampton June 1976."

"Which one is James, the Sandman?" asked Lisa.

Roy studied the faces and pointed to each in turn. "That's me, Danny Kaye, Simmons, Turner and Paulson. Paulson was killed in the Falklands, bloody good bloke, really good shot as well." The five marines were smartly turned out in green berets, shirt sleeve order, polished boots and big smiles. The sixth man was dressed in a full ghillie suit, so he looked like a walking bush. His face was obscured by a face veil, so that only the eyes were showing. "Come to think about it," said Roy "we didn't call him James, we called him Sneaky Beaky, or Beaky for short. He didn't have a name."

Peter turned to Nicholas "Can you search your records for someone called Sneaky Beaky or Mr Beaky?" Comforted by the notion that he wasn't the dumbest person in the room, Nicholas agreed. Meanwhile both Lisa and Miriam were using their phones to get clear pictures of the man in the album.

Two weeks later the Chairman of Trustees of the Royal Marines Museum found a cheque for £25,000 in the mail, together with a letter thanking RSM Roy Strong for his contribution to historical research. "What yarn has Roy spun them?" he wondered.

Chapter 28

1979

10th September - Monday
Castleblayney Road B32. Northern Ireland
Keith.

Keith Murphy had driven over the border in a Ford Escort van. His instructions were to drive along the Castleblayney Road, until he saw Clea Lake on his right. Once past the large white house he was to look for a road leading to a picnic area next to the lake. He was told to wait there until a local volunteer turned up. The explosives were already at the picnic spot, buried in a small pit. The plan was for the local man to help him load the van with explosives and prime it. He would then drive into Keady. He was to set the timer, get out of the van and walk away. Calmly, without looking back, he had been told. The local fella would tell him where to meet afterwards and drive him back over the border.

When he got to the picnic area, he saw a young woman sitting on the front wing of a pale blue Hillman Imp. There was a shovel propped against the car boot. She was reading, but when she saw him drive in, she put down the book and gave him a smile. Keith liked what he saw. She was dark haired, fair skinned and pretty. She was wearing a denim jacket over a white blouse. Over her shoulder was slung a Nikon camera.

She walked over to his van, waiting while he wound down the window. "Keith?" she had asked.

"Yes" came the reply. He noticed her blouse was undone enough to show a crucifix and the curve of her breast.

"We have some time before we need to get going" she told him, as her left hand undid another button. She was not wearing a bra he saw. She smiled. He smiled and leaned forward to watch, as her left hand undid another button.

He didn't even see the thin bladed knife that had been concealed in her right hand. She drove the blade into Keith's eye and brain, then twisted it hard. She withdrew the knife, opened the car door and dragged her flailing victim onto the ground. Keith bellowed like a wounded animal, rolling and convulsing. Blood spurted from his eye. The woman watched his agony impassively.

A man had appeared from the bushes. He held a pistol in his hand. He fired two shots, in quick succession, into Keith's chest, then a third into his head. The noise stopped and Keith lay still.

The woman wiped the knife clean on Keith's jacket, then started to walk around the van, systematically taking photographs. The man went through Keith's pockets.

Neither spoke. When they were finished, they put Keith's body back in the van.

The two of them walked over to a clump of shrubbery. From behind it they carried a body. It was a middle-aged man, eyes still open, but dead. His throat had been cut. He was placed alongside Keith in the back of the van. The contents of a petrol tin were liberally splashed over the two bodies.

The black wig was removed and flung into the van. Blonde again, she scratched her head. "That damned thing has really made my head itch" she said. As they drove away in the Imp, neither looked back as thick black smoke rose from the fiercely burning van.

"Oh Isobel, what a naughty Iceman you are!" said Alex in his best mock scolding tone.

She saw Alex turn and grin at her. "Don't get any ideas, Sandman" said Iceman smiling back as she realised that her blouse was still all the way undone. "Let what happened to the last man to ogle my tits be a warning to you. Let's get a move on, we have a ferry to catch."

They drove on in silence. Alex realised he really knew very little about the woman sat next to him. At no point during training had their paths crossed. They had not compared notes, but he guessed she had been following the same path as he had. Just after graduation he had been contacted by a former tutor from the university and asked if he would like to be considered for a very particular line of work. More out of curiosity than anything else, he had agreed. An invitation to attend a selection event at a former stately home in Surrey duly appeared.

The course was designed to assess whether candidates were physically fit, able to operate in challenging environments and able to acquire a skill set appropriate to their intended role. After two days of discussions and interviews half of the candidates had disappeared, leaving the remainder to exhaust themselves with a day of running over an obstacle course. Some treated this as an individual challenge, to be mastered alone, others paired up and helped each other. Neither approach guaranteed inclusion on day three and the numbers reduced again.

Day four had been problem solving. Alex and his group of three fellow candidates were given a couple of oil drums and some planks with which to surmount an obstacle. Unfortunately, the path over the obstacle was blocked by a cat's cradle of painted wooden poles. As time wore on, they tried various balancing strategies using the planks and drums to form a seesaw like structure. The idea was to somehow crawl along the planks, through the poles and drop down on the other side. It didn't work.

As they were about to run out of time, Alex turned to the others and said, "This is on me, OK…don't let it ruin your chances." He had picked up a drum, hurled it at the structure and demolished the poles. The instructor looked on in undisguised horror as the group passed across easily with the poles removed. Alex was taken to one side. The instructor firmly informed him that the rules were implicit in the task. Surveying the wreckage, he hissed that the poles were NOT to be touched.

"Implicit, but not explicit?" Alex had responded. The instructor was NOT amused.

To his surprise Alex had passed the assessment and found himself recruited as a member of Britain's Secret Intelligence Service. He embarked on a rigorous training program. By its conclusion he was much fitter and well versed in the art of killing, weapons handling, tradecraft and surveillance.

Under the tutelage of some colourful characters, he became adapt at deception and distraction. Harry "the Killer" taught lock picking and burglary. Mrs B. taught disguise, turning up to every lecture looking unrecognisable from the previous session, yet having made only subtle adjustments to her appearance. Finally, there had been some very enjoyable time spent learning to be a professional photographer, his potential cover story. There were intensive sessions learning how to use the latest in electronic surveillance.

His first assignment was to be in Malta. He was briefed that NATO headquarters in Malta had started to leak secrets and he was to find out the source. He never got to Malta. In early February of 1979 he was told to attend a mission briefing.
The mission was Ireland and sat next to him in the briefing was a pretty, young woman, smartly dressed, with blond hair and a serious manner. They were introduced to each other. Not their real names, but "you are now Alex James Manning, workname Sandman; you are Isobel Claire Elliot, workname Iceman." The controller handed him a file of paperwork to read, it was the background story for his new alias.

It transpired that Isobel had been preparing for the mission for some time, with another person, who it turned out was a female agent. The task was to deploy state of the art electronic listening devices in hotels, pubs etc used by the Provisional IRA. The cover was to be two female photographers, taking pictures for a book, maybe working as wedding photographers.

Alex had asked how much of the cover story had been deployed already as he didn't fancy doing the entire mission in drag. Faint smiles suggested that they had anticipated that issue.

His predecessor had developed a serious medical condition, which with surgery, should be curable. However, she faced a long period of recuperation, and the "show" needed to be "on the road, pronto."

The solution was that they were to be a young married couple, both freelance photographers, effectively on a working honeymoon. Married; Alex and Isobel had exchanged looks.

"I suppose that could work," said Isobel.

"Beggars can't be choosers" rejoined Alex, smiling. Isobel had smiled back.

Chapter 29

1979

13th February - Tuesday
Monkey Beach, West Mersea, Essex, England.
Alex.

Mersea Island is one of those places that is only an island at high tide. The connection to Essex is the Strood causeway and the road disappears beneath the waters of the Blackwater Estuary for a few hours each day. Alex had been told to go to Nelson's View hotel in West Mersea, to await further instructions. The hotel looked out over the saltmarsh and the estuary. Squatting amongst the marsh grass were houseboats which had once been ocean going racing yachts, now de-rigged and sorry looking.

Alex had paid the taxi driver and made his way to the Hotel's front door. It was hardly grand enough to be a hotel, really it was a large house, weatherboarded white in typical Essex fashion, providing bed and breakfast. It looked tidy and well kept.

The owner let him in, introduced herself as Mrs Cranston–Smythe and showed him to his room. It was comfortable enough and he unpacked his few clothes and possessions.

He wandered downstairs to find Isobel, who had arrived the day before. They were the only two guests. He almost didn't recognise her. She now had her hair dyed golden blonde and pinned back into a ponytail. She was dressed in dungarees and a cheesecloth blouse.

She motioned for Alex to come to her, and she quietly pointed to a couple of framed pictures on the top of the piano. The first was a couple on their wedding day, the young man in Army captain's uniform, smiling, handsome and with an incipient moustache. The bride in her wedding dress was clearly their landlady in younger days. The second portrait showed their landlady alone, in uniform, wearing various medals. She did not look much older than in her wedding portrait, but especially around the eyes, her prettiness had gone, and she looked gaunt and tired. Isobel pointed to the medals, "George Cross" she whispered to Alex, "she was in SOE during the war."

Mrs Cranston-Smythe had entered the room. "Admiring the photos, I see. That's my husband Tony on our wedding day in 1941, oh and that's me just after the war."

"Will we be meeting Mr Cranston-Smythe?" Alex had asked.

"Sadly no," came the reply "he was shot by the Germans in Sachsenhausen, sometime in 1944. A great shame, he was a beautiful, lovely man. We were in SOE together, I suppose we shouldn't have married, neither of us expected to survive the war. But then again, why not marry. Better to have loved and lost... "

"I'm so sorry to hear that" replied Alex.

"We lost so many young men," she paused "and this is me, taken in '46 on my return to this country. They gave me medals, but it's no consolation for losing a husband. For a long time, I wished I had been shot also. The irony is that at the end we were both in the same camp and didn't realise it. Probably just as well that the Gestapo didn't make the connection either. Tony was caught in Holland, I was in Italy at first, then Austria where they caught me, so there was nothing to tie us together." She showed her wrist, which bore a tattooed number.

"What kept me alive was that I had trained as a nurse. They had me working in the infirmary. As the Russians got closer, they marched us all away, deeper into Germany. What kept me going was that I thought I was going to see him again, that I was marching towards him. Sad really, he was already dead in the ground where I had just come from." She returned the picture to its place on the piano. "Anyway, less of the past, down to business. Here are your papers. "

Mrs Cranston–Smythe handed each of them a large envelope. "Together you need to fully rehearse your new identities. Tell each other nothing about your real lives, stick to the legend we have created for each of you. Rehearse until it becomes second nature. Don't even reveal your real names to each other. If there are details you want to fill in, discuss it together. You have a couple of weeks and then you will be off. Incidentally, you will need to have answers to the usual questions that young married couples get, where did you meet? how did he propose? what happened at the wedding? stuff like that."

"Finally, you need to agree how you are going to handle sleeping arrangements. I've put you in separate rooms to start, but you need to get comfortable being in the same bed once you are deployed. Get used to holding hands in public, you know, like young lovebirds. Alex, we need to work on your appearance – more beardy hippy please. So don't shave. Before you go, I want you to look as un-military as possible. I have some new clothes on order for you, they will be here in the next day or two."

The next week was bitterly cold and blustery. They got into the habit of walking along the beach, past the slipway, oyster sheds and sailing club, then out into the marsh area. They were undisturbed and they talked through their legends, agreed little stories to tell, until it all started to get real. They were Alex and Isobel, how they met on holiday, stayed in touch, discovered a shared love of photography and how Alex had proposed. There were wedding rings already in the envelope, but they concocted a story to tell about shopping for the rings. They would joke about discovering their taste in rings did not match up and they had to compromise, or the wedding would be off.

There were yachts stored ashore, overwintering on the hard. Alex eyed them wistfully, "One day…perhaps."

After a week had passed, two vehicles appeared. One was a Hillman Imp, designated the clean car, which had nothing out of the ordinary. The other was more sinister. Within the yellow and white VW camper concealed compartments held their weapons, killing kit, communications equipment and other stores. They were given a day of familiarisation, then the vehicles disappeared to await them at the ferry port for Ireland.

Amongst the killing kit was a wickedly sharp narrow bladed fighting knife. This was to be Isobel's. She had told Alex about the women's silent killing course, which had taught them the realities of their trade. As a woman they were told to remember that a man would generally be stronger, taller and with greater reach. In a straight fight, the woman was more likely to be overpowered if they fought a man on equal terms. The instructor then showed them pictures of women who had been treated brutally by men. Pictures that made you sick to look at them.

The women were taught techniques to get in close, to incapacitate quickly and to kill without hesitating. The instructor had said "Before you make your move, remember the women in those pictures, use that image to make you ruthless, don't hesitate, kill. If you don't, you end up like this" said the instructor, holding up an appalling photograph. "If you are facing a man, watch where he looks, is he checking out part of your body? Use it to distract him, don't show him that you have a knife, flutter your eyelashes! Then stab him! Stab to incapacitate, stab to kill."

Isobel had hoped to get into Colchester to see some of the Roman remains, but the chance didn't arise. Piqued by Isobel's passion for all things Roman, Alex started to take an interest in Roman history. They had stuck to the rule about not revealing past lives, but it was clear to Alex that Isobel must have studied classics and possibly languages, somewhere that only took the brightest of students. He also realised that the Service had made a trained killer of her.

Mrs Cranston-Smythe watched them and reported back that good progress was being made. She sat with them and briefed them on known threats and potential responses. They were to evade at the first hint of suspicion, not to stand and fight; if in doubt, get out.

They were given a test exercise to hide a set of bugs in the wiring of the hotel. The next day, confirmation was received that the kit was working well.

On one of their walks, Isobel had stopped and looked seriously at Alex. "I don't believe this, married all this time and you still haven't given me so much as a cuddle…. are you frigid?"

Alex was lost for words, but then saw she couldn't keep a straight face. She was teasing. "In this wind, frozen rigid not frigid" he laughed, then in mock seriousness "wait till I get you home young lady."

They kissed.

That night Isobel crept along the corridor and into Alex's room.

As the end of their time came closer, they decided to go out for a meal together. Now they were fully in character. They walked hand in hand, slightly self-conscious of their new wedding rings. Dark clouds hung over the estuary. It was raining; the gusting wind blew icy drops into their faces. It felt as if it was about to snow. Unsurprisingly, there was nobody else about. On a night like this it made sense to stay home and watch TV.

A little bell on the door announced their entry to the restaurant and the owner looked up surprised. "It looks like you're my only customers, sit wherever you like." The place was empty. The owner had been on the point of shutting up early.

After a quick count of their combined funds, Isobel and Alex decided to have a treat, a bottle of wine. The owner of the restaurant wanted to know all about them, so they practised their roles as newlyweds.

In his turn the owner was happy to explain to them how Monkey Beach had got its name. In past centuries, the area had been rife with smugglers. The Revenue men had set up a tower on the beach to watch for passing boats. The three Revenue men who manned the tower were sometimes referred to as the three wise monkeys as their tower looked like a cage. It was also said that they kept an actual monkey, and it was the monkey that did the watching, having been trained to ring a bell if a ship came into view. Whatever the truth was, in time, locals referred to the Monkey Steps, that led to the Monkey Tower, which stood on Monkey Beach.

"Are you staying with Rosie?" he asked. Seeing their confusion he clarified, "Mrs Cranston-Smythe, at Nelson's View?" They nodded in agreement. "She's a local legend" he confided, settling into his story unbidden. "She's a widow, lost her husband in the war. Settled in here with her parents in law, it was them who originally owned the guest house and it became hers when they passed away. At first, she was a wild one. Losing her husband broke her. She was out in the marshes all hours of the night, gin bottle in hand screaming at the moon. Often you would see her lying unconscious on the marsh, gin-drunk and covered in mud. People would carry her back home."

"I remember one time, just after the war ended, the Royal Engineers were here, clearing the barbed wire and mines from the beaches. A group of them were in the pub having a pint when Rosie burst in. She was screaming at them that they were careless bastards and had not done their job properly. As they protested, she threw an anti-personnel mine onto the table in front of them, "You missed that one" she shouted, "That was in the area you have marked as clear." She stormed out leaving everyone lying on the floor of the bar. There was a lot of beer spilled that night!"

"Anyway, one of the engineers checked the mine and it turned out that Rosie had already defused it. It was safe. A few of them wanted to have a word with her after that, but the Sergeant told them to leave her alone. He had seen the tattoo on her wrist. He'd seen tattoos like that before, at Belsen. He had been amongst the troops who liberated the camp as the war was ending. "Leave her alone", he had said, "if she was in the camps, no wonder she has a mad streak in her."

After a long dark period, a new Rosie had emerged from the mud and tears. She had joined the sailing club when it restarted after the war and taken on the running of the Dabchicks, the children's section of the club. She poured all her energy into the Dabchicks. She could be seen out in all weathers, teaching them, running the races, mending boats and mothering them. Sometimes she would sail her little dinghy alone into the roughest of seas, when nobody else dared go out and even the club safety boat was reluctant to launch. "When you sail in these conditions, you can think about nothing else", she had said, "no time for memories."

One stormy night one of the oyster smacks had broken free from its moorings. As the boat was swept seaward, Rosie had sailed her little dinghy out into the gale alone, boarded the smack and dropped its anchor. When men went out to the smack in the morning, she was still aboard and had raided the larder. She was cooking eggs and bacon! In time, she took over the running of the guest house as well, so she filled up her time and the gin-rages subsided.

Isobel and Alex had finished their meal and gone back to the guest house. All was quiet and they had headed up to Alex's room without even thinking about it. The newly married part of the legend had fallen into place.

When it came time to leave, they were almost wishing they could stay longer.

"I shall come back here one day" Isobel had told Mrs Cranston- Smythe as they made their farewells.

"I hope so" came the reply, "I hope you do, take care where you are going."

"We will" replied Alex, then Isobel surprised Mrs Cranston-Smythe by giving her a big hug.

"Take care", repeated the older woman, "remember that the more you stare into the abyss..." she didn't finish the quotation. Isobel knew she had heard it before somewhere, but couldn't bring it to mind.

As they journeyed towards London Isobel was deep in thought. "If I ever have a daughter, I shall call her Rosie" she told Alex. Meeting Rosie Cranston-Smythe had been a mixed blessing for both of them. That glimpse of what their life could lead to. "This work can come at a terrible cost" said Isobel.

That night Rosie wrote up her appraisal of the couple's time with her and she commented favourably on their technical skills and how convincingly they had adapted to their new identities. It was a good report, they had worked well together, but something troubled her about Isobel. There was something deep and dark about the girl, well hidden, but undefinable. Something of the abyss...

Chapter 30

1979

11th September - Tuesday
St Patrick Car Ferry, Irish Sea
Gerald.

The St Patrick car ferry was in heavy weather, rolling and pitching. It was a night crossing, most passengers had rushed to their cabins, leaving the bar area nearly deserted. Gerald, or Gerry as he was known to most, was flush with cash and determined to get some drinking under his belt. The cash was to fund his latest trip to England. The Big Man had come to the hotel two days before, handed over cash and tickets and told him to meet a woman called Bridget in Liverpool next Sunday.

He noticed a young woman come across the bar room. She came over to stand next to him at the bar. He realised that she was the pretty, photographer girl from the hotel. She ordered a Bacardi and coke. He'd not heard her speak before and realised she must be English. She was going through her purse to find enough to pay for the drink, it looked like she was about to come up short.

"Let me pay for that" he offered putting a note down on the bar.

"Oh, thank you" she replied beaming a big smile at him. She didn't seem to recognise him.

"You were staying at the Black Bull Inn; I was there at the same time."

She visibly relaxed "It's such a lovely spot; we got masses of photographs for the book"

He liked what he could see. She was tipsy. "Where's your boyfriend?" he asked.

"Seasick" she shrugged. She had followed the direction of his glance, then looked back at him directly. "Shall we go up on deck, get some fresh air?" she asked.

He agreed. "Well, yes" he followed her, swaying with the ship's motion trying to avoid spilling his drink.

In the cold air on the deck she stood at the rail, looking at the sea. The deck lurched. She reached out and grabbed onto his arm to steady herself. She drained her drink then hurled the empty glass over the side. She smiled at him.

He smiled back. "Do you want to go somewhere?" he asked, "somewhere a bit warmer and more private?"

She walked towards the stern of the ferry. The aft deck was deserted. "Wouldn't it be fun if someone caught us here?" she laughed. He looked around. He reached forward.

She drew back, "Oh no, not so quick. Finish your pint first! I don't want it spilled all over me. Come on, down in one!" He raised the pint glass to his lips. In her right hand she shifted the grip on the thin bladed dagger and drove it hard into his eye. She twisted the knife, withdrew it and repeated the process on the other eye. Gerald thrashed on the deck. In an instant, Sandman had emerged from the shadows. Together they picked Gerald up and carried him to the rail. Gerald's body tumbled end over end before it met the sea with a splash. The sound was lost in the noises of the ship and the waves. In seconds he was lost to sight in the churning wake.

"Good riddance" spat Iceman after him. He's lucky I didn't chop his cock off."

Sandman smiled, "A small mercy, for which he is undoubtedly most grateful."

By the time the ferry docked they had been hard at work. Iceman now had hennaed hair cut in a bob and was wearing glasses. Sandman's beard had been shaved off and his long hair was now cut short. Both had a complete change of clothes. Apart from the hair blocking the cabin's sink, it was as if the two people who had boarded the ferry in Dublin had never existed.

Bridget in Liverpool waited, but Gerry never appeared.

Chapter 31

2024

26th June - Wednesday
Economic Intelligence Unit, Victoria Street, London.
Nicholas and Miriam.

Nicholas had managed to spring Miriam from the Shepherds Bush archive. She now sat alongside him in the Economic Intelligence Unit's open plan office. It had taken ages to get her building pass for the Victoria Office, network log-on and all the other bumf in place. Before she could work, she had to complete several online courses: Health and Safety, time and attendance reporting and security protocols. The last one was a newly instituted course on mobile phone security, instituted after some dick had handed over an unlocked phone to a prankster. "Some people never learn" she thought.

The initial work was to find out more about Sandman and Iceman. They now had names from the death certificates, from Sandwich. Sandman was Alexander Manning and

Iceman was a woman, Isobel Clair Elliot. Both had been in the system, as children who had died young. Both looked to have been re-activated in early 1979. Deep within the personnel files Nicholas had located copies of the documents created back in 1979. There were full driving licences, passports, a British museum reader's ticket and various travel details. If Alexander was shortened to Sandy and Isobel's initials were used, you got the derivation of their work names. Sandman and Iceman, it fell into place. He was now certain beyond doubt that both Sandman and Iceman had been created by the Service.

The death records from Sandwich recorded the death in accidents of both Alexander and Isobel. Miriam had requested copies of the original notifications. Alexander's death had been notified by Isobel. Isobel's death had been advised by Alexander, supposedly after his own date of death. This looked like a smoking gun. But when they reported it to Fiona, she had asked "How do you know that someone didn't kill them and then report the deaths using their stolen identities? Back then, someone could turn up at the Registrar's using a doctored passport photo and would probably get away with it."

The travel details were limited. It looked as if both agents had spent some time in Essex, having travelled by train to Colchester.

Chapter 32

1979

27th August - Monday
Dublin Road playing fields. Eire.
Bernadette.

The day had been fine up until now, then the cloudburst had come. It was raining heavily. The children clustered together under the bus shelter. The team for Saturdays under 12's girls netball match had been posted on the noticeboard. Now, Bernadette was eager to get home and tell her mother that she had made the team. Being a little taller than the other girls was an advantage at last. In her day, her mother had also been a keen netball player and competed in the Schools League. The two of them had practiced together in the garden at home, shooting into a hoop that her father had nailed to the back wall.

Bernadette realised she had left her sports bag behind. It was probably still in the changing room. She had run back, skipping round the puddles, found the bag and ran back to the bus stop. The bus and all her friends had gone without her. She was dripping wet.

Her parents had made it clear, never get into a car with strangers. But when the car pulled up, the two smiling men had seemed friendly and sympathetic. The man in the passenger seat had got out, opened the door and pushed the seat forward, so that she could climb into the back seat. "We'll get you home to your Mam", the driver had said. In her moment of hesitation, he reached out and gently took her bag. "Let me help you with that." He seemed nice.

She got in.

Chapter 33

2024

26 June - Wednesday
American Embassy, Nine Elms Lane, London
Lisa.

Lisa was looking over the latest note from the Irish authorities. She had sent them the names of Sandman and Iceman that Nicholas had supplied. To her surprise both Alex Manning and Isobel Elliot had been persons of interest in a historic enquiry.

In August 1979 a twelve-year-old schoolgirl Bernadette O'Brian had disappeared. She was last seen getting into a Ford Capri containing two men. There had been a massive hunt, her picture was in all the papers. Some weeks later, a Ford Capri that fitted the description was found abandoned. It had been abandoned in the carpark of the Black Bull Inn on the Dublin Road, which was about forty miles away from where Bernadette had disappeared. Two men, both staying at the Black Bull were associated with the Capri. They were

Gerald O'Bannon, the registered owner of the car and Keith Murphy, in whose name the room had been rented. At first, neither man could be found.

Both had criminal records. They had met in prison. O'Bannon had a previous conviction for indecent assault and Murphy had been linked to the attempted rape of a minor. Both had served short prison terms. They were low level members of the IRA. There had been some intelligence to suggest they were part of an IRA cell responsible for planting culvert bombs in the North.

Shortly after Bernadette's disappearance Murphy was dead. His body was found in a burned-out van close to Lake Clea in the North. At first, this looked like a terrorist "own goal", blown up by his own bomb before he could plant it. Detailed forensic work on the badly burned body had been needed to confirm Murphy's identity. The forensics also confirmed that Murphy had been shot two or three times. Alongside Murphy was a local man, also murdered, probably by having his throat cut. Subsequent enquiries have established that the security forces in the North were not involved in Murphy's death and the case remains unsolved.

O'Bannon had also disappeared, while travelling by ferry from Dublin to Holyhead. He boarded the ferry, but did not complete the journey. It was believed he may have fallen overboard during the crossing. The crossing was rough, and the police report suggested it was possible that he got seasick and fell overboard in the night.

Alex Manning and Isobel Elliot were staying at the Black Bull Hotel at the same time as Murphy and O'Bannon. No link between the two groups was established, however in 2000, during refurbishment of the hotel a covert listening device was discovered in the room occupied by Murphy and O'Bannon. The presence of recording equipment beneath the floorboards of the room occupied by Alex Manning and Isobel Elliot raised speculation that they had the two IRA men under surveillance. Examination of the surveillance equipment does not give any clues to its origin. The GARDA wished to interview Manning and Elliot to see if they have information relevant to their enquiries into the disappearance of Bernadette O'Brian.

The disappearance of Bernadette O'Brian remains unsolved.

Both her parents have since died.

"This looks like progress" thought Lisa. She now knew that Manning and Elliot had been in Ireland, under cover. She had reported her findings back to Langley. She was instructed to ask the British for all the information they had on Murphy and O'Bannon.

Chapter 34

2024

1st July - Monday
Brighton Marina, East Sussex, England.
Pauline.

Pauline and Jenny were worried about Pete. The nightmares had returned, and he woke them several times in the night, shouting incoherently. First thing in the morning Pete was on the phone. Jenny heard him asking for the duty desk. Shortly afterwards, he announced that they were leaving for Eastbourne. As they started to back Sea Bear out of the slip, the boat was tugged to a halt. In the confusion of leaving, they had left the shore power cable plugged in. Andy had been walking back from the showers and freed the cable, passing it up to Jenny. "Give me a call if you fancy meeting up again," said Andy.

"I will" replied Jenny "we are off to Eastbourne."

Andy was pleased "we'll see you later then, we will be going there later today."

Once they were underway her father still seemed agitated "You shouldn't have told them where we are going, it's none of their business." Jenny and Pauline exchanged glances, something odd was going on.

The tide was against them at first, but the wind was just right for a steady beam reach along the coast. They settled back into the comfortable rhythm of sailing the boat and they gave a big whoop as they crossed the prime meridian off Peacehaven. They had just sailed from the Western Hemisphere into the Eastern Hemisphere, so coffee and biscuits came out to celebrate. They sailed past Newhaven, watchful for the big yellow and white Transmanche car ferry that was just preparing to leave the port. Ahead they could see Beachy Head with its towering white cliffs. Jenny pointed out a bumblebee that had landed on their deck. "what's it doing this far from land" she wondered.

Looking back towards Newhaven, Pauline was startled to see a powerful black RIB heading straight for them. It was crewed by black clad military types with helmets, balaclavas, dry suits, flak jackets and sub-machine guns. As it approached, the guns were trained on her and a loud voice shouted, "Stop at once, keep your hands where we can see them."

Chapter 35

2024

1st July- Monday
Victoria Street, London. (morning)
Miriam.

"Nicholas, Miriam, get to Newhaven as fast as you can, there's a car waiting for you downstairs" Fiona was shouting "Go, go, go...briefing call on route, go, go, go!!!

They had rushed down in the lift and jumped into the back of a blacked-out Range Rover. They were propelled through the London Streets at speed. The driver was not hanging about. He used his blues and two's whenever he needed to shift someone out of the way. Looking over the driver's shoulder she saw they were doing well over 100 mph on the clear sections of road. They both learned that you had to hang on for your life around roundabouts.

"Do you know what this is about?" Miriam asked Nicholas.
"Not a clue." The phone rang.

It was Fiona "you have been scrambled to Newhaven; you will intercept a yacht called Sea Bear. When you get there, meet up with a team from Border Force and a couple of our specialists will be joining you. Get the people off the yacht and get them up to London as quickly as you can."

"Your primary task is to retrieve a person who has been in witness protection since 1980. His name is Peter Thomas. He is a retired Police Superintendent from Cronulla in Australia; he is on a sailing holiday with his wife and adult daughter." Miriam chipped in "why are we doing this, what's the link to our work? "

Fiona's reply was succinct. "He ran into Sandman at Brighton yesterday. Apparently, the Sandman was waiting for him when they arrived. He thinks Sandman has recognised him. He says the Sandman is a man calling himself Martin. His worry is that Sandman aka Martin is going to kill him, as he will want to cover his tracks!"

Once at Newhaven they were introduced to the two heavies Josh and Ranulph, who were kitted out in tactical gear. From their Range Rover they dispensed drysuits, balaclavas and helmets. Nicholas and Miriam struggled into the unfamiliar gear.

"What do you want to tool up with" asked Josh "we've got MP5's or Glocks."

Miriam was first to respond "MP5 for me"

Nicholas followed suit and was surprised to be handed a sub-machine gun. Miriam expertly checked the weapon and then removed the magazine, which she tucked into the front of her flak vest.

Nicholas had no idea what to do, so handed the weapon back. "I could do more harm than good with that" he admitted.

Within 15 minutes of arriving in Newhaven they were on their way, a jolting stomach-churning ride. The RIB belonged to Border force, three of whose staff were aboard. The RIB jumped over every wave flinging them up and then down, with each crashing descent like jumping off a wall onto concrete.

After about twenty minutes they came up to the yacht, told its occupants to stop and then collided heavily with it. After a certain amount of confusion, Nicholas and Miriam were aboard the yacht, together with Ranulph.

The two women, Pauline and Jenny, were bewildered. The man, Peter Thomas, was adamant that they were in danger and that he needed to be evacuated. Reluctantly, the two women packed their things, and the family piled into the RIB. They left Ranulph and one of the Border force guys aboard, with instructions to sail it round to the Sovereign Harbour Marina at Eastbourne.

About half an hour later the two Range Rovers were whisking towards London, Josh ready for action and the rest feeling damp and weary.

Chapter 36

1979

30th August - Thursday
Black Bull Inn. Drogheda, Eire.
Alex.

Alex had never seen Isobel cry like this before. Now she sobbed, tears ran down her cheeks.

They had been away for a few days. Once they had unpacked and settled in, they removed the recorder from its hiding place. They were reviewing a recording from two days back. They could recognise Keith and Gerry, together with a third man who they could not identify.

There was another voice, a young girl. She pleaded to be allowed to go home. They gave her drink. Isobel had forced herself to listen as the men took their turns with the girl. The tape automatically stopping and starting for each grunt or moan. It seemed to go on for ever. The girl was desperately pleading for her Mam and crying as they hurt her.

The sound of choking and convulsions followed. The sound of the child being strangled to death.

"Mihi vindictam ego retribuam" said Isobel solemnly, "Vengeance will be mine, I shall repay." She wiped away the tears.

Chapter 37

1979

20th October - Saturday

Wessex helicopter. Somewhere above the Irish Sea

Alex.

The crew of the Wessex had waited, engine running, just long enough for the sagging body bag, the hooded prisoner and his captor to be loaded aboard. The take-off was quick and purposeful, the flight out fast and swooping. In bandit country it didn't pay to be slow and steady, that could invite a burst of gunfire.

Over the headset Sandman had asked the pilot of the Wessex to divert, so they could pass over the Irish Sea, "preferably a very deep bit."

"This should do" he had called back after about ten minutes. "Hover please." Looking back over his shoulder the pilot saw the body bag tumble from the door. It vanished below the surface. The Sandman came over the headset again, "Home James and don't spare the horses!"

Chapter 38

2024

1ˢᵗ July - Monday
The English Channel, off the Seven Sisters.
Martin.

Ranulph and the Border force chap had happily been left on the yacht, each assuming the other knew how to sail. After a while they discovered that they had no knowledge between them. At one point, they sailed round in a circle, sails flogging and the boom flailing across the boat. They tried pulling on the ropes that controlled the sails, but that made the boat heel alarmingly, sending books and plates crashing about down below. The yacht seemed to be steering itself, in any direction except the one they wanted to go in. After a while another yacht came up and shouted to them, "Ahoy Sea Bear, are you Ok?"

It was Martin's boat, Wanderer. There was a shouted conversation in which it became clear that the crew of Sea Bear had no idea where they were or what to do. After a little while and some careful manoeuvring, Martin managed to bring Wanderer alongside and the two boats were temporarily tied together. The younger of the Wanderer's crew jumped aboard Sea Bear, introduced himself as Andy and put them to work. The first step was to switch off the autopilot. Andy cast off the lines that held Wanderer and Martin set off towards Eastbourne. With the sails dropped, Andy started Sea Bear's engine.

He steered out to sea, following Wanderer's track. Ranulph protested that they wanted to take the quick route to Eastbourne. In reply, Andy pointed out the huge breaking waves of the overfalls ahead of them. "You were going to sail into that", he explained, "we need to go the long way round, as it's safer. Those waves have been known to swallow fishing boats, not a place to take chances when the tide is running like this."

The two boats locked into Eastbourne's Sovereign Harbour without undue difficulty. Wanderer had led the way between the breakwaters. On the green light they had motored into lock and tied up to the floating pontoons. Berths were already allocated, so in about half an hour, both yachts were tied up, tidied up and the two temporary crew were trying to arrange a taxi back to Newhaven.

The two Range Rovers were on the outskirts of London when Jenny heard her phone give a ping. It was a text from Andy. His message read "Is all ok? we had to rescue Sea Bear. It had two paramilitary types aboard, both unable to sail."

She texted back, "all well, medical emergency, catch up soon." Not strictly the truth, there was no medical issue, but it was a convenient excuse for the moment.

"Did anyone know that the two guys we left aboard Sea Bear couldn't sail?" she asked.

Everyone in the car looked round at Jenny "How do you know?"

"Text from Andy."

Josh seemed to get into a flap. He called Ranulph. He was reassured that Ranulph was still alive, safe ashore and about to go for a curry in Newhaven with the Border Force guys.

Chapter 39

2024

2nd July - Tuesday
Sovereign Harbour Marina, Eastbourne, East Sussex.
Martin.

The next morning at 6.00, Martin and Andy were rudely awoken by the sound of someone climbing into Wanderer's cockpit. There was the sound of knocking on the coach roof. It was Josh and Ranulph. They informed a very sleepy Martin that they were to take him to London immediately to answer questions. Andy wanted to know what was going on but could get no answer. He was particularly irritated by their manner and that both were carrying submachine guns.

Martin seemed relaxed about it. He reassured Andy that a lawyer probably wasn't needed and got dressed ready for the journey. Martin was walked along the pontoons, pausing only for him to point out a family of swans, complete with cygnets. They went through the car park to the waiting Range Rover. As an afterthought, Martin called back to Andy

"Son, can you book some extra days in the marina." They had originally planned to return to Brighton that day.

There was a delay while Ranulph retraced their steps. When he returned to the boat, Andy asked him what was going on. It transpired that both Josh and Ranulph had somehow mislaid the magazines from their submachine guns.

"Are you sure you had them in the first place?" Andy had asked, "it seems unlikely that they would just fall off."

The Range Rover finally set off, heading for London, while the magazines settled gently into the mud at the bottom of the marina.

Martin dozed off on the journey, leaving Josh and Ranulph to bicker quietly over how the magazines could have been lost and why they had needed to go fully armed in the first place. As Ranulph pointed out, Martin and Andy had come to their rescue the day before, so he was slightly embarrassed at holding them at gunpoint the next day.

On arrival in London, Martin was taken to an interview room. He was observed for a while, but he simply sat quietly, occasionally looking round the room.

The interview team went in and sat facing him. It had been agreed that Peter Griffin would lead the interrogation, Lisa would take notes. Miriam and Nicholas would act as observers.

The four of them filed into the room and sat in a row opposite Martin. Peter Griffin had decided that there was no need to pussyfoot around.

"So, Martin, do you know why you are here?"

"I'm here because two gentlemen came to my boat this morning, woke me and escorted me at gunpoint, at speed across the country to this room."

"No, the real reason you're here…"

"No, I don't, do you know why you've brought me here?"

"Yes of course."

"In that case why are you asking me? The question seems superfluous. I would be most grateful if someone could arrange a cup of coffee, milk, one sugar please. I'm prepared to pay for the coffee if necessary."

"We're not here to get you coffee. Let's start with you giving some answers, firstly, what is your full name?"

Martin gave Peter a puzzled look and then looked at the others "Are you suggesting that you dragged me from my bed and all the way here, yet you don't know who I am? Josh and Ranulph asked for me by name. I would also point out that your receptionist has issued me with a visitors' badge which has my name printed on it. Can I also refer you to the first question you asked me, which you began by addressing me by name."

"Have you ever been known by any other name?"

"No"

"We have brought you here to ask you questions about your period of service in the army."

"I've never served in the army."

"Alright then, the military?"

"I've never served in the military."

"Our records say differently."

"Really! your records are incorrect. I have never served in the military."

"Ok, maybe not military in the strictest definition, but I think we both know what I'm talking about"

"I'm not sure we do. Just to be absolutely clear, I have never been in any military organisation, army, navy, air force, marines, or any secret squirrel organisation, for any country. Hopefully that's clear. Although, thinking of secret squirrels…I was once in the Tufty Club."

"OK, so you were in this Tufty Club, tell me more, when did you join, who did you report to?"

"I don't remember when I joined, I was young. However, the big squirrel of the Tufty club was called….Tufty."

Peter turned to Lisa, "we need a full briefing from the Brits on the Tufty Club."

At that point the phone rang. Miriam answered it, they all looked at Miriam, who listened, nodded, then put the phone down. "I am advised that the Tufty Club and the identity of Tufty are not relevant to the matters at hand. Please follow other lines of enquiry."

At that point there was a knock on the door and a young man bought in a tray with cups of coffee and biscuits. There was much faffing around serving the coffee. Martin addressed the ceiling, "thank you" he said, "glad to know someone else remembers the Tufty Club."

Peter placed a picture of Collins on the table. "Do you know this man?"

Martin studied it carefully, he looked up. "No, never seen him before."

"Does the name Martin B Collins mean anything to you?"

"No."

"What if I told you that Martin B Collins was a wealthy young US citizen who disappeared in 1979, in mysterious circumstances?"

"No."

"Look at the photograph again, please, think, does the name Collins mean anything to you?"

There was a long pause. "Was he the one who was lost in a mysterious balloon accident? A hot air balloon?"

"No, not a balloon accident. There was no balloon accident."

"But mysterious?"

"Yes", Peter was beginning to wonder where this was going, so he tried another approach. He placed the photograph of the M60 on the table. "Do you recognise this?" He asked.

"It looks like a machine gun, I'm sorry I don't know enough about guns to tell you more." Martin picked up the photograph and looked more closely. He turned it over in his hands. "It would appear to be an M60 machine gun, 7.62 mm, belt fed."

"So, you do know about guns…"

"Not really, that's what's printed on the back of the photograph", Martin held it up for Peter to see.

"Would it surprise you to learn that this weapon was in the possession of the Royal Marines in Ireland in 1979"

"No."

"Interesting, why is that?"

"Because the Royal Marines have guns, isn't that the sort of thing they do, shooting and stuff?" Martin looked around the others to see if they agreed. Evidently, they did.

"Would it surprise you to learn that we believe that this weapon or one like it may have been involved in the disappearance of Martin B Collins?"

"Yes, it would surprise me"

"Why is that?"

"Because I don't believe the Royal Marines would shoot down a hot air balloon with a machine gun, or in fact any gun."

"There was no hot air balloon…"

"So why did you say that there was?"

"I didn't."

"Wouldn't shooting down a balloon be more of an air force sort of thing?" asked Martin. "You really are asking the wrong person here, shouldn't you talk to the RAF, perhaps they have an anti–balloon squadron."

Peter tried to get back on track, "Tell me, do you have any knowledge of guns being smuggled into Ireland."

"Yes, I think I do."

Peter leaned forward; this could be crucial he thought. "Tell me more…"

"Well, we were in Falmouth about two years ago and Dulcibella was there, or possibly a re-creation, anyway she was in lovely condition, clearly had a lot of money spent on her…."

"What is her full name?"

"I don't know but given her age she was probably on Lloyds Register, maybe they would know, it will probably be Dulcibella of somewhere."

"Her age?"

"I would guess she was built sometime before the First World War…"

"What are you talking about?"

"She's a classic yacht"

"I asked you about smuggling, what are you talking about…?"

"Well, the chap who owned her was involved in smuggling guns to Ireland"

"And how do you know this"

"I think it was well known at the time; I don't think it was a big secret or anything"

"I don't imagine that you can remember his name, that would be just too helpful" Peter sneered

Martin paused, as if thoughtfully registering the sarcasm, "Funnily enough I do remember his name, would you be interested in knowing it?"

"Obviously, yes,"

"It was Erskine Childers…"

"Progress at last," said Peter. "Lisa, make a note, we need to find out everything about this Childers."

At this point the phone rang again. Miriam answered and relayed the message in a somewhat exasperated tone. "Childers was shot by the Irish Free State Government in 1923" she advised. "We have been asked to conclude the interview."

Peter was distinctly angry. He stood up and shouted at Martin, "Are YOU The Sandman?"

"No"

"The Iceman?"

"No"

"Really??"

"Yes really, I am not the sandman, the iceman, the snowman, the postman, the pie man, the gingerbread man, the yeoman, I am not Tony the tiger, I am not Tufty the squirrel, I am not a washerwoman, I am not Alfredo the Great of Spain, I am not…"

"Either you get with the program or I am going to shoot you in the face, DO YOU UNDERSTAND!"

Martin seemed unimpressed, "I would say that your tone is completely uncalled for and if I may so…"

Peter was reaching under his jacket about to draw his gun from his shoulder holster.

Martin sat watching impassively as Lisa, Miriam and Nicholas jumped up to intervene. However, it became clear that Peter did not have the gun. Miriam turned to apologise and saw to her horror that Martin was holding Peter's Glock in his hand.

Martin removed the clip from the weapon, cleared it and handed it to Lisa. His tone was deadpan "Your colleague must have dropped this on the floor, I picked it up, but there wasn't a convenient break in the conversation for me to tell you that I had it."

The phone rang again. The voice at the other end told Miriam to announce that the meeting was now definitely over. Martin collected his belongings and was escorted from the building. He was not happy about having to travel back to Eastbourne at his own expense.

After Martin had gone, Miriam went to watch the video of the meeting. She had to watch it several times before she was able to spot the moment when Martin had used the distraction of the coffee arriving to lift Peter's gun unnoticed. About an hour later it was announced that Peter's briefcase had been handed in at reception. He evidently had not noticed that it gone missing from outside the interview room. He also was puzzled that his wallet was in the briefcase, when he thought he had it in his jacket.

Miriam was now convinced. This was old school. She had heard that, in the distant past, agents had been trained in skills such as lock picking, pickpocketing and various techniques for disarming opponents without them knowing using distraction. Skills picked up in the war from SOE, from professional criminals and the like were taught to trainees. Clearly, Martin had learned his lessons well.

Lisa was getting her ears bent. That she allowed her "ride along muppet" to walk round London with a loaded Glock was considered to be unprofessional and discourteous to her hosts. To be handed the gun back by the person being questioned was extraordinary. Her colleague was to return to the USA at once, Presidential appointment or not. A strongly worded note was to be sent.

Finally, to add insult to injury, she was informed that Britain had operated a Secret Service since 1570. The interview conducted by her colleague was judged to be the worst in the Service's history, a new low, an absolute benchmark setting catastrophe.

Chapter 40

1979

27th August - Monday
Bunduff Strand, Cliffoney, County Sligo, Eire
Alex and Isobel.

It was the August Bank Holiday. Alex and Isobel were watching a small section of beach and the quay beyond. They were hidden, but if someone had stumbled upon them, they might have appeared to be a courting couple engaged in a little al fresco mutual gratification. It had been raining for the days before, but the sun was now out.

To be fair, it was now more than an illusion. Alex and Isobel had grown remarkably close given the circumstances and how little time they had known each other. They had settled into a comfortable, passionate closeness. Perhaps it helped that neither knew anything about the other, they truly seemed to be living in the moment.

There had been a suggestion on the intercepts that something was being planned on a boat kept in the harbour, but no clue as to what. They had been asked to observe and report anything of interest. So far, it had been an unremarkable day.

Short legged birds, brown bodied and white bellied were running along the water's edge. Their little red beaks probed for food in the sand.

To pass the time they were listing composers in alphabetic order. Isobel had gone with Mahler, Alex with Mozart,

"Mendelssohn"

"Mazursky"

"Massenet"

Alex paused "MMMM, ok I quit N…."

They were both stumped on N.

Alex was feeling mischievous. "Wouldn't it be easier if you could tell how intelligent a woman was simply by looking…for example blondes are all stupid, brunettes are brainy or maybe, size related. The bigger the brainier perhaps. A for ignoramus, DD for genius. I guess you would be somewhere in the middle of the range…ahhh!"

She had grabbed him, "on the size scale of big equals brainy, I would describe you as possibly the least gifted intellectual I have ever met." She released her grip on his groin, with a final squeeze.

"Bloody hell Isabel, that bought the tears to my eyes, that's a very firm grip you've got there."

"Offenbach"

"Oldfield"

"Who?"

"Mike Oldfield, Tubular bells…"

"Pachelbel"

"Prokofiev"

"Puccini"

"Pag….what the hell?"

The birds burst into the air and whirred away.

A small fishing boat that had just left the harbour had exploded, blown into tiny fragments. A cloud of fire had shot up and they watched in shock as splintered bits of the boat rained down on the water.

"Let's get out of here," said Alex." There's going to be police all over this area in no time, we don't want to get caught up in their search."

On the news that night it was reported that Earl Mountbatten had been on the fishing boat, together with his family and various friends. Meanwhile, over the Border, an ambush at Warrenpoint had cost the lives of 18 soldiers, with as many as twenty wounded.

Things were taking a turn for the worse. Isobel and Alex decided to adopt a lower profile.

Chapter 41

1979

7th October - Sunday
Forest Lodge, Sligo. Eire.
Isobel.

Forest Lodge was a new development, a golf course with a club house and chalets scattered through the woods for guests. The developer had made the mistake of thinking that it made sense to charge American prices for an Irish golf course, so business had been slow. There had been no sign of the golf mad Japanese tourists that had featured so prominently in the developer's pitch to the bank. The chalets were still as new, having had few occupants.

The furthermost chalet was occupied, Alex and Isobel had been there for about a week, although neither had expressed any interest in using the golf course. Even the offer of half price tuition had been declined, gracefully. "I rank golf amongst the perversions to be avoided, like incest and Scottish Country dancing" Alex had told the manager.

"Ignore him" Isobel had laughed "he just knows he'll be rubbish at it." The manager had concluded that they were young and in love, with better things to do with their time.

The strange thing about Isobel and Alex's relationship is that by now they did look like a couple in love, because perhaps they were. They would probably not have admitted it at first, but somehow their instant marriage worked. In pretending to be married, all their cover story required of them was to sleep in the same bed and to go no further. Somehow, they short circuited the courtship process, first cuddles, then kisses and then sex. What made it strange was that neither knew anything about the other. It was if they had come into existence, as Alex and Isobel, in an instant in the briefing room and nothing beforehand mattered.

The stay at Forest Lodge was intended to allow them to duck out of sight for a while and keep a low profile. There was the risk that they might be stopped at a checkpoint, there was now a lot more police activity. They relied on the Imp for day-to-day travel. The Imp was clean, unmodified, so even the most careful search would find nothing incriminating.

Parked deep in the woods, the VW bus was well away from prying eyes. Whilst the VW looked innocent, they knew that a thorough search might give the game away. The camping gas cylinder had been carefully modified, so that the top held enough gas to fool casual inspection, whilst the base unscrewed to reveal pistols and ammunition. The radio was tuned to receive Radio Caroline, but a subtly concealed switch turned it into a transmitter. A hidden compartment in the rear quarter contained the electronics, the little boxes at the heart of the mission.

There were meeting rooms amongst the chalets, into which Alex had installed some of these electronic boxes. For once the wiring was new and the job was quick and easy to accomplish.

Chapter 42

1979

19th October - Friday
Forest Lodge, Sligo. Eire.
Isobel.

A message had come from control and Alex needed to head North. There had been a lead that a remote farmhouse close to the border needed watching. The thinking was that the people behind the Warrenpoint ambush might be using it as a safe house or store. Surveillance was needed, possibly with a view to a cross-border SAS raid.

Unfortunately, access from the Republic side was difficult. It would be too easy for someone to see you on the way in or out. Alex was tasked with getting to the farmhouse, seeing if there was a power supply and if possible installing listening devices. Alex had decided to go in from the North. He had slipped away, taking the Imp and by a circuitous route, headed North. Arrangements had been made for him to be flown into one of the forward bases overlooking the border.

Isobel was alone in the chalet, spending her time reading. She had gone to the clubhouses for lunch and noticed a couple of newcomers. The woman was dark haired, brown eyed, about 5'8", slim and pretty. The man, slightly taller, well built, blue eyes and dark hair. They matched the description of Anna and Eion who had checked up on them in their absence from the Shannon Hotel, so Isobel was immediately on her guard.

After Alex had driven away in the Imp, Eion had rushed to his car and driven after him. "Far too eager" Isobel had thought to herself. Alex would be parked up somewhere, watching the cars that passed, alert for a tail. She took her silenced pistol and knife from the hiding place in the van, returned to the chalet and waited.

After about an hour or so, she heard movement outside. A quick peep through the window revealed Anna walking around outside. Isobel quietly moved to the bathroom, leaving the door slightly ajar so she could watch.

After a while there was a knock on the door. "Housekeeping" called Anna. Getting no reply, Anna waited, then knocked again. Isobel heard a key turning in the lock and Anna entered the lodge. Barely breathing, Isobel watched Anna as she searched the room, looking through their suitcases, then sitting on the bed to read their letters. Anna carefully opened one of the boxes of photographs and looked at them one by one.

The silence was broken by a crash. From her hiding place, Isobel watched in surprise as two men flung the door open to burst into the room. Anna had sprung to her feet, but was punched hard in the face, flailing unconscious onto the bed. The two men quickly looked around the room, bound Anna's hands, taped up her mouth and placed a bag over her head.

They carried her out of the chalet and into the wooded area. Isobel followed at a distance, slowly, keeping herself hidden. By the time she was close enough to observe again she could see that the men were trying to beat a confession out of Anna. They had stripped Anna to the waist, her top had already been torn away. Her hands and feet had been bound with cable tie, her arms were tied behind her back. Anna was defenceless.

Isobel watched as the men took turns to punch and kick Anna. They did not say a word. They dragged her to her feet, punched her back to the ground, then lifted her back up to repeat the process. It was a brutal beating designed to break her will, to make the eventual interrogation easier.

The older of the two men was evidently in charge. He was heavily built, dressed in jeans and leather jacket. His slicked back hair and beard already showed signs of grey. Isobel noticed that he was missing two fingers from his left hand, perhaps a legacy of a past mishap. The younger man was slightly taller, thinner, with permed hair and a faint moustache. He was wearing tight jeans and a denim jacket. Both wore heavy work boots; the steel toecaps thudded into Anna's ribs.

Now the older man was issuing instructions. The hood and tape were removed. Anna was pulled up into a sitting position. She was dazed, bleeding from the mouth and nose. She was gasping for air.

"Who are you"? The older man's accent was harsh. Sounds like he's from Belfast, thought Isobel.

Anna looked wildly around; she was trembling violently. "Anna", she replied, "Anna"

"Why are you here?"

Anna shook her head and got a savage blow across the face in response.

The younger man took hold of Anna's hair and pulled her back upright.

"To check on the Brits" she mumbled

"Who sent you?" his fist was poised, ready to strike.

Anna flinched in anticipation of the blow, "We were sent to check on two Brits who might be here…"

The men paused. The hood was placed back over Anna's head. They stepped away from Anna and briefly conferred.

"She's lying, must be, she's trying to put us off the track…"

They went back to Anna. As they did this, Isobel moved a bit closer.

The hood was removed again. The older man put his face to Anna's. "You are as good as dead. In a few minutes we will kill you. How we do it depends on how cooperative you are. Listen carefully to my questions. Every time you lie, I am going to cut your pretty face."

Anna nodded, wide eyed.

"Was it you that followed two volunteers, shot them and burned their car?"

"No, that's what we were sent to find out."

"I don't believe you" the older man was holding a Stanley knife up to Anna's face.

"It's true…" she gasped.

The younger man took a firm grip on Anna's hair. She struggled, but the older man held her by the throat. He took the knife and pressed it into her forehead.

"No" cried Anna. She winced as the knife was slowly drawn down cutting into the flesh of her forehead, then down across her cheek to her chin. Blood poured.

"How did you know who they were? Who told you where they were going?"

"I don't know" she flinched as a second cut opened up her other cheek.

"Are you the Sandman?

"I don't know who that is…I don't." Another cut, this time diagonally across her face. Blood was pouring off her chin.

"Where is the Sandman?" the older man shouted.

Anna shook her head "No..."

He slapped her hard, blood spattered "Are you the Sandman?"

"I'm Anna, Anna, stop, please stop. Stop!"

He hit her again. "Talk, bitch, why are you here?"

The man punched her again. He raised the knife to Anna's eye.

Isobel decided she had heard enough. She stepped from the bushes and shot the younger man as he stood watching. The bullet entered his thigh, making him roll screaming in shock and pain to the ground.

The older man struggled to get to his feet, turning, reaching for the gun from his waistband. He was too slow. Isobel walked over to him, pressed her gun against his thigh and squeezed the trigger. He rolled away in agony, the shattered bone grinding painfully. Isobel looked down at him. She shot him in the other thigh. She leaned down, took his gun from his waistband and hurled it away. She walked over to the younger man and kicked his pistol well out of reach. Both men struggled in agony.

Isobel now freed Anna, cutting the cable ties with her long-bladed knife. Anna rose unsteadily, bruised, wild eyed and angry.

"Do you know these men?" Isobel asked her.

"No" came the reply, wide eyed and spitting. She wiped her face, the cuts stung painfully, she realised she was bleeding heavily.

Anna was looking warily at the silenced pistol in Isobel's hand; a grim realisation came to her. The younger man was beginning to get to his feet. Isobel shot him through the other thigh. He tumbled back down. It was an almost casual movement. Anna realised she was in the presence of a professional killer. This was no rescue. She was not going to get out of this alive.

Anna looked down at her nakedness. "Can I ask you a favour, before you kill me?" She gestured at the two men. "These bastards deserve to suffer…"

"Be my guest" replied Isobel, "take your time."

Anna took the knife that Isobel proffered. It was as sharp as a razor.

Anna went over to the older man and stood over him. She looked back at Isobel, hesitating. Isobel held out her left arm, her hand making a fist. Her thumb was held horizontal. Isobel smiled. She turned her thumb down, "Death" she said.

Anna turned back to the man. Once released, her rage was uncontrollable. She could feel the searing cuts on her face, the pain to her ribs. Now the pain fuelled her hatred. The hatred burned in her, bright, hot, pure and fierce. "You fucking bastard" she spat bloodily; she knelt over the older man and sliced off his nose. The blood gushed. She held it in bloodied hands in front of his face, his eyes were wide with terror.

"No" he screamed. He was panting and gasping. Blood spilled down his throat, choking him.

"See how you like it" she hissed, as she pushed the knife into his stomach, slitting it across. Steam rushed up and blood spurted all over her. She reached in and pulled out his intestines. She heaped the steaming mass onto his chest, leaving the man clawing at the ground.

She staggered over to the younger man who was rigid with shock. As he struggled, she pulled down his Y fronts and took hold of his penis. "Enjoy yourself, did you? Then enjoy this..." She slowly drew the blade across, cutting off his penis with a slow deliberate action. The man howled. Anna used the penis like a brush, wiping blood on the man's face as if to write a message. She slowly pushed the blade into his cheek, pushing up until she had burst the eye. She forced his mouth open and cut his tongue out. Anna stabbed him repeatedly in the chest. At one point the knife became stuck. She hammered at his chest, twisting the knife free, to stab again and again.

Once both men had ceased twitching and writhing, Anna collapsed exhausted to the ground. There she paused for breath, composed herself and shakily rose to her feet. She stood facing Isobel. Anna's body was spattered from head to toe in blood, her hair was matted with it, she held the knife in one hand, a severed penis in the other.

"Wow....Hell hath no fury..." said Isobel.

"Thank you," said Anna, she was breathing hard. She shuddered, "You can kill me now, please make it quick." She took a deep breath and closed her eyes. She fainted.

When Anna awoke, she was back in the chalet. Isobel was running a bath for her. Anna sat in the bath; the water took on a deep red colour as the blood washed away. Isobel helped her to wash her face and hair. Her face was burning in pain. When Anna was sufficiently cleaned, Isobel pressed bandages to her face. Isobel had a first aid kit open and had already used a whole tube of ointment on the cuts to Anna's face. Isobel lifted her from the bath and put her on the bed then helped dry her.

Isobel gave Anna tablets. "Painkillers" she said, then lowering her voice, "tell me, were you raped? Take these" she said, "we don't want you falling pregnant."

Anna was about to protest, as a Catholic, but the sin of contraception was the least of her worries having just killed and eviscerated two men. She shuddered.

Isobel dried and combed Anna's hair. "These cuts are nasty; you're going to have a bad black eye on this side and there's teeth missing. Does it feel like they broke any bones?

Anna was bruised all down her side, but she couldn't tell if her ribs were broken; all she knew was that she was in pain.

"Those men, why did they attack you?"

Anna didn't know. The younger man had repeated the phrase "English bitch" over and over again as he had pounded into her. "I heard them say that they wanted some fun before they killed me, they asked about the Sandman, then something about payback."

"But you're not English, are you, why would they think you were English" Isobel gently asked.

"They were after you" said Anna, "not me." Anna confessed that she had been searching Isobel's chalet when she was snatched. "We were told to check you out. The Leadership thought you might be Brit spies." Anna remembered the gun, the coldly efficient shooting. "Are you Brits?" she asked.

"What leadership?" asked Isobel.

Anna hesitated. "The Provisional IRA, both Eion and I are members of …"

Isobel hugged her. "Someone has a vivid imagination" she said. Isobel explained that she and Alex worked for an American corporation run by a man called Big Don. He was into property, building hotels and golf courses around the world. Some of this Don's associates were dodgy, mafia types and they could be pretty ruthless. They might try to muscle in and because much of the money was being laundered, going to the police was not an option. "It's the American way of business" she explained, "I carry a gun in case someone turns unpleasant, like the two men you just slit open."

Anna was confused, "So you're American?"

"No darling, Alex and I are both Russian." That surprised Anna. Isobel looked at her calmly. "Anna, you can tell whoever sent you to check us out; that we are not British spies. We are Russians, freelancers, working for an American organisation, from New York, US of A. Any interference with us would be bad for business. Big Don knows people who you wouldn't want to meet down a dark alley."

Chapter 43

1979

20th October - Saturday
Forest Lodge, Sligo. Eire.
Isobel.

Alex had returned to the chalet late on Saturday. Anna was there, awake in the bed. She watched as Isobel greeted Alex in Russian. Alex took the hint and replied in Russian. They went outside, there was a whispered conversation that Anna could not hear. Alex rushed away.

Eion too had been away, attempting to follow Alex. He had lost him almost straight away and spent the next day searching in vain for him. He had returned to the chalet to find it empty with no sign of Anna. To his surprise, Alex wandered past shortly afterwards, he must have been close behind him, unseen all along. Minutes later, Alex had come back, knocked on Eion's door and simply said "Your wife has been hurt, come at once."

They ran to the chalet, where Isobel was waiting at the door. To Eion's relief Anna was inside. She was tucked up in bed, her face heavily bandaged, her body badly bruised, smiling weakly at him. She was wearing some of Isobel's clothes. She tearfully explained what had happened and her ordeal at the hands of the two men. She told Eion that she had expected to die.

"Who were they?" Eion had asked, his face contorted in tears of anger.

Anna whispered back, "I think they were two of our men, I think they mixed me up with Isobel."

Eion wanted revenge. "They can't get away with this, I want to track them down and kill them."

Isobel tried to calm him, "Already dealt with, by Anna."

Eion gently lifted the bandages from Anna's face. He looked in horror at the cuts, they were deep and bloody. She would probably be scarred for life. He was panicking, "We must get an ambulance at once; a doctor needs to look at your face. Why have you not called an ambulance?" asked Eion.

Isobel stopped him. "You have two bodies to tidy away first. If you call an ambulance, the police will come, and you will have to explain why your wife has just hacked two men to death. First things first!"

"You boys have got some digging to do", said Isobel leading them to the small clearing where the two bodies lay, hastily covered with leaves. Eion was badly sick; it looked like both men had been butchered. When he was told Anna had done it, he was shocked to his core.

The flies were gathering on the bodies. As they watched, a dragonfly moved slowly towards the bodies, jewel like, hanging in the air. It darted forward and snatched a fly, paused to tighten its grip, then rushed away.

They went off to look for some shovels. A little later the two women watched as a mini digger drove past. Alex and Eion had "borrowed" it and in no time had dug a very deep pit, tipped in the bodies and covered it all in. They drove the mini digger away.

"What is it with boys and their toys?" said Isobel, "you're lying there in agony and they're clearly having fun."

The two men returned, having enjoyed playing with the digger. "It was a bit of luck finding that" Eion had shouted, "otherwise we would have been digging for hours." Isobel watched Eion, he was behaving strangely, evidently something had snapped in his head and he was not coping with the reality of this mess.

That evening the four of them sat in the chalet.

Alex spoke quietly and slowly. "Those two men probably came here to kill Isobel and me. It was just bad luck for you Anna, that you were in our chalet when they came. On the other hand, it was fortunate that Isobel returned when she did and was able to help you."

They nodded in agreement.

Alex continued "I realise this is all difficult to get our heads around. But, taking into account what Anna has told us, it seems to me that those men may have been sent here by the same people who sent you to spy on us. Nobody else would have known we were here. So, Anna, Eion, if you are part of some IRA kill team looking for Brits, we understand. However, as you now know, we are not Brits, but everyday Russians, working for Big Don and the good old US of A."

Isobel took up the proposition "If you can persuade your bosses that we are not to be worried about, we would be grateful. We don't want to be faced by another pair of thugs coming to find out what happened to the first pair."

She turned to Anna, "You have killed two men, and you, Eion, helped hide the bodies. You do rather owe us a favour in return for all we have done. If this comes to light, we will all be in the shit. Just tell your bosses, whoever they are, that you checked us out and all is well. Say nothing about the two men that came."

"Anna," said Isobel," we need to talk. In the eyes of the law, you are a murderer. If you end up in court, a jury of men is not going to sympathise with you. They will look at you and think you led those men on. When they hear that you then sliced them up and disembowelled them, they will think you are a monster. Some sick pervert. A man hater."

"They will put two and two together and you will be in the frame too, Eion. A pair of sickos hunting down innocent men and butchering them for fun. We have taken a big risk helping you, one that could get us killed."

"We are going to disappear now, back to America. Maybe at some point in the future, we may need to call in our favour" Alex had said. "When we do, whatever it is, do not hesitate, just do it."

"That's all we ask. We keep your secret; you give us time to get away to the US and so far as the rest of the world is concerned, those two men never existed."

They nodded in agreement. That night Eion phoned in his report. He said that all was well, and that the couple were not Brits. They had discovered that they were Russians, working on dodgy property deals for an American called Don. The voice on the other end of the call seemed dubious. He asked about two fellas who had been sent down from the North, to add some muscle. Eion stayed on message and said they had seen nothing. Isobel and Alex listened in to the call, relieved.

However, they snuck into one of the empty chalets that night, leaving their own looking like it was occupied. They took turns to watch, but it looked like Anna and Eion were true to their word. At 3.00 in the morning, Isobel had difficulty staying awake. As they sat in the darkness, Alex made her recite the Twelve Caesars in order, "full name and cause of death."

"Gaius Julius Caesar, murdered. Gaius Julius Caesar Augustus, known as Octavian, natural causes or poison, Tiberius Julius Caesar Augustus, poison or shagging, Gaius Caesar Augustus Germanicus, known as Caligula, murdered; Lucius Domitius Ahenobarbus, later known as Nero Claudius Caesar Augustus Germanicus, or Nero, suicide; Servius Sulpicius Galba, murdered; Marcus Salvius Otho, suicide: Aulus Vitellius murdered; That's enough, I'm too sleepy now." Alex made sure she was covered by the blanket and resumed his watch, gun at the ready.

Before breakfast Alex paid the bill, the Imp was loaded, and they drove away.

Alex drove, Isobel map read and watched behind. They knew they were blown, and the top priority was to get out as fast as possible. The last few days had been too close for comfort. Alex had run into the two men with the machine gun, Isobel had come close to being raped and murdered. They knew that someone would work it out. Even if the cover story about being Russians was believed, sooner or later someone would put it all together.

"What pisses me off, "said Alex "is that we were supposed to be under deep cover. Nothing gory. Just install the boxes, that was all. Instead, it's been one corpse after another. I make it eight so far. This whole thing could go wrong at any moment, and we will end up dead in a ditch."

Isobel had been quiet up till now. "I'm a monster" said Isobel, "a fucking monster."

Alex looked at her questioningly.

"In the chalet, I was there when the two men burst in. Anna was there purely by chance, a freak co-incidence that she chose the same moment as her own side's kill squad. I had a gun, I could have shot them all straight away, but I didn't. I realised they had come for me, I waited. I waited because I wanted to see what would happen."

"I wanted to watch. There was a thrill of anticipation. Like the crowd in the Coliseum before the fight, I wanted to watch someone else suffer and die. What made it so tasty was that she was going to experience the death that fate had served up for me. I watched and I waited. I watched them knock her unconscious. I watched as they dragged her to the woods, I watched them take turns to beat her. I listened as she regained consciousness, screamed and choked and struggled. I just watched."

"What's more, I don't recall feeling anything, other than perhaps curiosity. When they questioned her, I just wanted to hear their questions. In fact, I was disappointed at the level of questioning, it was "Who do you work for?" "Who are you here to meet?" I didn't feel any need to help her, I just wanted her still alive afterwards, so we could get her to talk if need be."

Isobel was staring at her hand. It was steady as a rock. "What clinched it was when they asked, "Where is the Sandman?" Then it was interesting, as I realised, we were blown. So, I shot them, to hobble them."

"Alex, you should have seen Anna, she was wild, like an animal. She cut those men open gleefully, screaming, yelling, it was raw, savage, like nothing I could have imagined. She became a fury. And I just watched, it was fascinating, when she pulled out the first one's guts and put them on his chest. I thought it was brilliant, now the second one would talk for sure."

"But she didn't want him to talk, it was just revenge. Once she had cut his dick off, I knew he wasn't going to talk. She just tortured him for the hell of it. I just watched; it was

wonderful. I watched her pop his eyeball and was fascinated by the way he squirmed and twisted and spat blood. You should have seen her, Alex; she was covered in blood from head to foot. She was like a Roman priestess who had just performed a sacrifice to the gods.
She just stood there, my dagger in one hand and a severed cock in the other. Alex, when it was over, I just felt disappointment that there wasn't more. It was beautiful. Alex, when it was over, she asked me to kill her."

"Why didn't you?"

"I don't know, I just took her back to the chalet and cleaned her up."

"Probably just as well, they seemed like a nice couple. What's more they owe us a favour, we might be able to use them in the future, turn them."

"You got on well with Eion, you were like a couple of kids playing with that digger."

"I couldn't work them out, they weren't professionals. He clearly was bright, but just seemed unprepared for what we had to do. He was very ill when we got to the bodies. His face was a picture when you told him that Anna had cut them up. It was unreal, he couldn't process what was happening."

"We had the strangest conversation. He asked me about football, apparently, he supported Liverpool. You should have seen his face when I said I supported Dynamo Kyiv as a boy. As for her, she didn't check every room of the chalet before searching, she came alone with no-one on overwatch, unarmed; they made basic errors. I think they were sent out to check on us as a training mission, maybe a test, with the killing to be done by the other two."

"They are the babes in the wood, and you're right, we are blown …it's time for us to get out. The two heavies were asking about Sandman. If they used the name Sandman that means that someone from our side has given us away. The IRA shouldn't know our worknames. We need to hide, go dark until we can find out what has happened."

"Time to leave the Grove and let some other slave become the King. The time has come for Sandman and Iceman to flee the world of men, to descend into Hades, the Abyss, the underworld, "

"Could you be a tad more specific…?"

"We need to go somewhere anonymous, somewhere where nobody will notice us. I have phoned ahead and booked us into the Travelodge Motel at Newport Pagnell services on the M1 for the next five days, under the names of Mr and Mrs Smithers."

Chapter 44

1979

22nd October - Monday

Travelodge Motel, Newport Pagnell Motorway Services. England.

Isobel and Alex.

The journey to Newport Pagnell had been surprisingly tense. At one point as they drove towards the ferry, a motorcycle appeared to be following them. They pulled into a side road, stopped and prepared to shoot it out. The motorcycle had just driven past, but later they noticed him drive back in the opposite direction.

On the ferry they had seen one or two suspicious characters. But nothing materialised. They had driven by a circuitous route until they took a short section of the M1 to the service station. Once booked into the hotel, they watched their car, kept to the room and generally looked for any potential trouble.

It's fair to say that they soon got bored. The walls were thin. It was evident that the next room was being used by two women to entertain gentleman callers for commercial gain. They recorded the activity and soon fathomed out the women's system. They took turns to use the room. The first woman they termed Miss Big, as she would pant out her catchphrase of "you're so big, Oh! Oh!." They timed her: meet punter in car park, financial arrangements, walk to room, time 5 minutes 27 seconds on average. From door closing, preliminary manoeuvres, to first bed spring creaks average two minutes 45 seconds. From first creak to "You're so big" average 6 minutes, although with no significant range from quickest to longest as Alex had observed. Post coital disengagement, shower, departure of client, then bed making and tidying, average 12 minutes 6 seconds.

Broadly speaking her co-occupant ran to the same 30-minute schedule, which they must have co-ordinated when they passed each other down in the foyer. The second woman they christened Loretta, simply because one of the punters had called that name out at around the statistically significant two minutes and 45 seconds mark. Isobel and Alex took to photographing Big and Loretta's punters as they paid in the car park.

They tried to estimate annual earnings, both gross and after tax. Alex had drawn up a graph of asset utilisation. They had been fascinated by the regular cessation of activity at certain times. The working hypothesis was that the breaks coincided with the screening of Coronation Street on ITV. Alex and Isobel were very bored.

What eluded Alex and Isobel as they listened and timed, was that the noises through the wall were in fact tape recordings.

The transactions going on in the next room were not carnal, but something more sinister. As the tapes played the noise blanketed whispered conversation and the rustle of documents being photographed.

Despite the boredom. Isobel and Alex could not get a decent night's sleep. Alex would lie fitful and uncomfortable on the bed, drifting in and out of wakefulness. The slightest noise outside would force him awake. When he did finally fall asleep, the dreams would come. His first two killings, the couple who had stayed at the hotel and driven into the North.

The nightmare took him back to the desperate drive in the camper-van. The worry that they would be spotted. Catching up with the car at the filling station. Watching the woman buy petrol. Seeing her look around. "Had she seen us?"

Following them again. Seeing them in the lay-by, driving past. They're meeting someone. Parking up and waiting, relief when they drove past again. Following. Watching.
Driving past the end of the alleyway. "Where's the man going? Is that a rifle under that blanket. Think! Think. Cause a distraction. You block her in, I'll go round the back. If I'm not clear sound the horn."

"Check it's loaded." Quick, quick. Walk walk! Good. She's blocked in. Cock weapon. Walk, walk. Bend down. She looks up surprised to see me, starts to smile. First shot, second shot. Her face. Shock. Her eyes, she's trying to speak. Third shot head snaps back. Blood, brains. Reach in. Pull her head upright. She's trembling, little twitches. Eyes are staring. Put her hands on the wheel. Feel the warm hands through the gloves.

Back behind the wall. Isobel is driving off. Rifle shots from somewhere behind. Hide. I can hear him coming. Car door is opening. Step out. He turns. Shot one. Shot two. One for luck. Quick! quick! Isobel beside me. Isobel saying, "look at her pearls." Wearing pearls, pearls, blood on the pearls, "she was wearing pearls."

Alex would fight his way back to wakefulness. Bathed in sweat, trembling. Isobel would be beside him looking concerned. Isobel would stroke his hair, rub his shoulders. He would lie awake looking into the darkness. He could see that moment over and over again. The woman in the car sees him. She looks up, starting to smile. The thump of the bullets in her chest. The look of surprise. What was she trying to say?

They talked about their nightmares, but it didn't help. Nightmare followed sleep until sleep became an ordeal to be avoided. They both got very tired. They read to avoid sleep. They talked to avoid sleep. When one slept the other would watch, hear the mumbled words, knowing where they were, in the dark torment of the dreamworld.

Alex had watched Isobel. For her, sleep took her back to the clearing behind the cabin. Anna stood before her. Anna puts her hands to her sides and says "Thank you, you can kill me now, please make it quick."

Isobel looks around. The crowd is roaring "Kill! Kill!" She is in the Coliseum in Rome, there is sand beneath her feet. The crowd chant "Kill! Kill!" She sees the bodies at Anna's feet. She looks around. She looks up to the Emperor. She watches as the Emperor stands, looks around the crowd and puts out his hand. The crowd falls silent. The Emperor looks at her. She watches as his thumb turns down. The crowd roar. She turns to Anna. She is smiling, holding out the knife for Isobel to take. Isobel takes the knife from Anna's hand. She reaches down and slits Anna's belly open. Anna continues to smile. Snakes pour from her stomach. They writhe upwards and surround her head. Anna smiles and takes hold of Isobel. She leans forward and kisses her on the lips, passionately. The snakes are in her hair. Isobel cannot breathe. She struggles. She fights. There is a crash as a pillow flies across the room, scattering the coffee cups. She is awake. She can't get back to sleep for hours. She reads.

They extended their stay to a fortnight, then turned up unannounced and unexpected at Sandwich. The man on the gate took some convincing, but he took in their envelope. The last batch of films was handed over and Sandwich control was formally advised that Sandman and Iceman had decided to retire.

It was if two pawns had decided that they no longer wanted to be on the chess board. No more waiting to be taken or sacrificed, time to quit.

Arrangements for the cover story went into play at once. It took a few days, but London provided new papers and identities.

Chapter 45

1979

19th December - Wednesday
Channel Lights Guest House, Deal, Kent. England.
Isobel and Alex.

For a few weeks they were kept in a guest house in Deal. They had been de-briefed separately. Of course, their stories matched, as well they should having been carefully concocted and rehearsed back in the Newport Pagnell motel room. There was no mention of any of the extra-curricular killings.

They were advised to be indoors at all times. The weather was atrocious, rain showers and gusty wind, so staying in was no problem. They had sat in the guest house's lounge and talked, mainly about their future. Isobel, in particular, was planning out a future together, "maybe Pompeii, if we can get on a dig", she had told Alex.

However much they talked, for Alex, something was wrong. It was hanging over every conversation. Alex was questioning how he felt about Isobel. Increasingly, he worried that their relationship was built on lust, not love. Somehow, they had been swept up in the whirl of the mission. Now that it was over, there was time to think. To think clearly about what he wanted and what he really knew. He kept trying to imagine how their life together would be; would it last?

They sat in the lounge, next to the tall windows that looked out over the well-kept garden to the sea beyond. The lights of a Christmas tree blinked in the corner of the room. There had been a long period of silence.

"I think we should go our separate ways" Alex had said after much thought.

Isobel flashed an angry look at him. "Really? Why? Where did that idea come from?"

"I don't know why, I can't put it in words, somehow I think we are bad for each other."
She was not happy "Bad in what way, where, in bed?

"Yes, in bed, but not the way you are implying. When I am with you, I can't sleep. All I get is bad dreams, it's torture"

"So I'm torturing you…."

"I didn't say that; I'm torturing myself, but being with you is what triggers it. Also, when I do doze off, you wake me with your own nightmares. You thrash about and call out. And there's something else"

"Do tell…." Isobel was looking angrier than he had ever seen before.

"In my dreams I'm frightened of you. I can't help it, it's there, it's fear, it's clawing at me in the dark. I think I love you, but I'm scared of what you might do. I can't get over what I have seen you do. I'm sorry, I just can't"

Isobel was tearing up "so I am a fucking monster…"

"No, you're not" he replied gently. He took her in his arms and held her. There was a long pause. "You need to tell me something…I want to know"

She pushed him away "What? What is so important to you?"

"Isobel, why did you use such a risky way to kill those men. I don't get it. We could have just shot them, but you always wanted to go through your…." Alex struggled for a description "seduction."

She scoffed at him, "Seduction…" her tone was mocking.

He stared at her, "No, don't wave it away, you know what I mean…why lead them on, why the flaunting of your body, why a knife in the eye? What's going on in your head, for Christ's sake. Do you enjoy it? Is it some sort of weird game? Are you getting your kicks…?" He had gone too far; he left the rest unsaid

Isobel turned away. "You bastard…" Rain beat down on the window. "Ok, yes, that's how I get my kicks, I'm a weirdo, a psycho…"

Alex spoke quietly, "No, you're not; tell the truth. Why did we set up those men like that, why kill like that, what was going on?"

Isobel looked at her hand. She was still wearing the wedding ring. "I need it" she looked back at him. "I need it, it's like a fucking drug, I can't explain. It's like I'm an addict. Just shooting them wouldn't satisfy me. I've told you; I'm a monster, I need blood to be spilled...like an alcoholic needs booze."

Alex knew he shouldn't ask the next question, but he couldn't help it "Before we met? Did you kill others?

"Yes"

"How many?"

"God knows, why ask? It's like asking how many pawns you have taken in chess games. Who cares?

"I care" replied Alex softly "how long have you been doing this...I assumed this was your first assignment."

"Assume nothing, Moscow Rules, you fucking idiot. I killed my first man when I was fourteen. He was a fat and ugly Turkish bastard. I was supposed to befriend his daughter who was my age and get close to the family... I was asked to get information on him, but I couldn't....then I discovered, the hard way, he had a taste for underage girls

"Fourteen?"

"Yes, fourteen and never been kissed! They told me it would be alright, that it would be fun, that I needed to be brave. To listen. The bastard got serious with me and there was a knife by the bed, so afterwards, as he slept, I just.... "

Alex watched the tears running down her face. "There have been more?"

"Yes, of course there have been more. More than I can remember. Sweaty bastards, bleeding to death in front of me, under me, with me astride them. Usually a knife in the eye, one time a pair of scissors, another time I used a poker – right after we fucked on a rug in front of his fireplace." She eyed Alex "You disapprove?"

"I don't know. In fact, I don't know you at all. I thought we got into this together, now it turns out that all along you were... "

"What? Say it, you bastard, a whore? A murderer? A psycho? That's the business we are in; what did you expect? You are no better than the bastards who got me into this in the first place. Send the sweet little girly! Oh dear, did someone get a knife in the eye! Oh, how shocked they are! Not so squeamish that they don't send me back out there again and again. You wonder why I'm fascinated by the Coliseum, Caligula, Rome...Gladiator...that's what I am. Trained to kill or be killed. Sent out into the arena for their amusement. How I kill is my concern, it's the only pleasure I get from the whole bloody business."

"Pleasure?"

"I don't mean pleasure; satisfaction is more like it; it fills up a hungry space. Except now it's something different. Something happened. I snapped, when Anna was stood before me, asking to be killed. I should have killed her, I wanted to, but I couldn't. I saw her as a person, not a target. She wanted to die. She didn't need to be seduced; she was willing me on, to kill her. Now the bitch is in my nightmares. Every night! Over and over again! I can't go on with this!

There was a long still silence. They sat and looked at each other.

In the end, it was Isobel who made the first move. She took off her wedding ring. She placed it firmly on the table. With a resigned look, she withdrew her hand slowly.

Alex watched her, he sighed. "You're right. Let's get this over with." He removed his wedding band and placed it next to hers on the coffee table.

"I'm sorry, truly sorry"

Isobel and Alex, put on coats and braving the weather, set off towards the beach. Hand in hand, they walked across the lawns, crossed the deserted road and made their way to the water's edge. One wave came a yard or so higher up the beach, soaking their feet.

"Should have worn wellies," said Isobel. From her coat she drew out her knife. She held it up, slowly turning it over in her hand, watching as its blade caught the light. "It ends here!" she shouted to the winds. She hurled the knife as far as she could, out amongst the waves. The knife vanished with the merest splash. "I half expected a hand clad in samite to emerge to catch it" she said, "like Excalibur." Her smile was back.

Alex smiled weakly at her. He hurled his wedding ring into the waves.

Isobel followed suit. "Done" she said.

"Done" replied Alex. It was over.

Chapter 46

2024

22nd July - Monday
Economic Intelligence Unit, Victoria, London
Fiona.

Fiona Perry was giving some serious thought to the issue of gender mismatch. Specifically, the gender mismatch at the Scottish Country Dancing and Reeling Society's last events. There was a surplus of lassies and not enough laddies. It was also clear that a number of the laddies had attended under duress and had deserted at the first opportunity.

She looked up to find that Geraldine the Fat Controller, plus acolyte were heading towards her office, looking for all the world like a ship of the line under full sail. White with cream accessories was probably the least slimming colour scheme that she could have chosen, but she had been colour profiled some time ago by a consultant. White clothes convey trust, she had been told. Behind her back her staff had likened her to the Sydney Harbour Opera house, Moby Dick or the

Iceberg that sank the Titanic, nevertheless nobody had the courage to pass comment to her face. Now she was in Fiona's office, a startling and unprecedented descent to the Economic Intelligence Unit.

"Ms Perry, members of your team are assisting our American colleagues in their enquiries into matters of ancient history, specifically the 1970's. From what I understand this has included a somewhat chaotic interview with a member of the public. I also understand that one of our American colleagues managed to make a complete prat of himself. You will be relieved to know that said prat is now back in the USA, where he will be whining to Mummy, who in her turn will be whining to the President, who will no doubt whine to the PM and the whole process will conclude with the Service looking for scapegoats. Unless a line can be drawn under this sorry affair, you may consider yourself the designated scapegoat."

Fiona noticed the acolyte was rolling his eyes at her. She resisted the temptation to lash out and, biting her lip, listened to the rest of Geraldine's diatribe.

"Your mission is to send Ms Lisa Simpson of the CIA on her merry way back to the USA, job done, mystery solved, with no more hares set running. So, Ms Perry, set your elves to work and find out why the Americans are chasing this hare. Also, get Sandman and Iceman in here to meet Ms Simpson and to tell her, from the horse's mouth so to speak, exactly what happened."

Fiona was puzzled, "But we think SANDMAN and Iceman are dead, killed in a car crash in 1980."

The Fat Controller looked at her with scorn, undiluted and evident, "In that case, how is it that you tried to interrogate SANDMAN in these very offices only a few days ago and why is it that Iceman regularly appears on Channel Four doing a programme about ancient Rome? Do keep up, dear…"

With that The Fat Controller set sail, leaving her acolyte to hand over a thin file of information. The first page was a list of topics to be investigated. She had never heard of any of them. Nicholas and Miriam were summoned and set to work.

Chapter 47

2024

23rd July - Tuesday
Wroxeter Roman City, Shropshire, England.
Carolyn.

The film crew had parked Professor Carolyn Suttcliffe's motorhome in the carpark of Wroxeter Roman City. They were moving around the ruins, filling the filming schedule for the day. In truth, there was not much of the Roman city left to be seen. Generations of Shropshire locals had robbed out most of the stone and used it to build elsewhere. The ruined wall of the Roman bath house remained, together with excavated shop foundations and a section of hypocaust. There was a reconstructed Roman villa, which was enough to provide context as she discussed the progression of Roman expansion across Britain, standing as she was at the onetime frontier and furthest extent of Watling Street.

Carolyn had completed filming for the day and her assistant was making a cup of tea before they moved on to Anglesey to film another segment. She was irritated. There had been sheep walking about in the back of shot and she needed to get the piece to camera in one continuous take. Otherwise, the sheep would appear to magically jump from place to place when they cut segments together. Every time she thought she was about to "get it in one", a car horn would sound, or a helicopter would fly over or in the penultimate take there was the sound of a truck rattling by.

As she walked back to the trailer, she had noticed a man sitting on a low wall. The hood of his jacket obscured his face. He held a bunch of red roses. "Probably just a fan" she thought. Something from the past switched into gear. "What did they say in training all those years ago? Assume nothing. Trust your gut instinct" she thought; "Moscow rules."

One of the runners came to the door, "Professor Suttcliffe, there is a man here asking to see you, says he's a fan and would like a quick word."

"I'm not in the mood for this" said Carolyn, "tell him perhaps another time."

The runner disappeared but returned looking slightly frustrated. "He's very charming, has a bunch of flowers for you and says he would like to talk to you about the Iceman."

Carolyn looked at the runner "Are you sure he said the Iceman?"

The runner was sure "Perhaps, he means the Otzi iceman who was found frozen in an Austrian glacier …"

"Maybe," replied Carolyn, "go on, send him in."

Once the runner was gone, Carolyn quickly went to her bag and took out a long, thin bladed knife. Holding the handle in her right hand, she concealed the blade behind her wrist, ready for use. The knife was a copy of a Roman original, kept razor sharp. Technically it was illegal to carry such a weapon. If challenged, Carolyn had always intended to pass it off as a prop for her lectures.

The man appeared at the door, beaming and holding a bunch of flowers. "Professor Suttcliffe, thank you for seeing me" he enthused, "please accept this small token of my appreciation" He held out the flowers.

Carolyn smiled in surprise and recognition. "Can you please find some water for these" she asked the runner, who scurried off.

"You haven't changed" he said, smiling.

"Hardly", she replied, "you will note that my hair is now grey, my face wrinkled, and lack of makeup or grooming has become my trademark look."

He gestured at her hand, "I was referring to the dagger hidden in your right hand, perhaps your original trademark..."

"We need to talk" he continued. "For some reason the CIA are digging into the past and trying to find out about Sandman and Iceman. Are you sure that you cleaned out everything from our files before we did the disappearing act?"

"Yes, pretty certain" she replied.

"They have already tracked me down and called me in for questioning. It turns out that one of the people I nabbed has been in witness protection. He came to the UK and we bumped into each other by chance. You're on the telly virtually every night, surely someone might recognise you. Has anyone made contact?"

Carolyn put the knife onto the table. "Nobody has ever even hinted that they recognised me. Most of the time back then, my hair was dyed, which makes a big difference. When I picked up my academic life, I simply told everyone I had been on an extended gap year, mentioned a few digs and nobody ever suspected. Why would they recognise me now as having been Isobel, I'm nothing like the slender, hippy girl from back then? I'm older and fatter, don't dress like a hippy anymore and in many respects a completely different woman. Do I look like a spook or a killer?"

"Perhaps not," Martin smiled, "It was all a long time ago. I suppose it was our version of the gap year, something to fill in the time between university and proper career. Hopefully not typical, given the number of people we bumped off."

Martin looked around the mobile home. "This is nice, a definite step up from the old VW bus. I see you stuck with your interest in Ancient Rome and turned it into a career. You were so keen on the Romans, always wanting to dig them up! You positively lusted after a posting to Italy! Pompeii, if I recall, just so you could get your hands dirty digging, rather than just reading about them in books. Did you ever get to dig at Pompeii? You were so keen to get there and instead we ended up in Ireland, where the Romans never settled. I remember our long chats in the car. All our time wasting, listing the reasons why the Romans never got to Ireland."

"Hibernia" corrected Carolyn. She thought for a while, "anyway, back to the point. I genuinely think that there is nothing anywhere that could link you or me to our past lives. If they found the right people, they might be able to point the finger, but most of them are probably dead by now. What's the CIA's angle, why not let sleeping dogs lie?"

Martin explained what he knew, the M60 machine gun and the links to the wealthy American.

"Logically, the American must be the key, "said Carolyn. "The man on the ferry and Keith Murphy were low level, can't think what the CIA would want with them. Even if they were CIA agents, I can't believe they would want the fact that those two murdered a child to come to light. Which leaves lots of other stuff we did, surveillance and the like, but who cares. It's all history now.

Incidentally, speaking of the old days coming back to haunt us, did you watch the Rugby World Cup on the TV. At one point they showed the Irish crowd all singing "Zombie" and there they were, half the big men in the old IRA leadership together in one box, pissed and singing their heads off. The irony of it; an anti-violence song and they have the temerity to sing along as if they were a party of innocent choirboys."

Martin hadn't seen the rugby coverage, but he agreed the American must be at the heart of this. "Well," said Martin, "there were two men there that day, up by the border. They had the M60 machine gun that the CIA have now traced. One man had the misfortune to have his head fall off and I never saw the other one again. Until the other day, that is; it was in Brighton marina, he saw my son and given the likeness between us, thought it was my ghost. The thing is, the man in Brighton is an Australian, possibly originally from Ireland, but I didn't think he could be an American. I suspect the missing American that the CIA is after is the man I shot."

"You have a son?" asked Carolyn.

"Yes, he's called Andrew, well Andy. He's all grown up now, but every now and again he comes sailing with his old man. Evidently, he looks enough like me to scare the poor man witless. What about you? Husband? Family?"

"Well, I met my husband on an archaeological dig in Dorset. He is now a professor, specialising in Bronze age settlement, so we don't quite overlap in our areas of study, but we have a lot in common. And we have three daughters, they were all little madams, obsessed with being pretty and popular. The eldest, Rosie is into horse riding, eventing. The middle daughter is Becca, who is the bookworm of the family and the youngest, Clare, you may be interested to learn has taken up dinghy sailing."

"Three daughters, wow, how did that happen…?"

"Oh, you know, the usual way, the stork bought them…and we didn't send them back in time" she was laughing.

There was so much to catch up on. The last time they had spoken was in Deal in 1980. They had agreed to go separate ways and never see each other again. One last kiss on the beach, the two wedding rings hurled into the waves and they had walked out of each other's lives.

Carolyn called the runner back. "Sophie dear, change of plans, please book a table for two at the Mytton and Mermaid restaurant, preferably somewhere quiet."

"Before we eat, we are going to the graveyard," said Carolyn. "Bring the flowers." As they stepped from the motorhome a swirling flock of jackdaws flew over. They watched as the birds settled on the telephone wires next to the road. Carolyn gestured at the road, "that's the Roman Watling Street, it ends here. At the other end of Watling Street is Richborough, or as it is now known, Sandwich. Apt somehow"

They retrieved the flowers from the runner and drove the short distance from Wroxeter to Atcham. Ten minutes later they were outside the Mytton and Mermaid, a hotel standing on the banks of the Severn in the tiny village of Atcham. The river was in flood and the hotel gardens on the riverbank were underwater, as were the fields that lay just upstream. Twin bridges crossed the Severn here, the original now relegated to duty as a footbridge, whilst its twin roared with traffic on the road into Shrewsbury.

At the rear of the hotel was the church of St Eata, square, ruddy and silent. In the failing light they walked past the green and mossy gravestones, to the furthermost part of the churchyard. Most of the gravestones dated back centuries, but amongst the newer stones, Carolyn picked out a child's headstone. It read "Isobel Elliot, swept away from our love, aged 3." The date was 14th November 1957. Carolyn gave the gravestone a quick wipe with a tissue and laid the flowers on the grave, pausing to arrange them tidily.

"Your legend, Isobel Elliot" said Martin quietly.
"Yes, some time ago I looked up her details. She lived a little way upstream. Her body and that of the man that took her washed up here, just by the bridge. Her parents must have buried her here, because it is so close to where she was found, in the river."

"You say she was taken by a man..."

"As far as I can find out he was a disturbed young man, he took her from outside a shop, for some purpose that was never established. They both entered the river and were swept to their deaths. The river would probably been in flood as it is now, so they didn't stand a chance."

"It's strange to stand here and look at a grave with your name on it..."

"It's not just the name. I grew up not far from here. I was probably left outside the same shops by my parents, maybe even on the same day. I used to wonder what chance led to her being picked and not me. I also wonder what it was that made him take her, what did he do. It's grim, bloody grim. "

"I suppose you did take a dim view of rapists..." he mimed a knife being pushed in and twisted.

"I suppose I did. But that was for other reasons, I never told you the details, but let's just say I had troubled teenage years! Just to be clear though, I stopped killing when I stopped being Isobel, those days are behind me."

"Same with me. I've enough bad memories without wanting to add to them."

Carolyn looked at the grave "Sleep little Isobel...rest in peace"

They turned and walked back to the Hotel. They passed the spot where little Isobel would have washed up, pausing to look at the swollen muddy river. The garden furniture was just poking out of the water. A fallen branch carried by the water rushed through the arches of the bridge. The current was fast here, a person in the water would have not stood a chance. A child would be as good as dead once in the river.

Once inside, they took their table. The bar and restaurant were full, but the runner had asked for a table with some privacy, so they could talk without being overheard. They weren't troubled, but Carolyn got warm smiles of recognition from fellow diners. The place had obviously just been through a refurbishment, new paint, lots of prints and paintings around the walls. They ordered from the menu and settled back into their past familiarity as if they had been apart for days, not decades. Carolyn had one interesting item of news; Martin was not the only person from their past to have surfaced.

"I was doing a talk at the British Museum" she recalled, "afterwards there was the usual gaggle of people wanting to ask questions or have books signed. Once they left, one woman remained. She came over and told me she had studied classics and now was taking a particular interest in the frumentarii..."

Martin gave her a quizzical look,

"The frumentarii were the secret police of the Roman empire, dating from Domitian or maybe soon after, anyway we had a very strange conversation about secret police and the like. I played it straight, the old classics don, listened to what she had to say. As we were finishing, she told me of her favourite item in the museum's collection, a patera, decorated with the head of Medusa. I went with her, and we looked at it together.

The weird thing about it is that same image had haunted my dreams for years, the nightmares I had about Anna. For a horrible moment, for some reason I thought she might be a stalker or worse, about to do me harm. Had this woman been manoeuvring me to a spot where there were no witnesses? I wondered if I was about to be assassinated, but the woman looked at the patera and said it was her favourite thing. She had first seen it years before, when she visited with a friend. She said the strangest thing. She said that she was living in exactly the same grove that I had once lived in. She repeated it, same grove, on the same side. She said "Thank you, Professor" and started to walk away. Then, she turned back and said, "thank you Isobel." She was gone."

"Who do you think she was?"

"I'm fairly certain it was Moira Shannon, grown up and working for the intelligence service of one country or another. She had the look of Moira Shannon, especially the eyes, do you remember Moira had very striking eyes. For whatever reason she was wanting to talk to me, to confirm that I was the woman she knew as Isobel. What I don't understand is why."

"So, you have had no contact with the Service since we both "died" in 1980?"

"That's right, not a peep. I disappeared into academia and would not have been seen again if the telly job had not come along. What's more I would not have welcomed an approach. I didn't see the point of risking my life and sanity for a government that was wrecking the country and pursuing a hard line against anyone who they didn't agree with. Bloody Thatcher…"

Martin nodded in agreement, "For me it was the same, I was having a rough time of it. I suppose now it would be termed PTSD. At the time I had nobody to turn to, I was forced to muddle through it on my own, unable to tell anyone what I had done. In the end I just threw myself into work, always looking forward, never back. Fortunately, it did ease off, I suppose I crammed my brain with so much other stuff that I smothered it. Of course, once there was a political solution and the Troubles ended, I didn't have cause to think about it. On the subject of the Troubles ending, I propose a toast…Mo Mowlem."

They clinked glasses, "Mo Mowlem."

Over the meal they considered their next steps. If all else failed, they could kill everyone and go on the run they laughingly agreed.

"If it comes to that I don't fancy the opposition's chances, you were the best with a knife I ever saw" he said.

"You were the best with a double tap to the chest" she replied.

With that they clinked glasses again.

More seriously, they needed an alternative narrative. A plausible alternative to actual events. Carolyn dug out her iPad and they started to try to fit events to dates. The date of the 1979 Fastnet yacht race fitted the bill. The entry read "A worse-than-expected storm on the third day of the race wreaked havoc on the 303 yachts that started the biennial race, resulting in 19 fatalities (15 yachtsmen and four spectators). Emergency services, naval forces, and civilian vessels from around the Western side of the English Channel were summoned to aid what became the largest ever rescue operation in peacetime. This involved some 4,000 people, including the entire Irish Naval Services fleet, lifeboats, commercial boats, and helicopters."

Martin started to lay out the plan. "There's no way they can be competitors in the race, those names would be recorded. Let's assume that for some reason they were out at sea at the same time, maybe fishing and they got caught in the storm. What if they got into trouble, but nobody came to rescue them because of the race taking all the rescue service resources? Could that work?

It is a truth universally acknowledged that when two or more people of a certain age get to talking, they will turn to the subject of pensions eventually. Both Carolyn and Martin had encountered problems, in part because the official records showed they had taken on the identities of dead children, then died themselves, then re-surfaced under other names. Both had been shortchanged on their pension entitlements, much grumbling ensued!

Chapter 48

1979

21st December - Friday
Sandwich Control: unit 7, Kent, England.
Kevin.

Kevin liked his job in the film processing lab. The lab was warm and clean. He had state of the art processing facilities, and nobody minded if he processed pictures of his own from time to time. As batches of film came in, he catalogued them and processed the film. He would run another machine to produce three copies of each picture, which he would label with reference numbers and date before sending them up to the analysts and interpreters. For nearly a year now he had been processing films from two agents, designated SANDMAN and ICEMAN. He had never met them, but he sort of knew them through their work. The first frame of a SANDMAN film would be a picture of a left hand, first frame of an ICEMAN film would be a right hand. If the fingers were crossed, it meant urgent processing. Judging by the hands ICEMAN was a woman, SANDMAN a man.

He liked their work, mainly because they were under cover as photographers producing a book. This meant lots of arty shots, mixed in with surveillance stuff. Guided by the analysts, Kevin produced good quality proofs, dodged and burned as appropriate, which would go back to the agents via a fake publisher. For these prints Kevin had use of a proper darkroom, a big old DeVere enlarger. He would watch the images come through in the developer tray, refine the images and happily while away the hours. This was his idea of proper photographic printing, the rest of the work was just keeping the machines clean and topped up.

SANDMAN was very formal in his approach to photographs, direct, carefully composed. ICEMAN seemed more relaxed and freer in hers, more playful. There had been landscapes, people, people with cats and pictures of a dead whale on a beach surrounded by a crowd of onlookers. They had built quite a portfolio between them. Kevin guessed that they were somewhere in Ireland, but it was better not to ask.

Every now and again there would be some tasteful nudes, of which Kevin had kept an extra copy, strictly for personal use. Sometimes pictures came in which the analysts would get excited about. There had been a big fat bloke, dead on the bed in a caravan or mobile home. There was a man and a woman, both shot through the head, sat in a car. These pictures came together with pictures of their driving licences, and other possessions. Kevin noticed how stylishly the woman was dressed, the dark lipstick. He found the look of surprise on her face and the hole in her forehead strangely unsettling. SANDMAN had sent in a full set of pictures, ten rolls of film, showing a funeral. He recognised the vicar who was presiding from one of the early cat pictures. It was clearly an IRA funeral with guard of honour. SANDMAN had managed to photograph all of the guard of honour, without their dark glasses and berets, by waiting until they had headed back to their cars. There were a lot of handshake pictures. The analysts would have a field day working out who A and B were in each of these pictures and logging that they had met. A later set had shown a dead man looking like he had been stabbed in the face, together with pictures of his van and personal effects.

Today's batch had been amazing. There had been pictures of two corpses. They looked like they had been blown up, but Kevin saw that they had in fact been cut up. He noticed a severed penis lying next to one body and shuddered.

The next film processed was a SANDMAN set. There was a set of pictures establishing a panorama. Kevin would need to stick these together. They looked like early morning pictures showing a section of road, a small farm, some hedges, a clump of trees. The next frame must have been taken from the same spot. A fox had been photographed looking towards the camera, it must have been walking across the field and just realised it was being watched.

The next two frames were nearly identical. It showed a light-coloured van parked by the farmhouse, the driver's door open and a man emerging. The next photograph showed two men walking from the van towards the camera. One man was wearing a very distinctive camouflage jacket and light-coloured boots. He was holding a machine gun, just casually, tucked under one arm. The second man was carrying an ammunition box.

The final batch of pictures were a mix of SANDMAN and ICEMAN pictures. They showed a car park, perhaps just outside a hotel or something similar. The pictures always had one of two women. One was very pretty and blonde, the other slightly darker and more curvaceous. One woman or the other would be shown meeting a man, sometimes with a kiss sometimes a hug. There were well over fifty different men. The photographs concluded with sets of timings and notes, all on stationery from the Travelodge, Newport Pagnell. Kevin realised that amongst the pictures was one of Margaret Thatcher's ministers, another he knew to be a senior member of the Service, a third was the man off the telly whose name he couldn't remember.

Kevin dropped off the prints with the analysis team, mentioning the faces he recognised.

About an hour later, all hell broke loose. He was called upstairs to see Sandwich Controller "At once." Kevin had never spoken with Sandwich Controller before, and he had been tempted to make a little joke by asking him if he oversaw picnic catering. He resisted the temptation and then faced a thorough grilling by Control as to where the pictures had come from, why weren't they marked urgent and a mass of questions about what he had received from SANDMAN and ICEMAN recently.

He was told in no uncertain terms that if he breathed a word to anyone about the pictures then he would expect to spend the rest of his life in the Scrubs, fulfilling every perverted wish of the worst cell mate they could find for him. This last threat was delivered with such menace that Kevin felt his sphincter tighten uncontrollably. He rushed back to the lab to run off the multiple duplicate sets that Control had ordered.

When he returned to Control's office there were half a dozen senior types looking at the photographs. He handed over the duplicates which they virtually snatched from his hand.

Control announced, "This is Kevin, one of our top people, he was the one who saw the potential of the material and flagged it up." The nearest man stood up and shook Kevin's hand, "Excellent work, excellent." The rest of the room followed suit. His hand was vigorously shaken. He was wished a Merry Christmas and a Happy New Year. Happy Year indeed! chortled one of them.

Kevin left the room with a warm satisfied feeling, matched only by his puzzlement as to what he had actually done.

Chapter 49

2024

23rd July - Tuesday
Chiswick High Road, West London
Gregory.

Gregory Fielding ran a successful antiques business. His premises in the Chiswick High Road had originally been a cinema. When he had taken on the lease back in 1983 the place had been a wreck. Piece by piece he had cleaned the place up, repaired the roof, restored the water damaged floor and after nearly six months of living on the dust filled premises, he had opened to the public.

Gregory had a good eye for what was on trend and what would sell. The business had grown, he had brought in partners and now he presided over a thriving internet business as well. Now, with forty years of ownership under his belt, the time had come to retire. He had the money and the inclination to find somewhere quiet, maybe on the coast. He had already taken a couple of trips to Whitstable to look at properties. Whitstable had changed a lot since he was last there, gentrified, fashionable, but still sufficiently "olde world" to be fun. There was a new art gallery, the Oyster company now had a very decent restaurant, the pubs had all gone up-market, making it a perfect place for him to see out his retirement.

He was sitting in his office, out of sight from the customers, looking at an estate agent's details of a house in Whitstable, when there was a knock at the door. One of the shop staff popped her head around the door and told him that someone was here, had some valuable items and that he had asked for Greg personally. Reluctantly he agreed and a sharply dressed man in his 40's came in and sat down. He held a small cardboard box. The man explained that the box contained some rare medals that he wished Greg to consider. There's not much of a market for medals in Chiswick, but Gregory humoured him as, "you never know what other stuff he might have."

The medals were an odd mix, British second war campaign medals, an Iron Cross, some medical medals and a cycling race winner's medal. Gregory was explaining that such medals had little financial value and it was best to keep them in the family as heirlooms, when the man drew his attention to a final item, a small red box. He handed it to Gregory, who opened it and saw it was silver, showing the portrait of Lenin, a tractor and a factory. "Ah," he said "this is a valuable and rare item. What you have here is the Order of Lenin, the highest honour bestowed by the former Soviet Union. It is probably worth more than £50,000, maybe more at auction. Do you happen to know its provenance?" The man simply told him to turn the medal over and read the inscription.

Gregory Fielding read the Cyrillic script on the back. It read "Grigori Kutuzov." He started, nobody had called him that since he was a boy. He looked at the man, "Is this a joke?" he asked.

"No, Lieutenant-General, this is not a joke, it was authorised by Putin himself and comes with the thanks of a grateful nation. You may consider yourself to be retired from the service. Your watch is ended."

"Is that what we say now, your watch is ended?"

"Well, no, that's from Game of Thrones, but I wanted to add something more personal. Let me say it has been a supreme honour, to meet the legend in person." He stood up stiffly, saluted, then left the room. A few minutes later the assistant popped her head around the door and asked, "Anything of interest?"

"Nothing really, just baubles"

When she had left, Gregory was on his feet doing a slightly arthritic one-man victory dance. "Order of Fucking Lenin, Ra! Ra! RA! Order of Fucking Lenin, Ra! Ra! RA!

Greg took the afternoon off. He bought a ludicrously expensive bottle of red wine at the wine merchant on the corner of Turnham Green Terrace and went home to his flat. He sat, savouring the wine, listening to classical music, just relaxing.

Eventually, as the room grew darker and he became more expansive, he imagined an article in the Brentford and Isleworth Gazette. "Local man awarded Russia's highest honour, The Order of Fucking Lenin." The reporter would ask "Do you have advice for any of our readers who wish to be awarded the Order of Lenin...?"

"Yes", he would say, "be very, very lucky..."

That would have been true. Young Grigori had grown up in an orphanage. The name Kutuzov was for the famous general, Grigori, simply the first name the nurses had agreed. He never knew his parents, the orphanage was his life, and he grew up happy enough, fed enough and was neither loved nor hated. He was bright enough to be selected for special education, which included learning English. He and his fellow pupils on the course watched films from both the British and Hollywood genres. After each film there would be a de-brief and discussion. However, the strangeness of the English Carry-On films remained a complete mystery, apparently beyond rational explanation.

Special education blended seamlessly into recruitment and training for the KGB. It seemed like a game, much better than anything else on offer. Finally, in 1977, he became Gregory Fielding, complete with all the documents and cover story to equip a newly deployed agent.

At first it was uneventful. He was supposed to be a courier within a long-term operation codenamed Crocodile. He was sent to Kent to investigate rumours that a new secret facility was being established. He was supposed to be based in Canterbury. It turned out that all the rented accommodation in Canterbury had been taken up by students. He ended up in a miserable little rented flat in Whitstable. It was there that he refined his accent, learned to drink pints of bitter and enjoy a fish supper.

Using the insight that a secret military installation would undoubtedly be in Military Road, Canterbury, he commenced surveillance of the facility. There were often students on the bus from Whitstable to the University, so he tagged along with them. This was his new cover, student. The beer was cheaper, so he grew his hair, adopted a beard and just blended in. He even went so far as to attend a few first-year lectures. He liked economic history, so attended those regularly. His one taste of statistics was enough to put him off for life. Sometimes in the evenings bands played. Life was good.

The surveillance proved to be less successful. He finally decided to just wander in and see what was going on. He found himself in a crowded waiting room. There was a cardboard box on the counter. A handwritten note on the box said, "Can you give a kitten a good home?" He investigated the box. It contained kittens.

A few days later he had used a side entrance to enter the building after the working day had ended. Security was lax. It was untidy. There were cakes and biscuits laid out on top of the filing cabinets. He was going to take a piece of cake, but the sight of mice scurrying away from it put him off. Perhaps that explains the kittens, he thought. There were files everywhere. He looked at a few, clearly, they were agent profiles, lists of payments, addresses, profiling information. He quickly photographed as many as possible, then realised the task was enormous. He had seen an operating manual and taken it. With a sigh of relief, he had exited the building and vanished into the night.

He had forwarded the films and documents to his handler. A message had come back suggesting his penetration showed good initiative, but the materials suggested that the building was operating as an administrative office as a cover for its true purpose. He needed to push beyond the disguise to get to the secret function. Fortunately, it dawned on Gregory before his handler that he was in fact trying to penetrate the Department of Health and Social Security, not MI6.

Chapter 50

2024

23rd July - Tuesday
Chiswick High Road, West London
Gregory.

The next time, he was lucky. He had heard a third-year student talking about jobs in a new facility at Sandwich, which were a hush-hush and secret squirrel. He went to Sandwich and took a room in a B&B and started his search by simply wandering around. Eventually, he found a new office building on the outside of town. It was next to a car showroom and a windmill. He wandered around the windmill and once he was sure nobody was around, climbed up on to the first floor of the windmill. He could see into the office building, and it looked very new. There appeared to be telephone switching equipment and filing cabinets. A few people were walking around. He casually walked back past the front of the building. The fence was high and topped with barbed wire. The entrance had a barrier. He had watched as a car drove up. The driver had to get out and go into the little security office at the gate. He could see the driver show a pass.

As he walked back towards the town, he noticed a young woman emerge from the gate. He followed her at a distance. For the next two days he made a point of watching for the woman as she left the office and followed her home. On Saturday morning he noticed her, stood at the bus stop. He took the same bus, which eventually got them to Canterbury. She took another bus up the hill to the University. At the University she headed into one of the colleges, then disappeared into the toilets. He had nearly missed her when she emerged. She had changed her clothes and hair for a "punkier" ensemble, nothing extreme, but a definite change of look.

Gregory had followed her to the bar and sat sipping a pint, studiously ignoring her. He had heard her order a pint of Bat's Blood, which surprised him. She had noticed his reaction, "It takes ten bats to make a pint" she told him, miming bats being squeezed into a glass. Seeing his puzzlement, she clarified that it was just lager and blackcurrant.

He went back to studiously ignoring her, but when he stole a glance back, she was looking at him. He looked away for a while, but when he looked back, she caught him again and smiled. He had smiled back.

She was there for the concert that night; a band called the Cure. He hung back, not wanting to be too forward. Later they took the same bus back to Sandwich. He pretended to read a book. He sat where she could see him, but he did no more than cast the odd glance and look away before she turned his way.

He watched her in the following week. She had regular working hours in the week. On Saturday she was off to the Uni again. This time he was in the bar waiting. He was just about to order, when she walked up. He saw her, turned and did an embarrassed smile of recognition. She smiled back. He had offered to buy her a drink and when it came, he had squeaked and pretended to squeeze a bat into it. She gave him a big smile.

And so, it began. Her name was Geraldine. There was a slow wooing process. Little hesitant advances towards friendship. His offer to take her out for a meal. They ate at Sweeney Todd's Pizza Parlour, just by the Cathedral. It was packed and noisy, full of students after a gig. They had sat together and noticed that the room was getting quiet. Two middle-aged women were talking loudly. One was comparing her husband's foreplay technique to the process of stuffing a Christmas turkey in the most graphic terms. The students had gone quiet to listen in. The woman had just referred to an onion being forced in, when she realised the extent of her audience. "You should know better than to listen in to peoples' private conversations" she had harrumphed.

"You've put me off onions for life!" one of the students responded and the general hubbub resumed. Gregory was beginning to notice that Geraldine could eat a lot, she had eaten all of her own pizza and pinched half of his.

They had more trips out. One slightly disastrous outing was to watch the film, Alien. When the monster popped out of the man's chest Geraldine had screeched and by the end of the film, she was unsettled. They had travelled back on the bus and before they parted to go their separate ways, she had kissed him.

Chapter 51

2024

23rd July - Tuesday
Chiswick High Road, West London
Gregory.

He never asked her about her work, but bit by bit he learned, as she chattered about her colleagues. One of them, Nigel, was a recurring topic as he always tried to look down her top. He had been bringing in the batches of photographs and he sort of stood next to her desk at an odd angle as he handed them over. Gregory had learned that most of the women were older than Geraldine and that they were more worldly wise. They weren't so shocked at what they heard on the tapes. Sometimes they would play juicy titbits aloud for everyone to hear. She recounted one where a couple were playing at being a nun and a priest. It was clear that they also listened to phone calls. She mentioned a call where a girl had told her mother that she was pregnant, and the mother had told her she was going to hell. For Gregory it was clear that the office was involved in surveillance. His handler was pleased and encouraged him to find out more.

Geraldine had sworn him to secrecy about these little morsels of gossip. Of course, he had agreed. One evening, as they sipped Bat's Blood and lager respectively, she informed him that she was now on the pill. He had continued to play the long game and said he didn't want to rush things. He respected her too much to do anything, he would wait until they were sure of each other.

It turned out that they were sure of each other by the next weekend and the affair progressed to the next stage. That Sunday morning, he sat by the bed and watched her as she lay fast asleep. He had pulled the curtains, and the Whitstable sunshine had played across her. He was so happy at that moment.

Now they were lovers, Geraldine told him more. He never asked, but she would chatter away, until as the months rolled by, a clear picture emerged. She was a clerical assistant to a team who were handling intelligence from multiple streams. There were surveillance photographs, processed by Kevin and Nigel.

There was also a large team of phone intercept analysts, who tended to keep themselves to themselves. One or two of them were having office romances, which Gregory noted.

The third team were listening to recordings of bugged rooms, mainly in pubs and hotels. It took a little while to establish that it was somewhere on the West coast of Ireland that was the hunting ground for one team of spies. Their work took up most of Geraldine's time, she filed index cards, each one bearing the summary of an intercepted call or bugged room.

One night in bed Geraldine told him in hushed tones that she had seen pictures from Ireland that Kevin had bought in. Two people, a man and a woman were in the pictures, both shot dead. The women in the office had remarked on how stylish the woman looked, dressed like a film star. They had said the bodies looked like the film Bonnie and Clyde. For the first time she let slip a name. It turned out the killer had been called Sandman.

Gregory looked forward to their time together. They had sat together on the beach, testing each other on the Highway code amongst the pebbles and oyster shells. They both passed their driving tests, within a week of each other and first time. He had found enough money for them to buy a second-hand FIAT and they took to roaming around Kent together.

He picked her up one day. As she got into the car, he saw immediately that she had a black eye, inexpertly concealed under a layer of foundation. She would not tell him at first, but in bed that evening Gregory coaxed the story out of her.

Geraldine cautiously explained, watching Gregory closely to gauge his reaction. She said she loved Gregory, but she was now sleeping with one of the senior managers at the office. They had been in bed together, when the man's wife had come home early.

Geraldine had stumbled out of bed, clutching the sheets to her to hide her nakedness. She had expected to be slapped. Instead, the furious wife delivered a full-bodied punch.

Geraldine had been knocked unconscious. She had awoken to find herself fully dressed and being fussed over. The wife had panicked. She had briefly believed she might have killed Geraldine and was full of remorse.

Geraldine had told the story as if it was all fun, but Gregory was appalled. She was the first girl he had ever slept with; in fact, she was the only woman he would ever sleep with. He had felt betrayed. He had wanted to push her away and shout at her, but as she soothed him, he realised that he had a job to do. He had said he understood. He said he didn't own her. That she must enjoy herself any way she wanted. He said he didn't mind sharing her so long as she was happy. In time, the senior manager's indiscretions would filter back to him through his pillow talk with Geraldine.

Gregory had asked for someone to approach the manager's wife and distract her. Under instruction from the Embassy, a young man from the staff was selected, given rudimentary golf lessons and sent to Sandwich. He caused a stir with the lady golfers when he appeared at the club. However, he stuck to his task and the wife soon had a new golf partner. If one was to map all golfers according to their looks and physical prowess, he would be considered a statistical outlier. Golf rapidly turned to passion.

Unfortunately, the wife was not a good source of information about her husband's work. However, she did have a predilection for risky liaisons in the bunkers on the golf course where, at any moment, they risked interruption. When it finally happened and they were caught "in flagrante", a grinning fellow golfer had simply asked "mind if I play through?"

For the young lothario this gave rise to performance anxiety. It didn't help that his golfing ability plateaued, so he spent a lot of time searching for lost golf balls, while the wife looked on tutting in evident irritation.

In time, the liaison between the manager and Geraldine had fizzled out. Geraldine had been supplanted by one of her bustier colleagues from the office. Thinking she resented being denied the pleasures of his bed, her manager had consoled her with promotion and an excellent appraisal.

It was Geraldine who told Gregory that Kevin's head had swollen to an unbelievable size! He had been getting praise for recognising various influential people up to no good. The photographs came from a Travelodge in a motorway service station. Gregory had reported this back, together with the information that the surveillance was the work of Sandman and, a new name, Iceman.

Of course, that was about the time when everything went to pieces. The Crocodile network was rolled up like a carpet. Gregory heard what was happening and expected the British to come for him any day. Gregory's handler was caught by the British, but Gregory was missed somehow.

Alone and without his usual network, Gregory fell back on the contingency plan. This meant infrequent contact, direct to Moscow. For a while he heard little. Moscow clearly had suspicions of him and anyone else who the British had missed. After a few years he started the antiques business, which gave him reasons to travel abroad without attracting suspicion. He dealt with the Embassies in Paris or the Hague, never London. He would make quick visits to drop off a parcel of films, receive money and instruction. He made no telephone calls, no radio transmissions and in time rejected any pressure to use text or email. Gregory was "Old School." What's more, Gregory's information was good.

As time wore on their careers prospered. Geraldine rose without trace through the ranks. She willingly tackled the crap that no-one else wanted: the dress code, the memos on excess stationery usage, the budgets, the archive indexes. She climbed the ladder: Clerical officer, then Executive Officer, then Higher Executive officer, then Senior Executive officer, then Principal. The years rolled by; she rolled upwards, at first in the Sandwich operation and then via outstations, to London.

Gregory had grown in stature within the KGB. He was an infallible source, he was promoted. He was also protected, he was the one tangible success from Crocodile in London, so while Moscow's eyes were increasingly on Afghanistan and then the Middle East, he was the key man in London. He started to nurture various sources of intelligence; he played the long game.

The relationship continued. They never discussed marriage. Geraldine wanted options, also she could be greedy. For a while she was in a menage a trois with two young men. They were builders who had been hired to work on her London townhouse. Of course, it had crossed her mind that Gregory might well have arranged them to suit her tastes. To have found two builders who were so physically fit was fortuitous. Any doubts she might have had didn't stop her from enjoying herself, and Gregory was pleased to see her so happy. The punky look soon disappeared. Soon she was in Jaeger or Country Casuals, power dressing to get the next job up.

Of course, Geraldine had worked it out long ago. She continued with her pillow talk, Gregory continued with the gifts, the lavish meals, the expensive wines, the companionship, the flowers and he just made her happy. Sometimes Geraldine hinted that she would like something or someone new to dally with, Gregory would oblige, she would be alone at a hotel bar and a young man would smile, come over to her, offer to buy a drink and afterwards take her to his room.

Gregory often wondered about what made Geraldine tick. At first, he had even worried that she might be a honey trap, set for him. Over time he began to see her for what she was. She was greedy. She would eat a whole box of chocolates at one go. She always wanted more. He had been pressured into finding a better flat, then expensive curtains, then new furniture. She had wanted a better car, so the old FIAT was traded in. She wanted to go to nice places: The Royal Academy exhibition, gallery openings, in fact anywhere that served free booze and canapes to hoover up. In all their time together, when they ate out, she never once declined dessert. There was no time when she had enough. He shuddered with the memory of her at a carvery, she had eaten so much she was sick in the street outside.

Gregory was puzzled that someone of mediocre intelligence and nothing more than two O levels had succeeded in the British Secret Service which was typified by the intelligentsia, the gilded youth of Oxford and Cambridge. He concluded that in any organisation that believes in excellence, you might recruit the most promising people. However, sometimes they are both gifted and lazy. The rot sets in when they can't be bothered to get their hands dirty with the grunt work. Like a mould that grows on a piece of cheese, there is a place for the mediocre to thrive. They take on the thankless tasks, the office moves planning, the procurement roles, the needless meetings specifying IT systems that will never work or hit budget.

He remembered with a smile Geraldine telling him that she had been put in charge of liquidations. He had asked if she would have to shoot people herself. She had laughed at him, explaining it was disposing of unwanted office furniture, no bloodshed was necessary.

In the fullness of time Geraldine became a Controller, primarily concerned with vetting. As retirement loomed, she was approached and asked to stay on as a member of an oversight board.

Chapter 52

2024

23rd July - Tuesday
Chiswick High Road, West London
Gregory.

As Gregory finished the first bottle of wine, then searched his kitchen for a second, he thought of his successes. How he had to tidy up after Salisbury. Novichok, for Christ's sake, what were they thinking? The panicked messages from Moscow asking what NATO might do. Then the relief when the full set of documents from the NATO meeting turned up in Moscow centre, courtesy of the British Foreign Secretary. Not copies, but originals. Then the disbelief that the Foreign Secretary had got away with it by simply saying he got pissed, lost the documents, didn't know where.

But what really irked Gregory and what kept Moscow in a state of constant worry, was the demise of Crocodile. It was ancient history, but it nagged and teased. A lot of careful effort had gone into building up the network of agents and informers that made up Crocodile. The structure of Crocodile was known to very few people, the most select and the most trusted. As part of the political preparations for the Afghanistan involvement, many of the Crocodile members had been pulled into a set of meetings. They chose a totally obscure location. It was organised at short notice; it was so carefully controlled that it could not leak.

Despite all the precautions, the British had a surveillance team in place. Geraldine had confirmed it was the British intelligence operation from Sandwich that were running the surveillance. Specifically, it was the mysterious Sandman and Iceman team that Geraldine had told him about. The logical conclusion was that someone well placed had betrayed the details to the British. Someone very senior or someone incredibly well informed; yet despite Moscow's best efforts, it was never clear who. A few people met early deaths, simply because they were suspected, but it was all guesswork.

Amongst some of those potential leakers were people who had gone on to become the most powerful in Russia, including the top jobs. There was a fear that, one day, the whole house of cards would come tumbling down. The knowledge that there was a traitor, hidden amongst Russia's most powerful players was a constant worry. It made for sleepless nights. To make it worse, the British files dealing with Crocodile were ultra secret. Despite her best-efforts Geraldine had never managed to get access to them.

In the last few days, Geraldine had told him that now the Americans had asked about Sandman, President to PM level and it looked as if she would get access to the files. This could be the long-awaited breakthrough, what a way to go out, on a high!

Gregory awoke the next morning with an absolutely blinding hangover. Order of Fucking Lenin Ra! Ra! Ra! he mumbled as he searched for paracetamol.

Chapter 53

2024

25 July - Thursday
Trafalgar Hotel, London
Martin.

Martin had been contacted and asked to be available for a meeting in London. Reluctantly he had agreed, and a car had been sent to drive him in from Brighton where the boat was now moored.

On arrival he showed surprise to see Professor Carolyn Suttcliffe. "So, they have called you in as well, any idea what they have got planned?"

Carolyn had been summoned from her college and had to rearrange her whole day's lectures and meetings. Her secretary was in a sullen rage at the extra work. She was already phoning around to cancel the morning's schedule.

Carolyn and Martin were waiting in the foyer of a small modern business hotel, just off Trafalgar Square. There appeared to be no guests. The staff looked as if they had all been recruited from the Parachute Regiment. They were armed.

After a little while, a uniformed guard, with a pistol on his hip, came down and asked them to follow him to the meeting room. Unfortunately, Carolyn's handbag caught a bowl of fruit and spilled the contents onto the carpet. An orange had rolled under the sofa, and it took a moment to extract it and put the fruit back. There was concern that one apple might still be missing, but the guard suggested that they were pushed for time and that he would look for the apple later.

"Do excuse me, I must be nervous although I can't think why. I suppose it's all part of getting old and doddery," said Carolyn.

Martin had protested, "hardly old and certainly not doddery."

Carolyn stopped to examine one of the pictures hanging on the wall. "Look at this" she said, "that's the Bay of Naples, see that's Pompeii." The guard had chivvied them on. Martin put his arm out for her to take. "Don't fuss," she waved him away.
They were led into the conference room. The meeting was presided over by Geraldine, the Fat Controller, who today was a vision of cream and peach. Around the table they were introduced to Fiona, Miriam, Nicholas and Lisa. Each of them had a smart document folder in front of them.

The room had pictures of sea battles. "Do you hold meetings with your counterparts in French intelligence here?" asked Martin. "This looks like HMS Victory at Trafalgar and this picture looks like the Battle of the Nile." Fiona realised he was onto something there. The French had seemed somewhat snarky last time they met.

The guard left the room to wait outside the door, but not before Miriam spotted that he had a banana in his holster, in place of his pistol.

Martin looked pleased, "We get tea and coffee this time, plus a decent selection of biscuits. This must be in your honour, Carolyn. Last time I had to beg to get a cup of coffee."

The Fat Controller had been in her element. She laid out the ground rules that had been agreed between the PM and the US President. Both Services had agreed to full and frank disclosure. It was explained all present had the highest level of clearance including Lisa.

Finally, she turned to Carolyn and Martin, "Can I just say that to have you here is a remarkable privilege. To have Iceman and Sandman present in person is a great honour. You may be interested to know that the surveillance techniques you used to bring down the Crocodile ring are still taught as a case study by the Service. It goes without saying that, for those in the know, you are both legends." As if to make a point she helped herself to a biscuit.

Carolyn had picked up a pen, written a note on the pad in front of her, it said, "Crocodile???"

Martin took the pen and wrote "No idea!!!!"

Carolyn nodded and put the note into her bag.

Miriam looked around the faces, not a flicker of recognition, clearly nobody knew what the Crocodile Ring was, or they were all poker players of the highest order. Miriam knew it was not taught as a case study, perhaps that seemingly throw away comment was intended to make it easier for them to open up.

Martin chose this moment to ask Lisa a question. He had noticed that Mr Collins was not present and asked her the reason.

Lisa had started to reply, then caught herself. "Do you mean Mr Griffin?"

Martin had been clear that he meant Collins, as that was the name on her colleague's passport and credit cards. Martin described how he had found correspondence in Collin's hotel room bearing that name and together with a semi-pornographic magazine, various personalised items in that name, including his pyjamas. "His mother is a US Senator, according to Google" he added. "Is it not something of a coincidence that you are trying to track down a missing person called Collins and the CIA send his nephew. I would say the Man from Uncle, but I suppose we are talking about the Man from Auntie."

Lisa explained that Mr Collins was back in the US under "something of a cloud." Clearly, she was getting the knack of British understatement.

Miriam's mind was racing. "The missing briefcase that was handed in at reception! Oh, they are a step ahead of us. And one of them now has a gun..." she thought. "These two could kill us in the blink of an eye"; she recalled the pictures she had been shown of their handiwork.

She looked around in case she needed to improvise a weapon. The best she could do was to move one of the bottles of spring water closer to hand. Carolyn noticed the movement and gave a slight nod of approval.

Martin continued, "in the interests of full disclosure and based on what I have read in the files held by Mr Collins, I think this has nothing to do with Professor Carolyn."

The Fat Controller ignored him and turned to Fiona, "For all our benefit, can you take us back to the beginning and, please, paint the full picture, for Lisa's sake."

Fiona began. "The British Secret Service established Project Pandora at a time when there was concern that the British Service had suffered significant penetration by foreign actors, in particular the Russian KGB and Bulgarian 1st Main Directorate. In the 70's, too much of the Service's established activity was being watched by the other side."

"For this reason, fresh assets were developed at a new facility in Sandwich, Kent. This operation was distinct and independent from our established organisational structure. It was hoped that this fresh approach would maintain secrecy."

"Two person teams were prepared, fluent in Russian and fully trained in covert operation under Moscow rules. They were intended to act as sleeper cells, deploying advanced signals Intelligence technology that had been developed in West Germany. The Pandora boxes had a capability to record either microphone or telephone conversations. Using public phone networks, the boxes retransmitted the condensed information in encrypted form, typically in the early hours of the morning. Any questions so far?"

Lisa was about to ask what this had to do with Ireland, but Fiona pressed on.

"During 1979, the intelligence picture for operations in Ireland was sub-optimal and political pressure to achieve greater penetration was intense. A decision was made at Cabinet level, to re-direct activity. One team, composed of Iceman and Sandman were urgently re-tasked from Iron Curtain and Mediterranean operations to the Atlantic coast of the Republic of Ireland. They operated with minimal supervision, under a hastily assembled legend of being a young married couple; freelance photographers working on a travel book."

"Pandora was a great success, the team built up a steady stream of SigInt as the boxes were installed, typically in hotels and pubs which were being used as safe houses or meeting places by the opposition. They also supplied a continuous stream of photographic material, both as part of routine surveillance and to endorse their cover story."
"The team remained in place for 1979 and at the end of the year withdrew. A narrative was established to extinguish the two legends. This included the publication of a limited-run edition of a book of photographs."

Nicholas leant down and took from his bag, a copy of the book. He had scoured the internet for it, only to discover that it was long out of print and about as likely to turn up as the Holy Grail. He had left messages with book sellers and even posted a message on a book finder website.

In the end, it was the Oxfam Book shop next to Turnham Green tube station that had come up with a copy. The woman behind the counter had taken a dim view of his trying to haggle down from the marked price of £50.00. He haggled on, eventually, she crossed out the marked price and changed it to £70.00. He had returned £70.00 poorer and a little wiser.

Carolyn and Martin looked through the book together. "I'm surprised you could find a copy", Carolyn had said. She had turned to the two facing pictures, Isobel on the beach Alex, rear view, unclothed. "Youth is wasted on the young." She turned the page and smiled, "Moira Shannon…"

Lisa looked at them "How does Martin B Collins fit into this?"

Miriam described her visit to Sandwich in search of the information originally supplied by Sandman and Iceman. She had spent a very long day with Kevin, formerly of Sandwich and now retired. Kevin's account of the work was substantial in terms of volume, but short in terms of relevance. He regaled Miriam with ancient office gossip, tales of affairs and intrigues, all of them petty. He had recounted his gripes about equipment shortages, the poor heating in the lab and the fundamental injustice that underlay the pay decisions throughout his career.

In amongst the dross, there were little nuggets. He recounted dusty old gossip about Geraldine. It would have been no more than an interesting diversion, until Kevin recalled that Geraldine had a foreign boyfriend who lived in Whitstable. She kept him secret. Kevin had seen them together and was convinced that one of the pictures from Pandora included someone very like him. But when he referred this to his manager, he was told not to gossip. The manager was protective of Geraldine, going so far as to accuse Kevin of an inappropriate interest in Geraldine. Despite his misgivings, Kevin had let the matter drop. When Miriam asked where the photo might be now, Kevin had explained that the photographic record from Pandora was probably still highly sensitive and, so far as he knew, nothing remained at Sandwich.

Miriam gave the meeting a quick précis of her findings, the files relating to Crocodile were not at Sandwich. She was careful to make no mention of the references to Geraldine.

On her return Miriam had never expected to see the Crocodile files. To her surprise, she had been given supervised access to a subset of the Crocodile material. In it was a very limited set of pictures. They recorded various corpses, none of whom resembled the pictures of Collins. However, there was a panorama, a picture of a fox and finally two men with a machine gun walking away from a van and towards the camera.

It was this picture that she now placed on the table. "This surveillance photograph appears to show Collins, seen here on the right, in camouflage jacket and light-coloured boots. To his left is someone who I can now confirm was captured, and was subsequently placed in a witness protection program, in Australia, with a new identity. His codename is Lobster. The photographs are attributed to Sandman. I think it reasonable to surmise that, shortly after these pictures were taken, Collins was killed by Sandman."

Lisa turned to Martin, "so you killed Collins in the Republic of Ireland. Did you have authority to kill him? You realise that when this gets out there will have to be a trial. "

Miriam moved the bottle a little closer. This could be about to go very bad.

Martin looked coolly at Lisa. "I operated at my own discretion. I was deployed in a purely surveillance capacity. When these two turned up, I watched them. They came and set up their machine gun about five feet from where I was hiding. I continued to watch. I could hear a helicopter approaching, I fully expected that they would open fire at it, so I took aim at the man behind the gun. My actions were taken to defend the individuals in the helicopter and potentially, I acted in self-defence. Let's be absolutely clear, these two were armed terrorists about to commit an atrocity. My response falls well within the established definition of reasonable force. No court would convict me, a trial would be an embarrassment for all concerned."

Lisa considered. "So, what happened next?"

Martin paused for effect "...Then his head fell off."

"Fell off?"

"Yes, fell off, I was unfamiliar with the rifle I had borrowed. The second pressure on the trigger was slightly lighter than I would have expected. So, I fired one round, which took me slightly by surprise. I think it hit the top of his head and ricocheted down the field. I instinctively fired a second shot in case I had missed and that hit him just below the base of his skull. His head exploded, blown to fragments, blood and brains went everywhere and he started to convulse. A 7.62 round at five yards range tends to completely compromise any enjoyment you will get from the rest of the day. He must have held the trigger down, as he fired a full belt of about fifty rounds of tracer all over the field and into the sky."

"I turned to shoot the second man, but he was sitting there in shock. He had no weapon, and he simply gibbered and cried. So, I didn't shoot him. I radioed the Marine Commandos who sent a squad to help me take away the body and the prisoner. One of them even managed to stand on me, I was so well hidden."

"So where is Collins buried?"

"Somewhere in the Irish sea, I dropped him out of the helicopter. It was very respectful, we had an archbishop, a choir, solemn music ...oh I beg your pardon, that was someone else's funeral, we were having a lot of funerals around that time. I think his one was over the side in a body bag, weighted down with a couple of breezeblocks. However, we didn't find his head, perhaps if you could re-assemble it ..."

It was Carolyn's turn to pitch in. "If this were ever to go to trial, I would be happy to testify that, as part of our surveillance activities, we monitored suspected bombers who were staying at the Black Bull Inn. It became clear to us that these two men, had kidnapped a young girl aged eleven, called Bernadette. Our recordings revealed that, together with a third man, they brutally raped and strangled the little girl. As I understand it her body has never been found."

Miriam looked at Carolyn in surprise, "So they got away with murder..."

Carolyn shook her head. "The first man was stabbed in the eye and shot and his body burned, the second man was stabbed in both eyes and fell from a ferry into the Irish Sea."

"What about the third man?"

"That was probably Martin B Collins; the man whose head fell off."

Lisa started to talk about subpoenaing evidence, when Fiona intervened. "Miss Simpson, have you ever reflected on the purpose of your investigation. Why was the President so keen for you and your ride-along to come here and investigate these matters. Admittedly, you have done a fine job and tracked down people who had remained hidden in plain sight for rather a long time. But ask yourself, what was the end game? Justice for a long dead relative? We are well past all of that now. The last thing either we or the Irish authorities would want is people looking into our murky past. Nicholas, could you talk us through your findings..."

Nicholas explained that he had looked carefully at the financial position of the Collins family in the US. He talked through the various inheritance arrangements which had been triggered by the recent passing of old Mr Collins, father to the headless corpse in the Irish Sea and his sister. As the older sibling, all financial assets would have passed to Martin

B Collins. Only in the event of his death without issue would the sister inherit. Her father had always presumed that Martin or maybe a child would turn up one day, so no attempt had been made to have him declared dead. In short, confirmation of death would release a substantial amount of assets, currently in trust. For the sister, this would release her from significant debt. For the President there was the promise of a much-needed financial boost for his re-election campaign.

Miriam was first to react. "All we need to do is confirm that he is dead, never mind the detail."

Lisa was not so sure "But what about the evidence…"

Martin spoke carefully and slowly "Write this down. We have found evidence that Martin Collins, together with two other men set out on a sailing trip from Wicklow to Pwllheli in Wales aboard a small yacht on 11th August 1979. They encountered severe weather conditions and although they succeeded in transmitting a Mayday message, their yacht was lost without trace. This was a period of exceptionally bad weather and a number of other yachts competing in the 1979 Fastnet race were also lost. There was considerable loss of life due to this storm. We are now satisfied beyond reasonable doubt that given the record of their departure, the Mayday and the failure of the yacht to arrive that it foundered with all hands."

Lisa looked around the room. "Can documentary evidence be supplied? If so, we have a solution. You said three men, does that mean we need two more names, has anyone else gone missing?"

"I can think of a couple of men who went missing at around that time. Also, the yacht can be given as having the same name as a yacht taking part in the race that also sent out distress messages. You can report that this confusion has only recently been identified by a journalist writing a book about the race. Say that the Coastguard thought they were looking for one yacht, when in reality, two vessels bearing the same name were in distress."

Lisa looked around the room. There were nods of agreement. She agreed, "Ok, that works for me, if it works for you guys. We just need to get enough documentation together to get a presumption of death drawn up. As soon as that's done, I can be out of here and on my way home."

"I think we can draw a line under this, once and for all." said Geraldine.

Lisa, Fiona and Nicholas left the meeting, tasked with producing a draft of the joint report that would go to the PM for onward transmission. They had left the book of photographs with Martin.

Chapter 54

2024

25 July - Thursday
London
Carolyn, Martin.

The Fat Controller asked Martin and Carolyn to remain, together with Miriam. She wanted an opportunity to debrief the pair of them in respect of Crocodile. Carolyn had asked for clarification, as they would be willing to help. However, she didn't know what the term Crocodile referred to.

Geraldine reached to her bag for a small dossier. Miriam had handed it to her just before the meeting started. Now, after a quick scan of the contents she realised she might have the information that Gregory had been so desperate for.

She opened the dossier and read aloud. "Summary: Crocodile. In January 1980 two agents, Sandman and ICEMAN, submitted a set of covert surveillance photographs and movement schedules detailing activity at the Travelodge

Motel at Newport Pagnell on the M1. Over the following months further surveillance measures were enacted, after which the team at Sandwich identified the following individuals:

Jonathan Northcliffe, at that time a senior member of MI5.

Bernard Trainer, a Junior Defence minister in the first Thatcher Cabinet.

Alexei Potemkin, a known senior KGB officer.

Three other KGB operatives, (designated Huey, Dewey and Louis).

A member of the Senior defence staff (MOD).

A member of the NATO maritime co-ordination command.

One senior official from GCHQ.

She could see the list was boring them already, so she cut to the chase. "A detailed surveillance plan was instigated. This revealed that all the above were apparently communicating with a Moscow run team, using as cover the services of two prostitutes based at the Travelodge.

More detailed work revealed that in fact the individuals were passing secret material to and from the KGB officers. In conclusion, the photographs led to the identification of twelve deep cover agents operated by the KGB, together with other persons of interest."

Martin was intrigued, "I assume you dealt with all concerned."

It was Miriam who answered, "Correct. According to our file, most were confronted, turned and used to channel disinformation back to the Russians. In time, the KGB cottoned on and liquidated the junior agents. Potemkin defected to the US. Some of the individuals retired. The Russian embassy was denuded of spooks. We declared a number of them persona non grata and withdrew their diplomatic credentials. They were sent home, of course the Russians responded in kind and sent home diplomats from our Embassy in Moscow. Back then, that was the game, tit for tat expulsions. Your surveillance effectively destroyed a spying operation that had taken the KGB years to put in place."

"Permanently dealt with?"

"Yes, some suffered unfortunate accidents. It is recorded in the file that Maggie Thatcher wanted to shoot Bernard Trainer herself when she found out."

"Did they let her?"

"No, he died of heart failure."

Carolyn wanted to know what value a debrief would be after all this time.

Geraldine was clear about what she wanted to know. She simply asked, "How is it that when you were supposed to be in Ireland, you came to be running a surveillance operation at Newport Pagnell? Who told you to go there? Why did you pick that particular time and place? "

"Oh, that's simple," came Carolyn's reply "pure co-incidence. We just happened to be there, and it was something to do." Her expression did not betray it, but Carolyn was already wondering why this question would be asked.

"Really, is it possible that someone at Sandwich or the Centre directed you there? What was your source? How did the Service know about Crocodile? Was the information provided by someone here or in Moscow centre? We need to document the sources of your information..."

"No idea" replied Carolyn. Now she was really curious to know what was behind these questions. She looked at Martin, he showed the merest hint of a frown.

Before they could proceed further, Miriam was thanking them, it was clear that the meeting was at an end. Geraldine was keen to get her answer, but something about Miriam's tone made it clear that there was to be no further discussion. Geraldine scanned the file further, perhaps there was a hint there.

Martin and Carolyn got up to go. Miriam showed them to the door of the hotel and thanked them for coming in. As they were about to leave the building, Carolyn turned back and said to Miriam, "be a dear and give this back to the guard, he's probably wondering where he put it."

"And where the banana came from" replied Miriam.

273

"Oh, so you noticed, here's the gun, it's cleared and safe, here's the clip. One final thing Miriam, there's always a reason for digging up the past, to look for some valuable insight. If Crocodile has been hidden all this time, who is now looking and why?"

Carolyn and Martin walked off into the night. "Fish and chips?" said Martin.

"Posh ones I hope" came the reply.

"Did you know", said Martin slipping into an Irish accent, "that in order to fry the very best quality fish and chips, you must use fresh oil, with a high smoke point and a neutral taste. Strong oils flavour the fish, which will never do, so I use a blend of peanut oil and sunflower oil...."

"Oh my god" said Carolyn, "Mr Shannon and his fish and chips...that man was obsessed, trust you to remember."

Chapter 55

2024

25 July - Thursday
London
Carolyn, Martin.

After the meal they had gone their separate ways, but neither slept that night. Carolyn dozed off only to be back in the Coliseum. As before the dream was brutally real, the Emperor turning down his thumb, the blood, the snakes, the panicked awakening. The bad dreams had dwindled to nothing over the years, but the day's events had somehow poured the colour back into the faded horror. She awoke, heart thumping, fighting for breath. She read until dawn and spent the next day weary.

For Martin also the nightmares returned. Once asleep he began to mutter, to talk. He was Alex again, back at the Forest. He had left Isobel alone in the cabin and had driven across the border alone and unarmed. Without her beside him to map read he would get lost, endlessly turning and returning along the same roads. He forced himself awake and got a cup of hot chocolate.

When he finally fell asleep again, he had no respite. The dream resumed. He was waiting in the agreed meeting spot. The undercover soldier from the Det pulling in. The agreed signal. Getting into the man's car leaving the Imp behind. Getting to the base. The squaddie on the gate being a prat about him not having papers and eventually the ride over the lush green countryside in the Wessex.

It bought back the feeling of worry, of hunger and the taste of bile in his mouth. He wasn't sick but it was touch and go. The smell and the hot oily blast. Getting off the Wessex and some twat being snippy with him. By then he was really wound up. The armourer pissed him off by giving him a piece of shit SLR that looked like it had never been cleaned. He found it hard to calm down. He remembered stripping and cleaning the gun over and over, to calm himself. He was irritated that he had forgotten to ask for a sling for the SLR. The sogginess of the borrowed ghillie suit. The slow movement out to the border in the dark. The tension rising as he made his way along one hedgerow, then across an open field. The breathless pauses as he stopped to listen. He had to stop to urinate. He struggled with the suit. He fumbled. He was getting anxious. This didn't feel right.

He had worked his way into the base of the hedge. The farm lay quiet in the darkness below him. It was too quiet; he had a terrible feeling that this was all going to go wrong. He waited. At one point he had dozed off then woken thinking something was moving around nearby. He kept still. The noise stopped. Then the morning came, and he took his photographs for the panorama and then the fox came. It walked across the open field, then stopped, looking directly at him, giving his position away. He took its picture, and the fox turned and walked on. He was so uncomfortable. His foot was going numb, and he was trying to stretch out the numbness.

Then the shock of noticing the van, its doors opening. How had he missed it driving up? The men getting out. One of them had an M60. Moving the SLR round, so he had them in his arc. Take pictures.

"Do they know I'm here? Are there more of them behind me?" A desire to get up and run. "Fight the urge." Stomach churning, then tightening. "Fuck, they are walking straight towards me. When do I fire? Not yet. They are close, yards away. What are they doing? They are setting up the gun. It's pointing away, towards the border. My mouth is dry. I can feel myself trembling." Move the SLR round. Infinite slowness. "How can they not hear me?" A twig creaks as he moves. They don't hear it, "I'm trembling. Control it."

"They are looking up, there's the sound of a helicopter, so that's their game. Aim at the one with the gun, the one with the light-coloured boots. The foresight is pumping up and down, control my breathing, control my breathing. Fuck! I've fired, have I missed, fire again. Hit. His body jumps, I see the head explode in a cloud of red mist. Fragments in all directions…He's pulled the trigger, a whole belt of tracer streaks at random across the countryside. After the silence of the night the noise is deafening. The man's body is convulsing. I can't move."

"The other man. Get sights on. It's slow, like I'm under water. Faster. I'm on. I can't pull the trigger. My hand is shaking uncontrollably. I must kill him."

"He's not moving. He's sat on his arse just looking at the corpse. He's crying. He's wet himself. He's not moving. I watch; he cries. I can't pull the trigger. I want to run away, I can't move. He sits there. I watch him. The backup team arrive eventually. When I emerge from the undergrowth in front of him, I see the man roll his eyes up into his head and pass out. As I stand, I am in agony from pins and needles. I rub my arms and legs. I walk over to look at the body. The head has gone completely. I want to run, but can't. There's a desperate urge to urinate."

Martin awoke and jumped up from the bed, staring wildly. He wiped his face. "Damn, that particular nightmare is back with a vengeance."

His heart was pounding wildly. He headed to the bathroom.

Chapter 56

2024

26th July - Friday
The Embankment, London
Miriam.

The Fat Controller had moved fast. She phoned the shop asking about an antique clock. The reply was equally prompt. It was their agreed emergency message, its meaning: "Meet Embankment tomorrow 8.30 am, usual place."

At 8.30 she was just about 100 yards from Cleopatra's Needle. She was certain she was not being followed. She had left home well before and taken a circuitous route. Gregory was waiting for her; he came up and spoke in a low voice. "What have you found out?"

She was unsure. "Firstly, I now know who Sandman and Icemen are. They are both still alive, but for whatever reason they didn't reveal why they were in the motel. Secondly, this is beginning to feel like a trap or a trick. There is no mention of a debrief after the Crocodile surveillance, in fact they pretend to have gone straight into deep cover afterwards. I can't believe that it was just a co-incidence as they claim. It was as if they didn't know about Crocodile at all. I've been given a dossier of information on Crocodile, but I don't trust it. I'm worried that I have been given a fake account of what happened, because they are on to me. I'm worried that I have been set up, that my interest in this has given me away."

"What are you suggesting we do?"

"Run maybe. If Crocodile was blown by someone in Moscow, it means SIS knows about you and if they know about you, they know about me."

"Run to where? Moscow? I've never been to Moscow, I was hoping to retire, to Whitstable."

"Whitstable? That's no good, they will track us down…"

Gregory felt a pang of regret. He wanted Whitstable, to be a retired English gentleman in a quiet seaside town. Walks on the beach, pints in the Neptune, not Moscow in the snow.

At the side of the road was a van. Its side door swung open; the noise made them turn to look. It was Miriam. She raised a silenced pistol and shot Geraldine twice in the chest, then as Geraldine lay sprawled on the pavement shot her once in the forehead.

Gregory looked at her in horror. He turned to Miriam. "Why? Why? Why did you do that? Who are you?" He looked back down at Geraldine, for an instant he remembered her, as the young woman, that first time, beautiful in the dappled sunlight on his bed in Whitstable. Now she was gone. He felt ill.

Miriam raised the pistol and pointed it at him.

"Stop, I am diplomat," stammered Gregory.

"Whatever…" replied Miriam. She shot Gregory twice in the chest and, after he had fallen on top of Geraldine, put a final bullet through the back of his head. Miriam stooped to pick up the brass shell cases from the pavement. She counted to make sure she had all six.

In seconds, two of Miriam's colleagues had emerged from the van, dragged the bodies in and they were driving away, towards Westminster Bridge. There were lots of people head down heading for work, but no-one noticed. Miriam had chosen her moment well. Apart from a few startled pigeons, there were no witnesses.

That evening, Miriam was sat in front of the Director. "Are you ok?" Bernard asked, for she looked wobbly.

She said that she was OK, just that she had never killed anyone before, and it seemed so personal to shoot someone who you had been in a meeting with just the day before. The Director had a big grin on his face that she found disconcerting.

"Don't worry" he reassured her, "it's very unlikely that you will have to do it again. This was a very special set of circumstances."

He continued to grin "Just this once we needed to send a message to Moscow…. whack a mole" He banged his hand on the tabletop. He was positively beaming at her.

As they spoke, away to the west of London, the fire brigade finished hosing down a crashed car. It had burnt fiercely, and the two occupants had been incinerated. Their two deeply charred bodies awaited extraction and identification. A week later the Brentford and Isleworth Gazette ran the story, "Local couple die in fiery car crash."

Chapter 57

2024

26 July - Friday

Flight BAO229 – 29,000 feet, Latitude 53'28.927 North, Longitude 5'56.642 West. Irish Sea

Lisa.

Lisa Simpson was on a British Airways flight. The seatbelt sign had just been switched off and the cabin crew were serving Piper Heidsieck Champagne to the business class passengers. Her London trip had been a success, and she was on her way back to Washington to await her next assignment from Langley. Hopefully, Senator Collins' son's idiocy would not damage her career. The Brits had been fired up about it but had been tactful in what they told her bosses.

At that precise moment, she was closer to the late Michael Brogan Collins than she had been at any time during the search. Twenty-nine thousand feet directly below her were the waves of the Irish sea. Twenty-one metres below the surface, the silt held a jumble of bones in a tattered body bag. Momentarily, she was about five and a half miles from the final resting place of the one-time heir to the Collins fortune.

Finally, she would be able to resume her real name and ditch the Lisa Simpson alias at last. This had been her first trip to Britain, and she had found it strange, just as she had found the British strange when she had served alongside them in Iraq and Afghanistan. What she had found most odd was that in all her time in Britain, she had not been asked out on a date once. This was weird; back in the States men were always hitting on her, yet the British not once.

No doubt the attention would resume. And then it struck her, the realisation. It was Garvey who had allocated the aliases for the trip. It was Garvey who had gleefully informed her that nobody in Britain had seen the Simpsons or Family Guy. It was Garvey who had handed her the passport with the less than flattering photograph. The same Garvey that, months before, had asked her out. She remembered the invitation, but why didn't it happen? The realisation that he must have been waiting for her at the restaurant. That she had bumped into Sheila and gone for a drink instead. Without meaning to, she had stood him up, leaving him to sit in an expensive restaurant on his own. She had completely forgotten, until now, sitting on the plane, holding a ticket in the name of a cartoon character.

Chapter 58

2024

29th July - Monday
Heathrow Airport, London
Yelizaveta.

Yelizaveta had cleared immigration and customs without problems, although even for a Russian, the time spent queuing seemed ridiculous. Her passport and identity for the trip had been that of a British woman, Megan Vaughan, who had been living in Spain for many years. As she queued, she noted that, in their haste, the documents section had forged an oldish passport but had used a recent picture of her. It was a rookie error which she would draw to their attention on her return. Fortunately, the Passport Control officer didn't seem to notice.

She made her way to the Piccadilly Line and headed into London. This was her first London assignment since the late 70's. The population had changed a lot in the meantime. More Indians, Africans, Arabs and Orientals, fewer whites.

More tourists too, she heard half a dozen languages being talked in her carriage alone. She was tired. The trip from Moscow to London had necessarily been via various cities before the final hop to Barcelona and then on to London. She went straight to her hotel; had a bath and that night she slept soundly. She would contact the London team in the morning.

Another change had occurred since she was last in London. Facial Recognition software now checked every arrival at Heathrow against a database of "known villains." Her arrival had not gone unnoticed.

Yelizaveta was in London to investigate the death of an old colleague of hers. He had been killed in a car crash alongside his principal source within the British intelligence service. She had breakfasted and made her way to Gregory's flat. She had walked around, waited and after several hours of careful watching, concluded that nobody else was watching. Her practised hands made short work of the lock. She let herself in. As she did so a small piece of folded paper fell from the door jamb. Old school, but effective, it confirmed that Gregory had been the last to leave the flat and nobody had been in since. Her search turned up nothing of note, other than a box containing Gregory's Order of Lenin. She read the inscription and wondered what foolishness inspired someone to send him this, or for Gregory to keep it. If the British had found it....but clearly they hadn't. A dark thought was forming. Could this have been someone on our side setting him up?

Out of the corner of her eye Yelizaveta saw something move. She turned. It was a little grey mouse. It scurried along, then stopped. For a moment they watched each other. The mouse vanished under the furniture.

Her next call was at the antiques business. Gregory's portrait, framed in black had been placed in the window. Yelizaveta had introduced herself as an old friend of Gregory's and had settled down for a cup of tea with the still teary assistant. She came away persuaded that Gregory had probably been the victim of a traffic accident, but somehow doubts remained.

The problem that confronted her was that the death didn't seem to fit with anyone's modus operandi. It was not like the British to kill a Russian agent in London, without good reason. As for Moscow, why kill one of their own who was considered a success and a valuable source of information. Neither motive made sense. She knew that Gregory had been pushing his source for information on Crocodile. She was nagged by the thought that this was somehow tied up with Crocodile, a disaster at the time, which Gregory had turned into an unexpected success in the long run. Yet that success had been known to very few people and of them, few remained, herself included.

She tried to think of the problem in chess terms. Crocodile had started all those years ago with a full complement of pieces. Somehow the British had wiped most of them from the board. But how? That piece of information they had guarded closely.

What of the pieces that remained? One pawn had become a king, the most valuable piece. Their piece, well placed on the British side of the board, shielded from view by a few Russian pawns: Gregory in London, herself in Moscow centre and ….who else?

Yelizaveta had travelled to Greenford by taxi and made her way to the Metropolitan Car Pound – Perivale. The pound was fenced off and there was no easy way in. She went around the corner and purchased a bunch of flowers. She rubbed her eyes to bring some tears and entered via the public entrance.

The police officer on duty was not expecting flowers! She explained they were not for him, but she had come to see her brother's car and she poured out her story. The crash, how he and a friend had died, burned and how she had travelled all the way from Spain. She sobbed out that she just wanted to see the car and leave her flowers. A Russian policeman would have quoted the rules, said No and only relented if bribed. An English policeman it seems, knows the rules, says no and offers you a cup of tea. She sat and sobbed, sipping the tea. After a while the policemen relented, let her in and stood respectfully next to her as she looked at the car.

The impact must have been at high speed, the front of the car was crushed into an unrecognisable mess. The roof had been cut away, to remove the bodies, he explained. She sobbed some more, while the policeman offered sympathy. He quietly offered that both occupants probably died due to the impact, so were spared the fire. She could see that the petrol tank had split. He knew few details other than that a colleague had suggested that the throttle may have jammed open. No other vehicles were involved, the driver lost control at speed. A tragic accident. She laid the flowers in the wreck, thanked the policeman and made her way back to the hotel.

Once she was gone, the policeman nipped out of his office and took the flowers away.

Chapter 59

2024

29th July - Monday
Economic Intelligence Unit. Victoria, London
Miriam.

Miriam sat at her desk in the Economic Intelligence Unit. A few desks away Nicholas was hard at work. She glanced over, he had an extremely complex spreadsheet open, so she didn't disturb him.

In the days since the killing, she had been mulling things over. Why had the Director selected her to do the killing? It was true that she was firearms trained, but that had been ages ago, and she hadn't handled a weapon since. It was weird that she had sat through the meeting with Geraldine and the others, knowing what was potentially to come next.

There had been no detailed planning, she was simply handed the silenced pistol and taken to the basement car park. There the three members of her team had been waiting.

Except they weren't her team. She had never seen them before; she would never see them again. They were soldiers, SAS or similar, who had come up from Hereford or somewhere that day. Their orders were simple: follow Miriam's lead, do whatever she tells you to do. Afterwards, don't breathe a word of what you have done.

They had introduced themselves to her as "One, Two and Three, not our real names Ma'am." They had a grievance. They had come up to town fully kitted out, only to be told they would be in civies and unarmed. After a pause Miriam had relented "just in case something kicks off" and agreed to one pistol apiece, hidden in the van. Soldier One, who was emerging as the spokesman of the trio had also tried to get the van swapped out for one of the Land Rover Defenders they had arrived in. The Defenders would be much more comfortable. Miriam said No, "too obvious for surveillance purposes, a Transit van would be much better for the job in hand." She didn't mention that they might need space for a body.

"Improvise" the Director had told her. "If Geraldine runs, if it looks like she is about to disappear, you are authorised to terminate her. Just do it as quietly as possible, no witnesses and make it look like an accident. I want no come back on this one."

In the back of the van Miriam had been tracking Geraldine's movements on an iPad. Slipped into the lining of Geraldine's handbag was a tiny tracker device. The handbag and owner were on the move. She was doing a runner! They had spotted Geraldine straight away and followed her at a distance. It became clear she was trying to shake any potential tail, about to meet someone. They parked up and waited.

A text pinged onto Miriam's phone. It simply said "Confirmed. Terminate Immediate"

It was unusually quiet. "Window of opportunity?" Miriam had asked. Her colleagues had looked around and agreed.

Miriam had checked her pistol was ready, stepped from the van, absolutely determined not to miss. She walked up, saw Geraldine's smile of recognition, then shock as Miriam took careful aim at her chest. Miriam had pictured exactly where the heart had been marked on the cardboard range targets and picked her point of aim. She held her breath and gently squeezed the trigger. The first shot was absolutely on target, so she had taken an instant to steady the second shot, which hit within centimetres of the first.

Miriam's sole emotion was relief that she had not missed. She didn't have specific orders to kill the Russian man, but it just felt like the right thing to do. He didn't try to run, he just stood there waiting to be shot. Afterwards she had collected the shell cases, picked up Geraldine's handbag and returned to the van. The three soldiers were looking at her wide eyed. Nobody had told them this was a hit.

As the soldiers dragged the bodies into the van, Miriam went through Geraldine's capacious handbag. It contained several files that should never have left the building. She noticed Geraldine's car keys; they were for the expensive Mercedes that was usually parked in the River House basement car park. She took out Geraldine's parking garage pass and handed it, with the keys, to one of the soldiers.

"Can you drive?" she asked. He nodded. "Then go to the underground carpark, collect this woman's car, it's a blue Mercedes AMG GT63 and meet us here as quickly as you can."

Miriam had improvised. They drove west on the M4, coming off at the Datchet exit. Miriam had in mind a particular sharp left-hand turn that came at the end of a long straight section of road on the far side of the reservoir. The road was little used, so they would not be disturbed. She sent two of the soldiers off with instructions to drive the Merc through a Gatso on the road at the back of the reservoir as fast as they could. "Just make sure your faces are hidden", she had told them. They came back grinning, "well over the ton" they assured her. They had seen the camera flash.

The next step was to load the two bodies into the Mercedes. The three soldiers had lifted the back wheels off the ground, Miriam had jammed the accelerator flat to the floor with a box of tissues and put the car in gear. The back of the car was dropped. The car squirrelled away, screeching. The car left the road with a roar, jumped the ditch, punched through the hedge, somersaulted several times into the field and came to rest upside down. Silence, then as if by magic, there were sheep scattering in all directions.

"Where did they come from?" Miriam had wondered.

"It won't catch fire on its own, ma'am" one of the soldiers had assured her as they walked towards the wreck. "That's just something that happens in movies." At that point the car had started to burn. The flames spread and after a short while, the fuel tank exploded. They stood and watched the blaze.

"Look at all the dead sheep," one of the soldiers observed "they must have been hiding on the other side of the hedge"

"Baaaaad luck, eh" replied one of his fellows. There were groans all round.

Miriam had an idea. "You two, take that dead sheep and put it at the side of the road, make it look like they were speeding, hit the sheep and went out of control into the field." There was slight confusion as she was talking to One and Three. She tried again "You two, that is One and Three, carry the sheep over there." It would be easier to use their real names, she had thought.

Once the scene had been staged to Miriam's satisfaction, they all piled into the van and headed back towards London. On a whim she decided to stop at the service station and treat the soldiers to hamburgers and chips.

The three soldiers were somewhat in awe of Miriam. They sat around the table, eating their burgers and stealing glances at her.

"Do you do this sort of thing often, ma'am?" one of them had asked.

She looked back at him coldly "If I told you, I would have to kill you." She smiled. They all nodded seriously, not sure if she was joking or not.

Number Two had been mulling a little joke that was too good to waste, "If you do, please remember, I wouldn't be seen dead in a Mercedes…." Groans all round. Cheekily, Soldier One asked if they could have another round of burgers.

She agreed, saying "Of course, my treat, and milkshakes all round?" Clearly, they had all managed to work up an appetite.

Miriam kept thinking about the events of that night. In the office there had been a lot of comments about Geraldine's death. People seemed ambivalent about her. As details emerged about the car crash, people were unsurprised; she had a reputation of being a bad driver, "God knows how many points on her license for speeding", they would confide. People said it was sad she had died so close to retirement and missing out on the pension. This tended to trigger a discussion about who would get the death in service lump sum "six times salary, tax free" they would say, but there was no idea who would receive it.

Geraldine was gone, the organisation moved on and nobody was any the wiser as to the truth. Except of course, Miriam, The Director and one other.

Chapter 60

2024

1st August - Thursday
Brittany Ferries Terminal, Portsmouth, England.
Yelizaveta.

Yelizaveta made her way to Portsmouth by train and then by taxi to the ferry terminal. She was booked on the ferry to Caen, with onward train and flight connections back to Moscow. As she waited in the terminal an official came over and asked her to pop into the office as there was an issue with her passport. She followed the official to a small room where two women were waiting. To her horror she saw that one was dressed identically to her, same coat, same hair, same glasses. The other motioned for her to sit down. "Good afternoon Yelizaveta, can we offer you a tea or coffee."

"My name is Vaughan" she replied. The woman persisted. "Yelizaveta, we know exactly who you are and why you are here. My name is Moira Shannon, and I am here on behalf of the UK Government. We believe that your life is in danger, and we propose a mutually advantageous arrangement that will mitigate the risk to you."

Moira continued, "Firstly, I propose that my colleague here takes your place on the ferry and continues your journey far enough to convince your local team that you have left the country and that you are en-route back to Moscow. In the meantime, I suggest you voluntarily come with me to a secure location where you can be de-briefed in safety as a preliminary to your placement in a secure witness program. You will have a new identity and proper financial support on an ongoing basis." Moira paused.

Yelizaveta started to protest that she was the victim of mistaken identity, so Moira passed her a typewritten document. It was headed UK eyes only and was a decoded message from Moscow to someone in France. It was a detailed itinerary of her return journey, her photograph and description, details of a tracking device on her phone. The message included an instruction that she be terminated and disposed of discreetly. She recognised the mandatory code word included in the message.

There was a long silence. Yelizaveta took her phone, tickets and passport from her bag. She held them for a while. She was undecided. Many years before, she and her colleagues had been summoned to watch a film in one of the training classrooms in KGB Headquarters. They watched as one of their colleagues confessed to camera that he was an American agent. He was shown strapped to a board. They watched in horror as he was slowly fed feet first into a furnace. When the film was over, they sat in stunned silence. A senior officer called for the lights to be turned on and stood before them. "We will not tolerate traitors" he had told them. Betraying the KGB was not to be undertaken lightly. The burned-out car in the police compound came to mind. "Cars don't usually burn" she thought.

Moira passed a second document to her. Another decoded message, this time from Moscow to London. It was a detailed description of Gregory, his address, his antiques business and other details. It instructed that he be terminated and disposed of discreetly.

"Someone is covering their tracks" said Moira.

Another long pause. Moira watched her intently. Yelizaveta went to hand the items to the doppelgänger woman next to her but could not bring herself to let go. She hesitated.

With a shudder, she decided. "Take my place" she said. In that moment a lifetime of service to the Soviet Union and the Russian Federation was betrayed. She momentarily recalled the image of the screaming man as his feet entered the furnace.

The woman got up and left without a word.

Yelizaveta turned to Moira. "How did you find me?"

Moira took back the two documents. "You must remember that Ukraine, who were once your friends, are now our friends" she replied. "Come, we have much to discuss."

Chapter 61

2024

1st August - Thursday
Brighton Marina, East Sussex, England.
Martin.

Martin had been strangely apprehensive about the day ahead. He had not slept well the night before, waking up several times as the boat rocked at its berth or there was the sound of activity in the marina. He had risen early, showered and set about tidying the boat. Tidying, then polishing and cleaning, so as to create a good impression for the visitors. He had walked over to ASDA to buy some decent coffee, tea and nice biscuits. He had exhausted the cleaning and tidying process, sitting down to wait, whilst checking his phone repeatedly.

The first arrival was Miriam. She phoned from the marina car park, and he went over to let her in through the marina gates. She seemed down, perhaps she too was having sleepless nights. Shortly afterwards Carolyn arrived, she was let in and joined them in the cabin of Wanderer. Martin made coffees in the cafetière, handed out biscuits and the three of them chatted about nothing in particular. Carolyn seemed particularly interested in Wanderer's gas stove and they reminisced about the stove in the camper van, which had always seemed as if it was on the point of either gassing them or blowing the van up.

Miriam had listened and when there was a suitable pause in the reminiscences asked for some time with them afterwards as there was something that she wanted to discuss with them.

Martin's phone rang. It was his son Andy, who advised he was bringing Pete to the boat, but would take Jenny and her mother into Brighton. Martin met Pete on the pontoon and walked him to the boat. The initial discussions were about sailing and a quick mention of Andy and Jenny. The two of them were seeing a lot of each other, despite the Home Office protection team's best efforts to hide Pete and his family. It turned out they had both enabled Find my iPhone to each other and had been meeting up regularly.

Martin took Pete aboard Wanderer and did the introductions. Pete recognised Carolyn from the television and Miriam he had already met aboard Sea Bear. Martin started the little speech he had rehearsed in his head over and over again.

"Pete, you were correct, I was the Sandman and the person who arrested you all those years ago in Ireland. Let me start by apologising for having disrupted your holiday and stirring up old memories. That was never intended on my part. Firstly, let me explain that shortly after our first meeting I ceased working with the Intelligence Service and have had no connection with them since. When we bumped into each other a little while ago, here in this marina, I had no idea what had happened to you, and it was pure chance that our paths had crossed again. You are under no threat from myself or anyone in the intelligence community. You are safe to continue your holiday, there is no need for the protection team or any other measures. Is that OK?"

Pete looked visibly relieved. He looked at Carolyn and Miriam, puzzled by their presence.

Martin continued. "Carolyn is here, because we are trying to tie up a number of loose ends that you may be able to help us with."

Pete had a question of his own though, "What I have always wanted to know is how you knew where we would be that day? I had told nobody, yet you were there in the hedge waiting for us. I chose the spot at the last minute, I was sure we were not followed, yet you were in the bottom of the hedge, yards from where we set up the gun. How did you know?"

Martin looked at Pete. "The honest truth is that we stumbled into each other. I was part of a team working in the Republic. Out of the blue I was asked to help with surveillance of a suspected farmhouse. At about that time there had been a number of culvert bombs in the area and the farmhouse looked like a possible safe house for the IRA team. It had only one way in, and we could not investigate it easily without being spotted. So, I was tasked with observing it. I went in the night before, from the North and had been hidden in that hedge for about 12 hours when you turned up. It was pure chance, bad luck on your part."

Pete had another question, but he struggled to ask it. "Why did you shoot...and why just one of us? Why didn't you ask us to surrender? Why kill the American and not me? Did you know who he was?"

Martin drew in a breath and paused. "It's really hard to explain. I shouldn't have been there; I had no authority to arrest you or to shoot for that matter. My intention was to kill you both. I took aim when I heard a helicopter approach, I thought that might be your target. I aimed at the man behind the gun first, then fired before I expected to. The weapon was unfamiliar, and the trigger pressure was less than I expected. In the confusion I thought the first round had missed, so I shot him again." Martin paused. The image of the convulsing body came back to him. He shuddered. "I put the sights on you, and it was clear that you were not going to fight, so I didn't shoot."

Pete was staring at him. "So, if I had made a move, you would have killed me?"

"Yes, two shots to the chest. You would have died instantly. But you didn't pose a threat, so you lived. I'm glad that's the way it turned out."

Pete asked, "What were the loose ends you mentioned?"

It was Carolyn's turn to ask the questions. "The same day as your encounter at the border, two men were sent to a place in Sligo called Forest Lodge. They were looking for Martin and me, with the intention of torturing us to obtain information and then killing us. Did you hear anything that might explain how they came to be looking for us?"

Pete realised that Carolyn was not just a television star, but a former spy as well. What little he knew had already been shared with his interrogators many years ago, but he repeated it now. "All I knew at the time was that the Russians were discreetly helping with information. They told us that two agents were operating in Sligo, a man and a woman. We had known for a little while and two volunteers had been close to finding them. I don't know what happened next."

Miriam picked up on the Russian angle. "How do you know the Russians were involved? Did you ever meet them?"

"I never met them, but I know that the contact was made in London. The Russians had a good source of information about British Intelligence, and they shared information from time to time. From what I heard it was often quite vague. However, some of it was very specific, I recall mention of two volunteers who were killed, a man and a woman. The source was very specific, right down to what the dead woman had been wearing. It was seen as quite a priority to track the two British agents down."

Miriam nodded and looked at the others. "That confirms all that we needed to know. As you would expect, all of this remains absolutely secret. Speaking of which, have you considered reverting to your former identity? As you will be aware, you are listed as one of the disappeared."

Pete was adamant, "I will never reveal my former identity, that's all gone, dead and buried in the past. I will never go back."

"In that case," continued Miriam " we would like to propose a solution to your unexplained disappearance. We are setting up a cover story, involving the loss of a yacht in the Irish Sea. We will create evidence that the American was aboard. We suggest that we add your original identity to the documents, with no hint of IRA involvement. It would simply be a tragic sailing accident."

Pete could see the irony that he was now a keen sailor, had met his wife through sailing and it seemed a fitting end. He agreed and in due course the "missing" yacht would retrospectively include him as a crew member and one less "disappeared" would be on the list. It also made sense as he came from a fishing family; to be out on a boat would not be out of character.

Pete left them and headed into Brighton to meet up with the family.

Miriam wanted to talk to Carolyn and Martin. "I'm thinking of leaving the service, but a recent event is troubling me. I've been offered counselling, but it doesn't seem to help. I can't tell them what I have done."

"How can we help?"

"During this investigation I've seen the evidence of your handiwork. Nowadays, we don't kill people, but the two of you were ruthlessly efficient. So much so, Martin, that I adopted your trademark two bullets to the chest and one to the head." She paused. The image came swimming back, the look of surprise. The sound of the bullets striking. The exhale of breath, the collapsing body. She was beginning to tear up. "I can't get over it, how did you manage to cope? I'm not sleeping, I see their faces, I 'm lost...."

Carolyn reached out and took Miriam's hand. "How many?"

"Two."

"Did they deserve it?"

"I don't know. One was a traitor...in fact she may have been the one who set the Russians on to you. We do know that she is responsible for whole networks being rolled up behind the Iron Curtain, back in the day. People died because of her..."

"And the other?"

"Her contact, Russian, well established, been in the UK for decades...."

"Do you expect retaliation?"

"We have covered it with a car crash, so no, probably not..."

"So, this was the woman we met in your offices?"

"Correct."

Carolyn spoke softly "The answer is not the one you want to hear I'm afraid. You never get over it. At first, you can't get it out of your head. You relive it. Sometimes, something happens and you feel like you are back in the moment again. The adrenaline, the rapid breathing the sense of urgency, it all rushes back. At times, you will have that feeling of anticipation, as if it is about to happen again at any moment. When it doesn't happen you are left nervous and shaky. Then there's the guilt. It's a big thing to kill someone, even a bad person. You keep being reminded that they were human like you, that they had life and hopes and a future. You took that away, whatever the rights and wrongs of it. Sometimes I would see someone in the street and for a moment think it was one of my victims, like a ghost come to haunt me. It's really hard to bottle it up and tell nobody, not even the people we love."

Carolyn could see the tears beginning to well in Miriam's eyes.

Carolyn continued "It does get better, trust me. Think about all those generations of people who went through the World Wars. They suffered worse than us, the bomber crews, waiting to go out over Germany, knowing they were more likely to die than return. The infantry man waiting to go into action. Paratroopers dropping alone into enemy territory in the dark, men escaping from burning tanks while their mates burned. Or prisoners of war, or our predecessors who faced torture and death at the hands of the Gestapo."

Martin took over, "They went through much worse than us and returned home, to rebuild, to become family men and to live on. Somehow most of them coped. They coped before there was the recognition or treatment of conditions like PTSD. I suppose they got on with life, filled their heads with dreams of holidays, packed the waking hours with distractions and just lived on. I suspect that the generations of men who filled their lives with obsessing over model trains, DIY, car maintenance or playing bowls did so to avoid those quiet moments when the darkness creeps back. I suppose others turned to drink or drugs, I guess you choose what gets it done."

Carolyn tried a more hopeful note, "In time, the memory fades and the dreams don't recur so often. However, every now and again, something will bring it all back. My advice is to quit. Do something else. Live your life looking forwards, keep busy, look to the future and try to draw a line under it."

"And take up sailing," added Martin.

Carolyn continued, "Unlike you, we were trained to live our lives a certain way, Moscow Rules, and it never leaves you. You don't have to do that. Have you heard Friedrich Nietzsche's quote about fighting monsters? "Beware that, when fighting monsters, you yourself do not become a monster... for when you gaze long into the abyss, the abyss gazes also into you." If you continue, you will become a monster, like I did. It takes a lot of coming back from. Trust me, I know."

Miriam didn't know it, but she was beginning to acquire almost legendary status. The three soldiers had been sworn to absolute secrecy. But the tale was too good not to be told to a select few friends. In turn, the friends would tell a few trusted confidants and with each retelling there will be little embellishments added.

Whether she would have recognised herself from their description it was hard to tell. She was now the anonymous assassin, glamorous as a supermodel, hard as nails and precise. Two bullets in the heart, so close together you could cover them with a beermat, was testament to her deadly accuracy.

The number of dead sheep increased at each telling, so that in time it was as if a whole flock had been slaughtered. Her reply to the pleading man, "Whatever", was her supposed trademark quip. In time, the number of men who could claim to have been amongst the original three also swelled. If you counted them all up it was as if Miriam had been accompanied by a whole battalion of wannabees who "were there."

Chapter 62

1997

21st June - Sunday
Forest Lodge, Sligo. Eire.
Anna.

Anna had travelled by bus and taxi to Forest Lodge. It had changed a great deal over the intervening seventeen years. The golf course was now busy, the car park full and it had been difficult to book a chalet for the date she wanted. The grounds around the chalets and clubhouse had been landscaped with shrubs and flower beds. The place looked established, prosperous even, not like how she had remembered it.

The chalet was almost how she remembered it. There was a big flat screen television now, the décor had changed, and it looked like there was a new bathroom suite. She caught sight of herself in the bedroom mirror. The scars on her face had never healed properly. The angry red lines, the way the flesh had puckered and drooped. She had once been pretty;

this was the place where her looks had been stolen from her. Now, she had returned.

She settled in and unpacked. From her bag she produced a bottle of vodka and poured herself a stiff drink. She had clawed her life back from alcoholism, so this was her first drink in years. Now it didn't matter what she drank.

She had arrived carrying a big bunch of flowers. Now, she took off the paper in which they were wrapped.

Anna took another drink. It felt good. She opened the packet of pills and popped them from the packaging, carefully, one by one to form a line on the tabletop. She refilled the glass; she broke the pills, one after another into the vodka. She swirled the mixture with her finger. She licked her finger, there was no bad taste, just the vodka.

Carrying her flowers over one arm and the glass in the other, she left the chalet and made her way to the clearing. She knew the way; she had retraced it countless times in her dreams. She was going back to where her life had changed. Her life was neatly divided onto before and after. After was hell; Eion leaving, despair, drunkenness, being lost to the world, the long slow climb back to a drab normality. Now she was back where it happened.

Anna sat upon the ground. Somewhere beneath her lay the two corpses. She shuddered at the memory of what they did to her and what she did to them. Anna had wanted to die afterwards, she had begged Isobel to kill her, but she had let her live. But it had been a life without pleasure or hope.

Anna drank down the vodka and sat looking at the trees. The sunlight slanted down through the branches; dust motes floated in the sunbeams. A large dragonfly hovered in the air close to her. It was jewel-like, a polished green. It hung there, watching her. "Hello there, wee fella" she said, "it's my birthday." She could tell her words were starting to slur.

It was time. From amongst the bunch of flowers she took out a long, thin-bladed knife.

The dragonfly watched as Anna slit first one wrist and then the other. The cuts hurt more than she had expected, making her gasp. In that moment she recalled her screams as the man had cut her. This time, she was quiet. Anna stared at her warm blood as it soaked into her dress. She carefully put the knife on the ground beside her, gathered the flowers up onto her chest and lay back.

She had intended to pray. Now the words of a song came to her. She had listened to the song on the radio in the taxi. It was about a woman who "realised she'd never ride through Paris in a sports car, with the warm wind in her hair." Such a sad song. The dragonfly flew over and briefly settled on the flowers. It flew away, up into the trees.

Anna died alone.

Chapter 63

2024

1st August - Thursday
Blake Hall, Lincolnshire
Yelizaveta.

Once she had accepted the British offer, Yelizaveta had spent a little time coming to terms with her decision. Now she worried that she had been uncharacteristically impulsive. Perhaps she should have declined the offer. Maybe she should have insisted they release her, taken her chances on the ferry and maybe even gone to her death a loyal Russian. She was also beginning to wonder if she had been tricked. The messages could have been faked and there wasn't a plan to have her liquidated before she got back to Moscow. The doubts were answered. Moira Shannon had asked that she surrender all her possessions for scanning. In the strap of her luggage, in her coat lining and in the base of her handbag were tracking devices. Yelizaveta had watched as they were found and confirmed that they were standard issue. Someone in Moscow was tracking her, which was ominous. All three devices were hurriedly sent after the ferry to complete the onward journey with her replacement.

As she was taken by car to a nearby airfield, she was already trying to anticipate what the British would do next. They could hardly expect her to return to Moscow and spy on their behalf, they had no leverage over her. She didn't want any of the usual inducements and she was not compromised in any way. Presumably she would be interrogated, but she knew she had little to tell. Once Moscow realised she had disappeared, any knowledge she had would soon be out of date. Agents and assets would be pulled out or discarded, depending on their value. She settled back and resolved to take what came with a dispassionate eye. From a professional point of view, it would be interesting to observe the British Secret Service in action. At the airfield she and Moira were transferred to a waiting helicopter. The flight took them North, skirting London and out towards Lincolnshire.

The helicopter landed on the lawn of an enormous stately home. They disembarked and made their way inside. Brief introductions were made to the three staff, and she was taken to her room. She was told to settle herself in and get some rest. The door was closed and locked behind her and she was alone. The room was grander than anything the Russian Intelligence service could offer. There was an enormous four poster bed, a luxurious sofa, antique writing desk and the walls were hung with oil paintings. The en-suite bathroom was marble lined and had a roll top bath, complete with gold taps. "I could get used to this" she thought. After a while there was a quiet knock at the door. Moira entered accompanied by Sophie, one of the staff she had just met.

Sophie was carrying a tray of food. "I'm afraid you arrived too late for the evening meal. On the off chance that you might be hungry we have rustled up a light meal for you to eat here in the room. I trust this is ok?"

Yelizaveta was hungry, but her professional instinct was to be wary. She herself had used tempting meals to give suspects a dose of SP-117, a psychoactive drug which acted as a "truth serum." Under its influence she had listened as deeply buried secrets were babbled out under the softest of questioning. It was not entirely reliable, but neither was torture. She was indeed hungry, so in the spirit of intellectual curiosity she ate the meal. The soup was leek and potato, which was delicious. She could not taste anything unusual. There were sandwiches: ham and tomato and cheese and pickle. There was tea. "Whatever they are using, it is undetectable by taste," she mentally noted.

Sophie returned after a little while to show her the button on the bedside table. This was to be pressed if anything was needed before morning. Sophie said that breakfast would be served 9.00, wished her a good night and left.

Yelizaveta changed into the nightdress provided and settled down to sleep. The bed was particularly comfortable, but she willed herself to stay awake, trying to detect the effect of the truth serum. Eventually, she concluded, correctly as it happened, that she had not been drugged and drifted off to sleep.

Chapter 64

2024

2nd August - Friday
Blake Hall, Lincolnshire
Yelizaveta.

She awoke early next morning and dressed. Looking out of the window, she watched as a herd of deer walked slowly across the lawn and disappeared into the shrubbery. At 9.00 Sophie knocked on the door and walked with her down two flights of stairs to the breakfast room. Moira was already there; they were the only two guests. They had a convivial breakfast; Moira's interest in her was confined to whether she had slept well, whether the room was comfortable enough and was the heating set at the right level. She had told her that they would spend the afternoon together, but the priority was to get her settled in.

Moira motioned to Sophie. "Could you take Miss Yelizaveta to see Mr Mason after breakfast?" she consulted a note "could you be both be back here by 11.00, I have arranged a session for Miss Yelizaveta with Mrs Dutton."

"So, it begins" thought Yelizaveta.

Sophie took her to a small room, where Mr Mason was waiting. He was a heavy-set, tough looking man, with the demeanour and appearance of a brawler. Yelizaveta noticed a small smear of blood on Mr Mason's cuff. Mentally, she prepared herself for the worst. She had not expected they would jump straight to torture and beating.

Mason was the cook. His questioning of Yelizaveta was primarily about any food allergies or preferences.

"Did she prefer tea or coffee at breakfast." He had laid out a meal plan for the week ahead and wanted her to confirm what she wanted.

"Was veal acceptable?" There was also the question of which wine to serve. Sensing her indecision, he had arranged with Sophie that later in the week he would lay on a tasting session. He promised three suitable white wines, from which she could take her pick. There was also the need to establish her preference as to which cheeses to buy in.

As they left the meeting room, Yelizaveta felt unsteady and visibly wobbled.

"Are you alright?" enquired Sophie, concerned and holding out a steadying hand.

Yelizaveta exhaled, "I'm sorry, that rather took me by surprise. I was expecting an interrogation; I was steeling myself for a beating and then that…"

Sophie was a mask of concern. "Oh, I'm so sorry, I hope I didn't give you that impression, oh dear, that's funny! I can't imagine Mason beating anyone, certainly not a lady like yourself." She laughed "unless you were a vegetarian perhaps."

Sophie took her towards her appointment with Mrs Dutton. As they walked, Sophie had words of warning. "I need to tell you that, amongst us girls, we refer to her as Chopper Dutton," she confided. "When she does you, she favours short styles, hair pulled back from the face, very 1960's, but not very flattering. Insist that she doesn't cut too much off and that she leaves you something to work with. Don't let her hack away at your fringe."

Yelizaveta had almost started to wobble again until she realised that Chopper Dutton was a hairdresser. In due course, Chopper Dutton gave her a new and different hair style, attended to make-up, nails and glasses. Other changes were planned.

"Make do with these glasses for now, I will have some others, including sunglasses for you to try in a day or two," said Madam Chopper. "The other change is that I have some new shoes for you. Strictly speaking, you don't need to wear them here, but it would make sense to get used to them. They will make you a couple of inches taller, you'd be surprised how much of a difference it makes. Furthermore, we need to adjust your overall shape, I will get some new under garments made up for you. We'll move some of your bumps around! I want you to carefully study the eye make-up I have applied, Western fashions like this are very different from the current Russian look. It makes a big difference to whether you will be recognised or not, so change it from now on. Don't go back to your old style."

Yelizaveta slipped on the shoes and glasses. In the mirror she studied her new appearance. "Very effective" she thought "I hardly recognise myself now."

Mrs Dutton had fussed over her with a tape measure, jotting down the details. "We will have a new wardrobe for you in a few days. A few basic items, which we can build on. In time we will develop a completely new look, a different colour palette from your habitual one, different shapes and cuts. Oh, one more thing, I will arrange for a dentist to visit. We will need some tidying up here at the front and maybe lose a couple of back teeth to change your jaw line a little."

Moira joined them for a light lunch. She listened to Sophie's account of the confusion over Mason and straight away set out to reassure Yelizaveta that all was well, she was safe and that no harm would come to her. Their program was to debrief her, give her a new identity and appearance, so that in time she would safely move on.

"With that in mind" Moira had continued, "We will need to re-name you. With your agreement I propose that we simply anglicise your name and call you Elisabeth for the time being. It's close enough to your Russian name to be familiar to you, but if anyone happens to mention Miss Elisabeth in passing, it's a common enough English name."

"Good enough for the Queen, so good enough for me you mean?"

"Yes Miss Elisabeth, good enough."

The interrogation began and it surprised her. Rather than go straight to where the "gold" lay the British team wanted to start at the beginning and record every detail of her life. Moira led the interrogation, asking her to start at the very beginning, to tell her life's story, omitting nothing.

"Have you heard that, in Imperial China, the interview for the civil service consisted of only one question?" asked Moira.

Yelizaveta was puzzled, "What was the question?"

Moira smiled at her. "Tell me everything that you know…."

Chapter 65

2024

2nd August - Friday
Blake Hall, Lincolnshire
Yelizaveta.

It began with Yelizaveta's childhood. She described at length her happy childhood. Her parents doted on each other and on their two children. She recounted her earliest memory, her mother singing in the kitchen of their little flat in Moscow as the first snow of winter fell. With her father they had built a T34 tank out of snow in the courtyard, which seemed strange to their neighbours. Muscovites build snowmen, ice sculptures maybe, but not a snow T34 the size of a car! But her father regularly travelled abroad, and the neighbours reasoned he must have picked up his strange habits there.

Her father was one of Russia's foremost tank experts. For him, it was more than just a technical job, it was his passion, borne of youthful experience. In the Great Patriotic War, he had started as a humble tank commander. Through luck and expertise, he had risen from commanding a single tank to a whole Guards Tank Regiment. He and his men had driven from Moscow, battle after bloody battle, to the gates of Berlin. He knew everything about tanks: how to maintain them, how to use them tactically and how to get the best out of his men. To him tank warfare was like chess. A game to be played with skill and precision.

On the road to Berlin, he had formed an attachment that would blossom into the other great passion of his life, Yelizaveta's mother. As a nurse attached to the Tank Regiment, she saw the worst that war can do to men's frail bodies: the burns, the torn limbs and the broken minds. Before every fight, she fretted about her man. She watched for his T34, marked out by its pennant as the commander's mount, but which also drew the aim of enemy anti-tank gunners. At the close of each day's fighting, she would anxiously wait for his return, dreading the day when it was his tank that was hit and burned.

Eventually his luck had run out, just outside Gubin, as the Red Army attacked the Seelow Heights, at the gates of Berlin. With a monstrous clang an anti-tank round had hit the T34 and butchered his crew mates. He had rolled from the turret, on fire and screaming. Then she was there, she had run forward through machine gun fire, to cover him in a coat and beat out the flames. She had dragged him into the ditch, away from the fierce heat of the exploding tank. She had cradled him in her arms, gently rocking back and forth. He had looked up, recognised her and simply said "Marry me", before passing into unconsciousness. So, her mother had gained both a medal for bravery and a husband in one day. It was a story the couple would never weary of telling.

After the war her father's expertise was much in demand and he was transferred to the KGB's technical section. He was not a spy as such, just a collector of information about foreign tanks and tactics. He travelled overseas, attended weapons trials, trade fairs and even wars. Sometimes he was accompanied by his wife and young family.

Yelizaveta loved her father. He encouraged her love of chess. He treated her and her brother alike, which appealed to the tomboy streak in her. Sometimes on their trips, they would stand looking out over a stretch of countryside. "How," he would ask the children "would you attack an enemy who held that position? Answer assuming you have a regiment of tanks at your disposal?"

He would critique their ideas.

"Where would you expect the enemy anti-tank guns to be situated?" he would ask; "where would he place his tactical reserve? If you push forward here, what will he do next?" His favourite saying was "Turn the chessboard around my children, see the ground as he sees it, anticipate his moves."

When she was nine, Yelizaveta had been in the first batch from her year to take the solemn oath and become a Young Pioneer. She had loved being a Pioneer. Whilst still a teenager, she was approached and asked to work for the KGB. She still travelled with her mother and father, but now wrote reports on the people she met. On one journey she had travelled with her parents to see a new tank being put through its paces on a proving ground in East Germany. She was instructed to wander through the nearby town, to "take the temperature", to monitor the sentiment expressed by local youngsters and to look for signs of dissent.

As they drove home, her father unexpectedly stopped the car. He got out and walked unsteadily to the side of the road. It was an unremarkable spot. A raised road, tree lined and running through open wheat fields. She went to her father, and, to her complete surprise, he was sobbing. Seeing her husband's distress, their mother had shepherded the children back to the car to wait. From the car she and her brother had watched as their parents stood together, impassive at the roadside. When they finally drove on, it was in absolute, oppressive silence.

The next day her mother took her to one side and explained what had happened. In the war, her father had been to that very place on the road. A German Tiger tank had ambushed his column as they pushed forward on the raised roadway. The German was at long range, yet deadly accurate. One by one, the tanks ahead of her father's were hit, some burning, others exploding. The surviving crews had tumbled from their stricken tanks, seeking cover. Her father ordered his tank off the road away from the menacing Tiger. He had not seen the wounded men who lay in his path. In his haste to get to safety, his tank had run over and crushed to death his best friend, a man he had known since boyhood. When he saw the place again, he had recognised it in an instant. The memory had come flooding back. There was a long silence. Finally, her mother said, "This is why there must never be another war, whatever you do little Liza, work for peace! We must become so strong that nobody dares to make war on us again."

As the interrogations went on, Yelizaveta realised she had been talking continuously for a while and that she had never before told anyone about her parents in such detail. She paused, wondering if this really was what Moira really wanted.

"So, what became of your parents?" prompted Moira.

"They are both long dead now," came the reply. "My mother died of cancer, she was ill for a long time and my father died soon after. He simply gave up and died. What surprised me was that both were given full KGB funerals, I had never realised my mother was in the KGB, yet there she lay in her coffin in a full colonel's uniform, with a chest full of medals.

When my father died, he too was in uniform, again with a chest full of medals and the uniform of a KGB General. It was the only time I saw either of them in uniform. Time had not been kind to the old tank men who came to the funeral. They shuffled past the coffin wearily, but afterwards they told tales of my parents that I had never heard. It's funny to think of it, but they were just my parents, I never thought of them as heroes. Or for that matter, senior KGB officers, even though I was a junior member of the KGB at the time, I never realised..."

"Tell me about your time at school, were you happy there?" asked Moira.

Chapter 66

2024

2nd September - Monday.
Blake Hall, Lincolnshire
Yelizaveta.

The days followed a similar pattern. The morning would be spent on some activity. Sophie had encouraged her to come horse riding. After some very tentative first lessons, Miss Elisabeth, as she was generally known, could be seen gently riding around the estate. Her mount was a big softie of a horse called Trooper. She looked forward to their rides, even taking on the work of cleaning out the stables and feeding Trooper.

Sophie accompanied her everywhere when they were out of the house. On one occasion, she had spotted a Glock pistol tucked under Sophie's padded gilet. Sophie was always armed.

In the afternoon the debrief sessions continued, gently wandering forwards through Yelizaveta's life and career. There was a microphone in plain sight on the table, every word was transcribed, analysed and noted by an unseen team of listeners. Every fact was being tabulated, checked and cross referenced. Every person she mentioned would be entered into a database, locations and timings were added.

As an interrogator herself, Yelizaveta knew that her best approach was to provide only facts and never to lie. To conceal, one must omit; her problem was that she could not understand what the British were after. She could turn the chessboard around, but she couldn't see the pieces.

After the evening meal she would sit with Sophie or one of the other team members and watch the TV. Much of the broadcast TV did not appeal, so they watched films. One particular set of films were guaranteed to make her chuckle. It was a film with plasticine puppets about a mad inventor and his long suffering, silent yet expressive dog. Yelizaveta had discovered Wallace and Gromit!

Aside from her love of Wallace and Gromit, she had acquired something even more quintessentially English. Her accent had become purest cut glass, absorbed as if by osmosis from Sophie. As they rode around the estate a casual observer might have assumed from their chatter, they were mother and daughter, Downton Abbey personified.

There were little snippets of news that the team could share with her about her former colleagues. One picture, culled from Facebook, showed a smiling mother proudly holding twin girls. They did not need Yelizaveta to tell them that the mother was one of Moscow's rising stars.

The team did not mention that the vacancy created by Yelizaveta's still unexplained disappearance was being held open awaiting the young mum's return to work after her maternity leave. By taking Yelizaveta out of the game, London had moved the new mother, one of its key assets within Moscow centre, another step up the ladder.

One night, Yelizaveta awoke with a start from a deep sleep. In the darkness she could just make out the shape of a person standing in her room. She screamed, dived for the panic button, pressed it and rolled off the bed onto the floor. Within moments the door burst open and one of the staff burst in gun at the ready. Sophie appeared, also armed and ready to shoot. Once the initial confusion was over, they reassured her that she was alone. The cameras had picked up nothing. She realised. The sinister shape she had seen was a dressing gown hanging on the back of the door. There was much hilarity before they left her, but she found it hard to get back to sleep. The British were taking her security very seriously. They also had cameras in the room.

Behind the scenes, the pieces of information were slowly being assembled into a picture. Sometimes a little fragment of information would open up a whole new line of investigation. Yelizaveta had corrected Moira at one point. Crocodile was not the code name of an operational group. It was simply a way of referring to a number of contacts developed by a single person, who was nicknamed "The Crocodile" because of his ferocious reputation. Linking activity to the "Crocodile's" known posting to London, which had ended with his expulsion, gave them another insight into who might be involved.

Perhaps unintentionally, Moira had confirmed something that Moscow had suspected, but Yelizaveta had not previously understood. The woman who had died in the same car crash as Gregory was indeed a member of the British SIS. Gregory had run two high value assets, PEARL and LYRE. To protect them, Gregory had never revealed the identity of either, even to trusted Moscow controllers such as herself.

Yelizaveta could not work out what information Moira was after. Moira treated every question and every answer with equal importance. Yelizaveta was trying to stay one step ahead but was making a classic mistake. She couldn't see the relevance or importance of some lines of questioning. She was actively considering whether any line of questioning might relate to PEARL or LYRE. She wasn't burying the secrets, instead she was actively considering them as she spoke. Like a chess player who keeps looking at where he will make his next move, all it would take was one slip of the tongue...and the game would be given away.

Chapter 67

2024

Autumn
Blake Hall, Lincolnshire
Yelizaveta.

After many hours of patient questioning, they were almost caught up to recent events. Yelizaveta had become comfortable in her new way of life. She had grown up as a member of an elite. At the time she had not realised it, but looking back she realised she had been privileged. Her parents had been respected, relatively well off and given freedoms that other Russians could not obtain. It was not the excess of later years, when the oligarchs had taken over Russia, but it had been comfortable.

Now she was slipping into the lifestyle and manners of a privileged English lady, not wealthy, but comfortable. The young woman, Sophie, who was both guard and companion, now seemed more like a friend or even a family member.

Sophie chatted to her about her own school days, university and the Service.

One damp morning, as they rode along one of the estate's lanes Yelizaveta looked across at Sophie. "Can I ask you a personal question, Sophie dear?" she had asked. "If I was to try and escape by riding off, would you shoot me?"

"Goodness! What a question," came the reply. "It would be like shooting my own Mum, not sure I could do it." Smiling she added, "You wouldn't get far on Trooper anyway, remember he's a member of the Service too. He would bring you back! He's a highly trained intelligence horse!"

Yelizaveta laughed, but she got the message. Sophie would shoot if she needed to.

The gentle interrogation sessions continued. Now the topic was her last few weeks in Moscow Centre. The preparations for her trip were discussed in detail. Yelizaveta had explained her frustrations over the shoddy work in preparing her alias and the lack of time to absorb all the details of her new identity. She was irritated that they had made her travel as an English woman, but at that time her English was rusty and accented.

She mentioned the rookie mistake over the passport photograph. To her surprise Moira had told her that the identity selected was that of a wanted criminal, yet another stupid mistake. The woman who had travelled onwards on the ferry had come close to being arrested in France when she had used the credit card Yelizaveta had handed over.

Moira set out the possible interpretations of the evidence. Moscow had either been careless and incompetent or that Yelizaveta was set up. "We are considering the hypothesis that someone in Moscow wanted you dead, but in a way that was completely off the books. It is likely that you were going to vanish, dead in a ditch somewhere in France, but carrying dodgy fake ID. So far as the French Police would have been concerned, the body would have been a British petty criminal, killed by fellow criminals."

Moira pressed the point. "If we are correct, your death would have been to achieve an objective. What we don't understand yet, is what that objective is. Is it likely that you have made enemies in the leadership who would want you eliminated in this way?"

Yelizaveta considered this carefully. "No, I don't think so."

Moira continued, "Let us assume that you are now dead. But you did not die alone. We have two other deaths to add into the equation. What can you tell us about Gregory Fielding? You came to London to investigate his death, why was he of interest?"

After a pause Yelizaveta decided to stick to her honesty approach. "He was a long time Moscow asset, put in place by "The Crocodile."

Moira's next question puzzled her. "When you were sent to investigate, were you aware that someone in Moscow ordered Gregory's death?"

"No, I was not. So far as I know there was genuine surprise in Moscow at what happened. That's why I was sent to investigate. There was a rush to find out what had happened and why. We thought at the time you might have killed him. We also considered other intelligence services, but Gregory was a very specialised asset. He dealt only in British material, taken from very selective British sources. Only a tiny number of people could have known of his existence."

"I can assure you we didn't kill him; as we now know, the order came from Moscow itself. Who might have originated such an order?"

Yelizaveta was reluctant to speculate, but when she thought about it, a few names came to mind.

Moira continued, "What objective could be served by killing both yourself and Gregory? What would have linked the two of you in the mind of someone powerful enough to have set this all up, powerful enough to kill two well established, loyal operatives? What had you and Gregory done wrong to deserve to be killed?"

"I don't know. What links us is that I was Gregory's controller in Moscow. He had very old school ways of feeding intelligence back, so he only trusted me. I was his sole point of contact. We had both been in London together, back in the early days, so he knew me. He sent me all of his information, strictly one way. I never communicated with him at all, I just received information and arranged for funds to be credited back to him.

He had set up an antiques business and we used to funnel funds to him, always in small amounts, directly linked to items he had shipped. Ironically, the antiques were always good quality, so we had a side-line selling them on to various customers. To any investigation, the whole set-up would have looked legitimate. The key to the operation was that Gregory ran his own sources. He was very selective."

"So, who in the Centre, other than yourself, knew that Gregory was the source of the information from London that you controlled?"

"That's what I have been wondering. I didn't think anyone knew. I always concealed his identity internally, because some of his information was of the highest value. But I think someone else did know, someone very highly placed."

"Why highly placed?"

"Because when I searched Gregory's flat, I found a medal with his name on it. It was the Order of Lenin."

"Why is that significant, I thought such medals were commonplace?"

"Not the Order of Lenin, to award it you would need Putin's personal sign-off and I don't think he would have awarded it to someone he had never heard of. It's also a bizarre thing to have happened. The actual medal engraved with his real name was in the flat. It wasn't even well hidden. Gregory should have destroyed it, not put it on his mantelpiece. It just doesn't make sense. We protected his identity all these years and then someone sends him the medal and he kept it, madness!"

"So, you didn't send it to him?"

"Absolutely not, that would be insane. You can't put an Order of Lenin in the post, maybe someone delivered it in person. Things started to go wrong. Have you read a book called Treasure Island?"

Moira looked up from her notes "Of course, Robert Louis Stevenson, it is a children's classic."

"Do you remember a blind man comes and gives the sea captain the Black Spot, so he knows he was doomed."

"So, you think Gregory was given the Black Spot, so to speak, in the form of Russia's highest order?"

"Maybe, perhaps it was an act of consolation. Someone's twisted logic, give the medal then kill them. They die a hero, no disgrace, a balance of outcomes."

"Are there people who think like that?"

"Of course. We have sent a generation of young men to die in Ukraine; for what? They get nothing from it, they stay poor, or they die. What do they get, a medal! Napoleon said that men are led with baubles. Like all psychopaths he knew that the prospect of a tin star was enough to make men risk life and limb, all for his own benefit. Your death is a sacrifice I am prepared to make!"

"If you are right, how does Putin benefit? Why kill Gregory and then kill you? What's the objective?"

"Perhaps, he was returning a favour. Maybe he was just closing down a source of information. Burning the pipeline, so it can never be found. It might have been the reward to one of Gregory's sources?"

"Could this be connected to the woman? It was her car that they died in. We originally thought it was just a crash, but we realised we had intercepted an instruction to kill Gregory. Did you find out why a senior member of SIS was in the car with him that night, was he kidnapping her"?

"On the contrary, I now think she was one of his sources, codenamed PEARL. Gregory was very protective of both of his key sources. He would not name them, even under pressure from the Centre. Only Gregory knew the identity of PEARL, but there was speculation in Moscow that she was a senior member of SIS. He had cultivated her as a junior employee and followed her rise through the ranks."

On her notepad Moira had written the word "Both."

"We struggled to understand what role PEARL might have. Some of the intelligence was first class: names, identities, other items were almost trivial. As an example, we spent ages trying to make sense of the various documents she supplied. They apparently involved a heated debate by memo about the definition of blue jeans and whether they could be considered as smart casual for the purposes of the dress code. It made no sense; it wasn't valuable yet wasn't chickenfeed. Nobody in their right mind would fabricate this stuff, so it had to be genuine, but why send it? It was almost as if the source had no idea what was of value and what was not. I don't think Gregory helped in this regard, he made big payments, irrespective of quality. Over the years, PEARL cost us a fortune, yet only gave us glimpses of what we needed."

"How many years was PEARL active, via Gregory?"

"Both PEARL and LYRE go back to the late 70's…" Yelizaveta stopped herself too late.

Moira looked up from her notes. "LYRE? Not sure you have mentioned him or her before…"

Chapter 68

2024

1st September- Sunday
Alfriston. East Sussex, England.
Martin, Carolyn.

Martin and Carolyn met for lunch. They drove towards Beachy Head. Martin was at the wheel and Carolyn stared out at the expanse of the Downland. Strong winds had driven the gulls ashore, they lined the fields.

Carolyn was feeling tired. "Why did we do it?" she asked.

Martin looked away from the road. "By it, do you mean join, or stay or do you mean why did we quit?"

"I mean join and continue doing what we did. We both could have gone into other careers, why become spooks? Was there no point in the training where you thought I don't want to do this?"

"Funnily enough, now you mention it no, there wasn't. I just did it as a challenge; I suppose I just wanted to master the skill."

"But think about it, why? Neither of us was particularly wedded to an ideology or a philosophy that would require us to go and kill."

Martin considered, "You won't remember this, but you once compared that life to the life of the Roman gladiator. Not a slave, but a professional fighter. You go out into the arena for your own gratification. The thrill of kill or be killed is pretty intoxicating, like an addiction, the classic adrenaline junkie."

"I do remember. It was on the beach at Deal…"

"And you moved on, broke the adrenaline habit, lived a normal life, it was just a phase, just one little piece of the puzzle."

"It's the historian's lot to never have the full picture and to want to know more" she mused. "Imagine a craftsman or woman back in, say the second century. They create an urn, perhaps a funeral urn, intended for someone's ashes after cremation. The urn is exquisitely decorated. Everything we could want to know about that person is recorded in a frieze that runs around it. Their birth, their childhood, their life, their loves, disappointments, triumphs and ultimately their death."

"Two thousand years later, we dig it up. It's been smashed by the plough, broken to pieces and scattered. Perhaps we only find a few fragments. We reconstruct the urn, perhaps its pieces are mixed with bits of other urns. We guess, we fill in the blanks, maybe we go and dig again and find more fragments. We have an incomplete story and it's not even the version told by the dead person themself; it is told by the urn maker."

Martin glanced across at her. "Not sure where you are going with this line of thought, is something worrying you?"

"Oh, I don't know, perhaps just that I'm getting old, and I want to make sense of it all. I feel like I haven't even got all the fragments of my own life and what I have doesn't feel like the full picture. Just to pick on one aspect of my life, I spent nearly a year of my life living as your wife, we slept together, created a book together, so far as the world knew then, we were a couple. The world thought we had died. By the end of our time together I thought I knew you, but in reality, I knew nothing at all. I didn't know your real name, your background, anything about the real you. Yes, I knew our cover stories, but they were just fiction… it troubles me that my life is made up of fragments that will never be fitted together. How can I make sense of my life if it's a jumble of broken bits."

"Why worry about it? Do all the fragments matter; why all of them?"

Carolyn paused, looking out over the fields. "Take the fragment I spent with you, it started on Mersea Island and ended with a funeral in Sandwich. It made me into a monster. I killed people. It seems we blew wide open this Crocodile thing, without ever realising what we had done."

Martin hesitated before interrupting, "I don't know what to say. Perhaps just live for the here and now. Forget about the fragments. Leave that for some other person to fret about, when they dig up your urn in two thousand years' time. Anyway, given your fame, how big an urn are you planning?"

"Acquaintance lessens fame", she responded "so perhaps a little urn?"

He looked puzzled. "Should I know that quotation, it sounds familiar?"

"Tiberius Claudius Caesar Augustus Germanicus, known to history as Claudius, a God in Colchester at least", she intoned "and another bloody historian, what are we like?"

"Bet he had a big urn...ooooh Matron!"

"Now you're being silly. Looks like we are here."

They parked up behind the pub. Martin had eaten there some months before, so this was his recommendation. In a field at the back of the pub were two donkeys. The donkeys came over to the fence, as if to say hello. Carolyn patted one donkey on the nose. The other pressed its nose to her and it was stroked in its turn.

"These are two very old donkeys" she said, "well past their prime and put out to pasture...to while away their days watching the world go by, just like us."

"They look happy enough" replied Martin, stroking the nearest donkey's furry ear. "It's better than the alternatives, anyway I'm a happy donkey!"

"It's nice that they've got each other to talk to" replied Carolyn, "someone to share your field with, who knows what it's like to be a donkey."

Martin was amused "Two donkeys, like us and all the other pairings we came up against. I suppose it's a natural combination for spying; one alone looks suspicious, three's a crowd. Two just works. It seemed to work for the other side as well, the man and woman who came to the hotel, the two in the Bull Inn who killed the little girl, Eion and Anna, the two men that Anna chopped up and we buried. Work together, hide together, kill together, get your cover blown together and then die together. Unhappy pairs. Unlike us, we are the happy old donkeys."

"Couples are also capable of the worst that people can do, remember. What about the Moors Murderers, Brady and Hindley, the Wests, all those Roman Emperors and their scheming wives? Perhaps it would be better if we get reincarnated as a pair of donkeys," laughed Carolyn.

"Surely you don't believe in reincarnation" came the reply. They were settling back into the old way of joshing with each other.

Carolyn was smiling. "Of course I do, I hardly remember my real life as a schoolgirl and student, then I was Isobel, married and a spook, and then I was dead. So, yes, reincarnation as Carolyn and then married again, also a new married name to get used to as well. I guess it's not the classic Buddhist path, but I've no complaints about going through existence as girl, then killer, fake corpse, keen student, loving wife, grungy professor, TV personality and who knows what comes next."

"Definitely a donkey. You're guaranteed to come back as a donkey after that lot, maybe a clever donkey with thousands of followers on Tik Tok."

"On that cheerful note, let's go in and get our nosebags. In this incarnation I will want something better than raw carrots."

"After you then, lead the way Madam Donkey, sorry Professor Donkey."

Chapter 69

2024

17th September - Tuesday
Thamesbank House, London
Miriam.

The election was over. A new party and a new government after fourteen years, so everyone was scuttling around, preparing briefs, setting out what the new masters needed to know in pithy PowerPoint presentations.

Miriam was nursing a hangover. The night before, she had been at a pub quiz. She didn't care much for the questions, but she had drunk until she did and then drunk some more. As she crept into the office she was intercepted by the Director's Personal Assistant. "You are wanted in the Head of Service's office now" was the message. "Comb your hair and smarten yourself up, he has a visitor. Get over to Thamesbank House as fast as you can – there's a car outside waiting for you."

Miriam was shown into the Head of Service's office and introduced to the visitor, the newly appointed Home Secretary. Clearly this was not the anticipated bollocking for coming in late, that would be well below the pay grade of a Minister of State. Miriam had only ever seen the Home Secretary on TV, but now here she was in the flesh. She looked somehow smaller than expected and tired. Miriam waited while the Home Secretary flicked through a file. It was Miriam's personnel file, which bore her name and photograph on the cover. The Home Secretary closed the file and looked directly at Miriam as if to weigh her up.

The Head introduced Miriam as if he had known her for years; in reality he had never seen her before. The Home Secretary smiled and told her to take a seat.

The Home Secretary was watching her closely.

"I would like to hear your thoughts on this individual," said the Home Secretary.

The smile was gone, the scrutiny more intense as she handed Miriam a file.

Opening the file, Miriam recognised the photograph at once. Characteristically tousled haired and open-mouthed, the former Prime Minister was probably still the most recognisable person in Britain. Miriam's face fell. The prospect of providing close protection for a duplicitous sex pest was the last thing she wanted.

"What are your thoughts?" asked the Home Secretary.

Miriam paused. "I would rather be assigned elsewhere" she replied. A deep breath, "I despise the man." Visions of a return to the archives swam into her head. "I don't think it would be appropriate for me to be involved in his close protection team." Her mouth had gone dry. She reached for a glass of water from the Director's desk.

The Home Secretary looked at her, unsmiling and direct. "Miriam," she said "you misunderstand. Your assignment is to kill this individual. He is a traitor. Look at the file. Appropriately the Russians codenamed him LYRE, a nice touch on their part"

Now the absence of the bag carriers and hangers on who attend such meeting made sense. This was on a need-to-know basis and very few people fell into that category for a matter such as this. The contents of the file were startling. Miriam turned to the Head, "How on earth did we miss this? Why did he do it, are we sure of our sources?"

Her boss shook his head, "We missed it because he was operating in plain sight, we mistook his antics for buffoonery. We underestimated him and his handler. They were very good; they used tradecraft of the highest order, very disciplined and focussed. It was by chance that we picked it up. You recall your little whack-a-mole episode? Our Russian friends sent someone senior and trusted, to sniff around, to work out what had happened."

"That senior person became convinced, at our prompting, that it was their own side that was behind the deaths. That someone in Moscow centre was covering tracks, someone friendly to LYRE perhaps. We were able to implant the notion that they would be next on the death list. So, when presented with certain "facts", they agreed to accept our hospitality, bringing us a treasure trove of information."

Miriam gulped down the glass of water. She was being told to kill again.

The Head of Service continued as if this was all routine, nothing to get excited about. "A team has been checking that information for some time, and we have waited until after the election for a more dispassionate assessment of the options. What we were told is that all those years ago, one of the people we missed when we rolled up Crocodile was an inconsequential young journalist. He was small fry, considered unreliable by Moscow, prone to making up stuff and consequently not debriefed as regularly as the others. Over the years he got into various scrapes, but Moscow had a soft spot for him, so they fed him scraps of work and paid him handsomely in return. Of course, you know how the story develops and that various doubts have been aired about both him and his advisors, but we never had proof, until now."

The Home Secretary took up the narrative, "To be clear, exposure of this issue would damage our relationships with our allies beyond repair. There can be no trial, just a sudden, accidental death, followed by a state funeral."

"Oh, and just to be clear, this needs to have watertight deniability. To use a well-worn cliché, this meeting never happened, you and I have never met, that file will disappear beyond recall in due course. If you are wondering why you have been selected to take this project on, I am assured that you have already proven yourself adept at unsanctioned and potentially illegal killing on behalf of the Service. If you get this wrong and word leaks out, you will be painted as a psychopathic bad apple, in effect a loose cannon, a rogue agent. On the other side of the coin, get this right and our gratitude will be immeasurable."

Miriam was already considering options, a drowning, alcohol induced car crash, sexual misadventure, when practicalities came to mind. She turned to the Head of Service, "What resources will I have available, do I have a team?"

"You will have no internal or official resources to draw upon. So far as funding is concerned, steps have been taken to place an account at your disposal." He handed her a bank card. "The card has no limit, no oversight, spend what you need, no questions asked. Whatever equipment or resources you need, buy it, nothing comes from within the Service. As for access to our systems" he handed over a file "This contains information that will allow you hack unseen into our systems, please be careful with it, use it only when necessary and destroy it afterwards. If discovered, we will attribute any activity you generate to a sophisticated hacking operation. However, in that event, be warned, the Service will be trying to track down and eliminate the hacker. There's no way they can know what's really behind this."

"For manpower, I suggest you take a trip to Oxford and then Brighton Marina. It's time to call in a favour or two. The Service has gone to a lot of effort to wipe the slate clean for those two. It seems that the Sandman and the Iceman can come back to life for one last hurrah. I leave the details of how it will be done to you and your new team."

"If you can, please make the circumstances of death," he smiled weakly "appropriately whimsical."

Chapter 70

2024

19th September - Thursday
BA Flight BA0293
Pete Thomas "aka Lobster"

"Christ" said Jenny "I wasn't expecting this."

She was peering over the top of her seat. Her mother and father were a picture of contentment in the unaccustomed luxury of the first-class cabin. The family were on their way home to Australia, taking the long way back via the States, Hawaii, New Zealand and then home. At the check-in desk they had been told their tickets had been upgraded from economy to first. Miriam had seen them off, she described it as "a parting gift to make up for all the inconvenience."

For Jenny the parting had been tough. She was already thinking about returning to the UK to see Andy. He was talking about a visit to Australia.

Jenny had a window seat; her parents were side by side in centre seats behind her. Beige partitions kept them distinct from the passengers around them and the comfortable seats turned into full length beds. Pete had discovered he could raise a little screen between himself and Pauline but had lowered it again for fear of causing offence. Moments before, the crew had come round with drinks and nibbles. Now, Pauline was reading the menu. This was a treat to be savoured.

There was the slightest of bumps as the plane was about to cross the Irish coast. Pete went over to Jenny's seat and looked down on the bright green land stretched out below. He guessed they were somewhere over Carlingford Lough. From this height he could see the whole curve of the bay. There was Dunany, he could see the coast all the way round to Dublin. He traced the line of the coast, until there it was, the glittering line of the River Glyde. He pointed, "that's the River Glyde and that village that's Annagassan." Jenny followed where he was pointing.

"Annagassan, that's where I was born."
Jenny looked round at her mother; both wore puzzled expressions.

"Are you sure, Dad? That's Ireland down there, I thought you were born in Suffolk."

"No, I'm sure, that's where I'm from and when we get home, I have some explaining to do."

In a few moments they would be high over the border. High over the place where Pete's life had hung in the balance all those years age. A fragment of time, when the slightest pressure on the Sandman's trigger meant death, torn apart by bullets. Yet the trigger wasn't squeezed, and he had lived. Spared to become a respected member of the community, a police inspector on the other side of the world. Propelled into a new life, to love, to marry, to have a wonderful daughter.

He pictured the cell the night of his capture; "almost like being born again" he thought. "Down there is the place of my birth and my re-birth, my two lives begin in Ireland."

"That army officer, the one who interrogated me, got it wrong. I didn't incur the displeasure of the Sandman. I experienced his humanity."

Afterword

Dear Reader,

There it is. The tale is told, cosy ending, neatly tied up with a tidy bow. All is resolved.

Or is it? Does it really seem likely that the Home Secretary would order the death of a former Prime Minister? Based on what information? Surely, she would be suspicious. She must remember the damage the WMD "dodgy dossier" did to a previous Government?

Come to think of it, Yelizaveta didn't know the identity of LYRE. How is it that now it's a certainty? Why did Moscow send Yelizaveta? They already had people in London, why not use them?

That text that Miriam received authorising her to eliminate Geraldine. Who sent that? Why did Miriam upgrade the Thomas family to First Class. Was it just to see what happened when she used that credit card?

Why is Miriam being asked to do the killing? The killing to be something whimsical. What on earth does that mean?

What's going to happen?
Read the next book in the series to find out.

Printed in Great Britain
by Amazon